Y0-BBD-974

TEMPE LIBRARY
1000265298

AUG 19

Bkm

TEMPE PUBLIC LIBRARY
TEMPE, AZ 85282

808.83874 S445

The Second reel west

THE SECOND
REEL WEST

THE SECOND REEL WEST

EDITED BY BILL PRONZINI
AND MARTIN H. GREENBERG

DOUBLEDAY & COMPANY, INC.
GARDEN CITY, NEW YORK
1985

All of the characters in this book
are fictitious, and any resemblance
to actual persons, living or dead,
is purely coincidental.

Acknowledgments
"Command" by James Warner Bellah. Copyright © 1946 by The Curtis Publishing Company. First published in *The Saturday Evening Post*. Reprinted by permission of Scott Meredith Literary Agency, Inc., 845 Third Ave., New York, NY 10022.

"Big Hunt" by James Warner Bellah. Copyright © 1947 by The Curtis Publishing Company. First published in *The Saturday Evening Post*. Reprinted by permission of Scott Meredith Literary Agency, Inc., 845 Third Ave., New York, NY 10022.

"Yankee Gold" by John M. Cunningham. Copyright © 1946 by Street and Smith Publications, Inc.; copyright renewed 1974 by John M. Cunningham. First published in *Pic*. Reprinted by permission of Knox Burger Associates.

"A Man Called Horse" by Dorothy M. Johnson. Copyright © 1949 by Dorothy M. Johnson; copyright renewed 1977 by Dorothy M. Johnson. First published in *Collier's*. Reprinted by permission of McIntosh and Otis, Inc.

"The Singing Sands" by Steve Frazee. Copyright © 1954 by Popular Publications, Inc. First published in *Fifteen Western Tales*. Reprinted by permission of Scott Meredith Literary Agency, Inc., 845 Third Ave., New York, NY 10022.

"Sergeant Houck" by Jack Schaefer. Copyright © 1951 by Jack Schaefer; copyright renewed 1979 by Jack Schaefer. Reprinted by permission of Don Congdon Associates, Inc.

"The Captives" by Elmore Leonard. Copyright © 1955 by Elmore Leonard; copyright renewed 1983 by Elmore Leonard. First published in *Argosy*. Reprinted by permission of H. N. Swandon, Inc.

Library of Congress Cataloging in Publication Data
Main entry under title:
The Second reel west.
1. Western stories. 2. Short stories, American.
I. Pronzini, Bill. II. Greenberg, Martin Harry.
PS648.W4S42 1985   813'.0874'08
ISBN: 0-385-23103-2
Library of Congress Catalog Card Number 85-4409

Copyright © 1985 by Bill Pronzini and Martin H. Greenberg
ALL RIGHTS RESERVED
PRINTED IN THE UNITED STATES OF AMERICA
FIRST EDITION

CONTENTS

Introduction	vii
The Outcasts of Poker Flat, Bret Harte (THE OUTCASTS OF POKER FLAT)	1
The Passing of Black Eagle, O. Henry (BLACK EAGLE)	10
The Two-Gun Man, Stewart Edward White (UNDER A TEXAS MOON)	19
Back to God's Country, James Oliver Curwood (BACK TO GOD'S COUNTRY)	30
Command and *Big Hunt,* James Warner Bellah (SHE WORE A YELLOW RIBBON)	53 64
Yankee Gold, John M. Cunningham (THE STRANGER WORE A GUN)	75
A Man Called Horse, Dorothy M. Johnson (A MAN CALLED HORSE)	98
The Singing Sands, Steve Frazee (GOLD OF THE SEVEN SAINTS)	111
Sergeant Houck, Jack Schaefer (TROOPER HOOK)	136
The Captives, Elmore Leonard (THE TALL T)	157

INTRODUCTION

The Second Reel West is a sequel to *The Reel West* (Doubleday, 1984), and like its predecessor is an anthology of exceptional stories which were the basis for notable Western films. In our introduction to that first volume, we made a point which bears repeating here: Some of the tales in these pages have not been faithfully transferred to the screen, while others contributed only the basic idea to the movies they became. All differ in varying degrees from their Hollywood adaptations, according to the whims (sometimes good, sometimes bad) of producers, directors, actors, and screenwriters. Readers may find it interesting—and occasionally frustrating—to compare the two versions of each entry.

A brief look at the films, first, in chronological order:

Under a Texas Moon (1930), directed by the great Michael Curtiz, is based on Stewart Edward White's 1907 story "The Two-Gun Man." Featuring Frank Fay, a very young (and beautiful) Myrna Loy, Raquel Torres, Noah Beery, Sr., and George Stone, it is among the very few *musicals* developed from a short story (and a reasonably serious story at that). Its basic plot, of a man (Fay) caught between two women (Loy and Torres), later became a common one in motion pictures, Western and otherwise; but the film is a good one and stands up as well as can be expected of a fifty-five-year-old early talkie.

The most enduring of Bret Harte's peerless tales of the California Gold Rush, first published in 1869, was made into *The Outcasts of Poker Flat* (1937, remade in 1952). The 1937 screen version was directed by Christy Cabanne and starred Preston Foster, Van Heflin, and Jean Muir; it has one of those classic Western plots in which a small group of people confined in one place—in this case, a snowbound cabin in the mountains—and suspense is derived from the relationships and conflicts that develop among them. The 1952 remake, which featured Dale Robertson, Anne Baxter, and Cameron Mitchell, under the direction of Joseph M. Newman, is no improvement on the earlier adaptation. There is also a silent version of *Outcasts*, made in 1919, which we have never seen.

"The Passing of Black Eagle" (1901) by the great American writer of short stories, O. Henry, is the basis of *Black Eagle* (1948), directed by Robert Gordon and starring William Bishop and Virginia Patton. Although seldom seen anymore even on "The Late Late Show," it is a good, action-packed B Western with better character development than the usual horse opera.

John Ford's *She Wore a Yellow Ribbon* (1949), with a huge cast headed by John Wayne, Joanne Dru, John Agar, Ben Johnson, and Victor McLaglen, is the second in Ford's big-budget "cavalry trilogy." Based on two *Saturday Evening Post* stories by James Warner Bellah, "Command" (1946) and "Big Hunt" (1947), it is distinguished by an outstanding performance by Wayne in the role of Captain Nathan Brittles, an "old soldier" seemingly at the end of his career. The cinematography is excellent and the Monument Valley scenery quite striking.

Back to God's Country (1953), from the 1920 story of the same title by James Oliver Curwood, is a pure adventure story, one of many that Hollywood filmmakers shot on location in Canada. The featured players are Rock Hudson as an ex-sea captain, Marcia Henderson as his love interest, and Hugh O'Brian and the much underrated Steve Cochran in supporting roles. Joseph Pevney's direction is first-rate.

Adapted from John Cunningham's 1947 novelette "Yankee Gold," André De Toth's *The Stranger Wore a Gun* (1953) is arguably the best Western ever made in 3-D. Randolph Scott and Claire Trevor had the lead roles; but as in so many Western films, it was the actors portraying the villains who stole the show—the great Lee Marvin, young and menacing; Alfonso Bedoya, the ultimate Mexican bandit (remember him in *The Treasure of Sierra Madre?*); and Ernest Borgnine, exuding nastiness with every breath.

Trooper Hook (1957), directed by Charles Marquis Warren (himself a writer of Western fiction) and based on Jack Schaefer's fine 1951 short story, "Sergeant Houck," is an important and powerful film, one of Hollywood's earlier attempts to deal with racism and miscegenation. The stars are Barbara Stanwyck as a woman hated by her fellow whites because she has lived among Indians and Joel McCrea as the brave soldier who helps her.

The year 1957 was a very good one for Western films, as evidenced also by *The Tall T*. Adapted from the then relatively unknown Elmore Leonard's novelette "The Captives" (1955), it is one of the talented Budd Boetticher's best films and features the prototypical Western hero, Randolph Scott, along with Maureen O'Sullivan as the middle-aged heroine and three more of the screen's top portrayers of villainy—Richard Boone, Skip Homeier, and Henry Silva. Both story and film provide considerable excitement and suspense.

Steve Frazee's "The Singing Sands" (1954) was the basis for the 1961 film, *Gold of the Seven Saints*. Under the direction of Gordon Douglas, this feature starred Clint Walker, Roger Moore (yes, the same actor who would later portray James Bond), Chill Wills, and Robert Middleton. It is an "odd couple" story that pairs the rugged Walker with the less-than-believable-as-a-Westerner Moore and is not nearly as good as its source.

Finally, 1970's *A Man Called Horse* was taken from the late Dorothy M.

Johnson's superb 1949 *Collier's* story of the same title. This film is best known for the powerful scene in which star Richard Harris hangs by his chest from the top of a hut during the Sioux Sun Vow Initiation Ceremony—and is one of several extremely violent Westerns made by Harris. Its most unusual characteristic is the casting of Dame Judith Anderson as a Sioux woman, a performance that brought both praise and derision from the critics. Elliot Silverstein directed.

And now—

We're pleased to present the stories that brought these films into being—stories we think you'll find every bit as, if not more, provocative and entertaining as the Hollywood productions themselves. Enjoy.

—Bill Pronzini and
Martin H. Greenberg

January 1985

THE OUTCASTS OF POKER FLAT
BY BRET HARTE
(The Outcasts of Poker Flat)

No one wrote better fiction about those hell-roaring days of the California Gold Rush than Bret Harte (1836–1902). He made a career of writing stories about that era, in fact, penning new tales of the mining camps and the men who inhabited them even as an expatriate American living in London in the late 1800s. "The Outcasts of Poker Flat" (1869) is probably his best known story; and the 1937 film version ranks with Tennessee's Partner *(1955), from the story of the same title (included in* The Reel West), *as the best screen adaptation of his work. Another of Harte's famous stories, "The Luck of Roaring Camp," was poorly filmed with an obscure group of actors in 1937.*

As Mr. John Oakhurst, gambler, stepped into the main street of Poker Flat on the morning of the 23d of November, 1850, he was conscious of a change in its moral atmosphere since the preceding night. Two or three men, conversing earnestly together, ceased as he approached, and exchanged significant glances. There was a Sabbath lull in the air, which, in a settlement unused to Sabbath influences, looked ominous.

Mr. Oakhurst's calm, handsome face betrayed small concern in these indications. Whether he was conscious of any predisposing cause was another question. "I reckon they're after somebody," he reflected; "likely it's me." He returned to his pocket the handkerchief with which he had been whipping away the red dust of Poker Flat from his neat boots, and quietly discharged his mind of any further conjecture.

In point of fact, Poker Flat was "after somebody." It had lately suffered the loss of several thousand dollars, two valuable horses, and a prominent citizen. It was experiencing a spasm of virtuous reaction, quite as lawless and ungovernable as any of the acts that had provoked it. A secret committee had determined to rid the town of all improper persons. This was done permanently in regard of two men who were then hanging from the boughs of a sycamore in the gulch, and temporarily in the banishment of certain other objectionable characters. I regret to say that some of these were ladies. It is but due to the sex, however, to state that their impropriety was professional, and it was only in such easily established standards of evil that Poker Flat ventured to sit in judgment.

Mr. Oakhurst was right in supposing that he was included in this category. A few of the committee had urged hanging him as a possible example and a sure method of reimbursing themselves from his pockets of the sums he had won from them. "It's agin justice," said Jim Wheeler, "to let this yer young man from Roaring Camp—an entire stranger—carry away our money." But a crude sentiment of equity residing in the breasts of those who had been fortunate enough to win from Mr. Oakhurst overruled this narrower local prejudice.

Mr. Oakhurst received his sentence with philosophic calmness, none the less coolly that he was aware of the hesitation of his judges. He was too much of a gambler not to accept fate. With him life was at best an uncertain game, and he recognized the usual percentage in favor of the dealer.

A body of armed men accompanied the deported wickedness of Poker Flat to the outskirts of the settlement. Besides Mr. Oakhurst, who was known to be a coolly desperate man, and for whose intimidation the armed escort was intended, the expatriated party consisted of a young woman familiarly known as "The Duchess"; another who had won the title of "Mother Shipton"; and "Uncle Billy," a suspected sluice-robber and confirmed drunkard. The cavalcade provoked no comments from the spectators, nor was any word uttered by the escort. Only when the gulch which marked the uttermost limit of Poker Flat was reached, the leader spoke briefly and to the point. The exiles were forbidden to return at the peril of their lives.

As the escort disappeared, their pent-up feelings found vent in a few hysterical tears from the Duchess, some bad language from Mother Shipton, and a Parthian volley of expletives from Uncle Billy. The philosophic Oakhurst alone remained silent. He listened calmly to Mother Shipton's desire to cut somebody's heart out, to the repeated statements of the Duchess that she would die in the road, and to the alarming oaths that seemed to be bumped out of Uncle Billy as he rode forward. With the easy good humor characteristic of his class, he insisted upon exchanging his own riding-horse, "Five-Spot," for the sorry mule which the Duchess rode. But even this act did not draw the party into any closer sympathy. The young woman readjusted her somewhat draggled plumes with a feeble, faded coquetry; Mother Shipton eyed the possessor of "Five-Spot" with malevolence, and Uncle Billy included the whole party in one sweeping anathema.

The road to Sandy Bar—a camp that, not having as yet experienced the regenerating influences of Poker Flat, consequently seemed to offer some invitation to the emigrants—lay over a steep mountain range. It was distant a day's severe travel. In that advanced season the party soon passed out of the moist, temperate regions of the foothills into the dry, cold, bracing air of the Sierras. The trail was narrow and difficult. At noon the Duchess, rolling out of her saddle upon the ground, declared her intention of going no farther, and the party halted.

The spot was singularly wild and impressive. A wooded amphitheatre, surrounded on three sides by precipitous cliffs of naked granite, sloped gently toward the crest of another precipice that overlooked the valley. It was, undoubtedly, the most suitable spot for a camp, had camping been advisable. But Mr. Oakhurst knew that scarcely half the journey to Sandy Bar was accomplished, and the party were not equipped or provisioned for delay. This fact he pointed out to his companions curtly, with a philosophic commentary on the folly of "throwing up their hand before the game was played out." But they were furnished with liquor, which in this emergency stood them in place of food, fuel, rest, and prescience. In spite of his remonstrances, it was not long before they were more or less under its influence. Uncle Billy passed rapidly from a bellicose state into one of stupor, the Duchess became maudlin, and Mother Shipton snored. Mr. Oakhurst alone remained erect, leaning against a rock, calmly surveying them.

Mr. Oakhurst did not drink. It interfered with a profession which required coolness, impassiveness, and presence of mind, and in his own language, he "couldn't afford it." As he gazed at his recumbent fellow exiles, the loneliness begotten of his pariah trade, his habits of life, his very vices, for the first time seriously oppressed him. He bestirred himself in dusting his black clothes, washing his hands and face, and other acts characteristic of his studiously neat habits, and for a moment forgot his annoyance. The thought of deserting his weaker and more pitiable companions never perhaps occurred to him. Yet he could not help feeling the want of that excitement which, singularly enough, was most conducive to that calm equanimity for which he was notorious. He looked at the gloomy walls that rose a thousand feet sheer above the circling pines around him, at the sky ominously clouded, at the valley below, already deepening into shadow; and doing so, suddenly he heard his own name called.

A horseman slowly ascended the trail. In the fresh, open face of the newcomer Mr. Oakhurst recognized Tom Simson, otherwise known as "The Innocent," of Sandy Bar. He had met him some months before over a "little game," and had, with perfect equanimity, won the entire fortune—amounting to some forty dollars—of that guileless youth. After the game was finished, Mr. Oakhurst drew the youthful speculator behind the door and thus addressed him: "Tommy, you're a good little man, but you can't gamble worth a cent. Don't try it over again." He then handed him his money back, pushed him gently from the room, and so made a devoted slave of Tom Simson.

There was a remembrance of this in his boyish and enthusiastic greeting of Mr. Oakhurst. He had started, he said, to go to Poker Flat to seek his fortune. "Alone?" No, not exactly alone; in fact (a giggle), he had run away with Piney Woods. Didn't Mr. Oakhurst remember Piney? She that used to wait on the table at the Temperance House? They had been engaged a long time, but old Jake Woods had objected, and so they had run away, and were going to Poker Flat to be married, and here they were. And they were tired out, and how lucky it was they had found a place to camp, and company. All this the Innocent delivered rapidly, while Piney, a stout, comely damsel of fifteen, emerged from behind the pine tree, where she had been blushing unseen, and rode to the side of her lover.

Mr. Oakhurst seldom troubled himself with sentiment, still less with propriety; but he had a vague idea that the situation was not fortunate. He retained, however, his presence of mind sufficiently to kick Uncle Billy, who was about to say something, and Uncle Billy was sober enough to recognize in Mr. Oakhurst's kick a superior power that would not bear trifling. He then endeavored to dissuade Tom Simson from delaying further, but in vain. He even pointed out the fact that there was no provision, nor means of making a camp. But, unluckily, the Innocent met this objection by assuring the party that he was provided with an extra mule loaded with provisions, and by the discovery of a rude attempt at a log house near the trail. "Piney can stay with Mrs. Oakhurst," said the Innocent, pointing to the Duchess, "and I can shift for myself."

Nothing but Mr. Oakhurst's admonishing foot saved Uncle Billy from bursting into a roar of laughter. As it was, he felt compelled to retire up the canyon until he could recover his gravity. There he confided the joke to the tall pine trees, with many slaps of his leg, contortions of his face, and the usual profanity. But when he returned to the party, he found them seated by a fire—for the air had grown strangely chill and the sky overcast—in apparently amicable conversation. Piney was actually talking in an impulsive girlish fashion to the Duchess, who was listening with an interest and animation she had not shown for many days. The Innocent was holding forth, apparently with equal effect, to Mr. Oakhurst and Mother Shipton, who was actually relaxing into amiability. "Is this yer a d—d picnic?" said Uncle Billy, with inward scorn, as he surveyed the sylvan group, the glancing firelight, and the tethered animals in the foreground. Suddenly an idea mingled with the alcoholic fumes that disturbed his brain. It was apparently of a jocular nature, for he felt impelled to slap his leg again and cram his fist into his mouth.

As the shadows crept slowly up the mountain, a slight breeze rocked the tops of the pine trees and moaned through their long and gloomy aisles. The ruined cabin, patched and covered with pine boughs, was set apart for the ladies. As the lovers parted, they unaffectedly exchanged a kiss, so honest and sincere that it might have been heard above the swaying pines. The frail Duchess and the malevolent Mother Shipton were probably too stunned to remark upon this last evidence of simplicity, and so turned without a word to the hut. The fire was replenished, the men lay down before the door, and in a few minutes were asleep.

Mr. Oakhurst was a light sleeper. Toward morning he awoke benumbed and cold. As he stirred the dying fire, the wind, which was now blowing strongly, brought to his cheek that which caused the blood to leave it—snow!

He started to his feet with the intention of awakening the sleepers, for there was no time to lose. But turning to where Uncle Billy had been lying, he found him gone. A suspicion leaped to his brain, and a curse to his lips. He ran to the spot where the mules had been tethered—they were no longer there. The tracks were already rapidly disappearing in the snow.

The momentary excitement brought Mr. Oakhurst back to the fire with his usual calm. He did not waken the sleepers. The Innocent slumbered peacefully, with a smile on his good-humored, freckled face; the virgin Piney slept beside her frailer sisters as sweetly as though attended by celestial guardians; and Mr. Oakhurst, drawing his blanket over his shoulders, stroked his mustaches and waited for the dawn. It came slowly in a whirling mist of snowflakes that dazzled and confused the eye. What could be seen of the landscape appeared magically changed. He looked over the valley, and summed up the present and future in two words, "Snowed in!"

A careful inventory of the provisions, which, fortunately for the party, had been stored within the hut, and so escaped the felonious fingers of Uncle Billy, disclosed the fact that with care and prudence they might last ten days longer. "That is," said Mr. Oakhurst *sotto voce* to the Innocent, "if you're willing to board us. If you ain't—and perhaps you'd better not—you can wait till Uncle Billy gets back with provisions." For some occult reason, Mr. Oakhurt could not bring himself to disclose Uncle Billy's rascality, and so offered the hypothesis that he had wandered from the camp and had accidentally stampeded the animals. He dropped a warning to the Duchess and Mother Shipton, who of course knew the facts of their associate's defection. "They'll find out the truth about us *all* when they find out anything," he added significantly, "and there's no good frightening them now."

Tom Simson not only put all his worldly store at the disposal of Mr. Oakhurst, but seemed to enjoy the prospect of their enforced seclusion. "We'll have a good camp for a week, and then the snow'll melt, and we'll all go back together." The cheerful gayety of the young man and Mr. Oakhurst's calm infected the others. The Innocent, with the aid of pine boughs, extemporized a thatch for the roofless cabin, and the Duchess directed Piney in the rearrangement of the interior with a taste and tact that opened the blue eyes of that provincial maiden to their fullest extent. "I reckon now you're used to fine things at Poker Flat," said Piney. The Duchess turned away sharply to conceal something that reddened her cheeks through their professional tint, and Mother Shipton requested Piney not to "chatter." But when Mr. Oakhurst returned from a weary search for the trail, he heard the sound of happy laughter echoed from the rocks. He stopped in some alarm, and his thoughts first naturally reverted to the whiskey, which he had prudently cached. "And yet it don't somehow sound like whiskey," said the gambler. It was not until he caught sight of the blazing fire through the still blinding storm, and the group around it, that he settled to the conviction that it was "square fun."

Whether Mr. Oakhurst had cached his cards with the whiskey as something debarred the free access of the community, I cannot say. It was certain that, in Mother Shipton's words, he "didn't say 'cards' once" during that evening. Haply the time was beguiled by an accordion, produced somewhat ostentatiously by Tom Simson from his pack. Notwithstanding some difficulties attending the manipulation of this instrument, Piney Woods managed to pluck several reluctant melodies from its keys to an accompaniment by the Innocent on a pair of bone castanets. But the crowning festivity of the evening was reached in a rude camp-meeting hymn, which the lovers, joining hands, sang with great earnestness and vociferation. I fear that a certain defiant tone and covenanter's swing to its chorus, rather than any devotional quality, caused it speedily to infect the others, who at last joined in the refrain:

> "I'm proud to live in the service of the Lord,
> And I'm bound to die in His army."

The pines rocked, the storm eddied and whirled above the miserable group, and the flames of their altar leaped heavenward, as if in token of the vow.

At midnight the storm abated, the rolling clouds parted, and the stars glittered keenly above the sleeping camp. Mr. Oakhurst, whose professional habits had enabled him to live on the smallest possible amount of sleep, in dividing the watch with Tom Simson somehow managed to take upon himself the greater part of that duty. He excused himself to the Innocent by saying that he had "often been a week without sleep." "Doing what?" asked Tom. "Poker!" replied Oakhurst sententiously. "When a man gets a streak of luck—nigger-luck—he don't get tired. The luck gives in first. Luck," continued the gambler reflectively, "is a mighty queer thing. All you know about it for certain is that it's bound to change. And it's finding out when it's going to change that makes you. We've had a streak of bad luck since we left Poker Flat—you come along, and slap you get into it, too. If you can hold your cards right along you're all right. For," added the gambler, with cheerful irrelevance—

" 'I'm proud to live in the service of the Lord,
And I'm bound to die in His army.' "

The third day came, and the sun, looking through the white-curtained valley, saw the outcasts divide their slowly decreasing store of provisions for the morning meal. It was one of the peculiarities of that mountain climate that its rays diffused a kindly warmth over the wintry landscape, as if in regretful commiseration of the past. But it revealed drift on drift of snow piled high around the hut—a hopeless, uncharted, trackless sea of white lying below the rocky shores to which the castaways still clung. Through the marvelously clear air the smoke of the pastoral village of Poker Flat rose miles away. Mother Shipton saw it, and from a remote pinnacle of her rocky fastness hurled in that direction a final malediction. It was her last vituperative attempt, and perhaps for that reason was invested with a certain degree of sublimity. It did her good, she privately informed the Duchess. "Just you go out there and cuss, and see." She then set herself to the task of amusing "the child," as she and the Duchess were pleased to call Piney. Piney was no chicken, but it was a soothing and original theory of the pair thus to account for the fact that she didn't swear and wasn't improper.

When night crept up again through the gorges, the reedy notes of the accordion rose and fell in fitful spasms and long-drawn gasps by the flickering campfire. But music failed to fill entirely the aching void left by insufficient food, and a new diversion was proposed by Piney—storytelling. Neither Mr. Oakhurst nor his female companions caring to relate their personal experiences, this plan would have failed too, but for the Innocent. Some months before he had chanced upon a stray copy of Mr. Pope's ingenious translation of the Iliad. He now proposed to narrate the principal incidents of that poem —having thoroughly mastered the argument and fairly forgotten the words— in the current vernacular of Sandy Bar. And so for the rest of that night the Homeric demigods again walked the earth. Trojan bully and wily Greek wrestled in the winds, and the great pines in the canyon seemed to bow to the wrath of the son of Peleus. Mr. Oakhurst listened with quiet satisfaction. Most especially was he interested in the fate of "Ash-heels," as the Innocent persisted in denominating the "swift-footed Achilles."

So, with small food and much of Homer and the accordion, a week passed over the heads of the outcasts. The sun again forsook them, and again from leaden skies the snowflakes were sifted over the land. Day by day closer around them drew the snowy circle, until at last they looked from their prison over drifted walls of dazzling white that towered twenty feet above their heads. It became more and more difficult to replenish their fires, even from the fallen trees beside them, now half hidden in the drifts. And yet no one complained. The lovers turned from the dreary prospect and looked into each other's eyes, and were happy. Mr. Oakhurst settled himself coolly to the losing game before him. The Duchess, more cheerful than she had been, assumed the care of Piney. Only Mother Shipton—once the strongest of the party—seemed to sicken and fade. At midnight on the tenth day she called Oakhurst to her side. "I'm going," she said, in a voice of querulous weakness, "but don't say anything about it. Don't waken the kids. Take the bundle from under my head, and open it." Mr. Oakhurst did so. It contained Mother Shipton's rations for the last week, untouched. "Give 'em to the child," she said, pointing to the sleeping Piney. "You've starved yourself," said the gambler. "That's what they call it," said the woman querulously, as she lay down again, and turning her face to the wall, passed quietly away.

The accordion and the bones were put aside that day, and Homer was forgotten. When the body of Mother Shipton had been committed to the snow, Mr. Oakhurst took the Innocent aside, and showed him a pair of snowshoes, which he had fashioned from the old pack-saddle. "There's one chance in a hundred to save her yet," he said, pointing to Piney; "but it's there," he added, pointing toward Poker Flat. "If you can reach there in two days she's safe." "And you?" asked Tom Simson. "I'll stay here," was the curt reply.

The lovers parted with a long embrace. "You are not going, too?" said the Duchess, as she saw Mr. Oakhurst apparently waiting to accompany him. "As far as the canyon," he replied. He turned suddenly and kissed the Duchess, leaving her pallid face aflame, and her trembling limbs rigid with amazement.

Night came, but not Mr. Oakhurst. It brought the storm again and the whirling snow. Then the Duchess, feeding the fire, found that someone had quietly piled beside the hut enough fuel to last a few days longer. The tears rose to her eyes, but she hid them from Piney.

The women slept but little. In the morning, looking into each other's faces, they read their fate. Neither spoke, but Piney, accepting the position of the stronger, drew near and placed her arm around the Duchess's waist. They kept this attitude for the rest of the day. That night the storm reached its greatest fury, and rending asunder the protecting vines, invaded the very hut.

Toward morning they found themselves unable to feed the fire, which gradually died away. As the embers slowly blackened, the Duchess crept closer to Piney, and broke the silence of many hours: "Piney, can you pray?" "No, dear," said Piney simply. The Duchess, without knowing exactly why, felt relieved, and putting her head upon Piney's shoulder, spoke no more. And so reclining, the younger and purer pillowing the head of her soiled sister upon her virgin breast, they fell asleep.

The wind lulled as if it feared to waken them. Feathery drifts of snow, shaken from the long pine boughs, flew like white winged birds, and settled about them as they slept. The moon through the rifted clouds looked down upon what had been the camp. But all human stain, all trace of earthly travail, was hidden beneath the spotless mantle mercifully flung from above.

They slept all that day and the next, nor did they waken when voices and footsteps broke the silence of the camp. And when pitying fingers brushed the snow from their wan faces, you could scarcely have told from the equal peace that dwelt upon them which was she that had sinned. Even the law of Poker Flat recognized this, and turned away, leaving them still locked in each other's arms.

But at the head of the gulch, on one of the largest pine trees, they found the deuce of clubs pinned to the bark with a bowie knife. It bore the following, written in pencil in a firm hand:

†

BENEATH THIS TREE
LIES THE BODY
OF
JOHN OAKHURST,
WHO STRUCK A STREAK OF BAD LUCK
ON THE 23D OF NOVEMBER, 1850,
AND
HANDED IN HIS CHECKS
ON THE 7TH DECEMBER, 1850.

↓

And pulseless and cold, with a derringer by his side and a bullet in his heart, though still calm as in life, beneath the snow lay he who was at once the strongest and yet the weakest of the outcasts of Poker Flat.

THE PASSING OF BLACK EAGLE
BY O. HENRY
(Black Eagle)

The border bandit known as Black Eagle is only one of the memorable southwestern desperadoes created by the native Texan named William Sydney Porter (1862–1910) who wrote as O. Henry. Two others are the wicked Cisco Kid, who was transformed, with typical Hollywood logic, into a dashing "Robin Hood of the Old West" in the TV series starring Duncan Renaldo; and the Llano Kid, the "villainous hero" of the story "A Double-Dyed Deceiver" (see The Reel West) *and the 1930 Gary Cooper film,* The Texan. *Although written while Porter was living in New York City just after the turn of the century, "The Passing of Black Eagle" (1901) is one of his best Western stories and demonstrates why he is famous for his surprise endings.*

For some months of a certain year a grim bandit infested the Texas border along the Rio Grande. Peculiarly striking to the optic nerve was this notorious marauder. His personality secured him the title of "Black Eagle, the Terror of the Border." Many fearsome tales are on record concerning the doings of him and his followers. Suddenly, in the space of a single minute, Black Eagle vanished from earth. He was never heard of again. His own band never even guessed the mystery of his disappearance. The border ranches and settlements feared he would come again to ride and ravage the mesquite flats. He never will. It is to disclose the fate of Black Eagle that this narrative is written.

The initial movement of the story is furnished by the foot of a bartender in St. Louis. His discerning eye fell upon the form of Chicken Ruggles as he pecked with avidity at the free lunch. Chicken was a "hobo." He had a long nose like the bill of a fowl, an inordinate appetite for poultry, and a habit of gratifying it without expense, which accounts for the name given him by his fellow vagrants.

Physicians agree that the partaking of liquors at meal times is not a healthy practice. The hygiene of the saloon promulgates the opposite. Chicken had neglected to purchase a drink to accompany his meal. The bartender rounded the counter, caught the injudicious diner by the ear with a lemon squeezer, led him to the door and kicked him into the street.

Thus the mind of Chicken was brought to realize the signs of coming winter. The night was cold; the stars shone with unkindly brilliancy; people were hurrying along the streets in two egotistic, jostling streams. Men had donned their overcoats, and Chicken knew to an exact percentage the increased difficulty of coaxing dimes from those buttoned-in vest pockets. The time had come for his annual exodus to the south.

A little boy, five or six years old, stood looking with covetous eyes in a confectioner's window. In one small hand he held an empty two-ounce vial; in the other he grasped tightly something flat and round, with a shining milled edge. The scene presented a field of operations commensurate to Chicken's talents and daring. After sweeping the horizon to make sure that no official tug was cruising near, he insidiously accosted his prey. The boy, having been early taught by his household to regard altruisitic advances with extreme suspicion, received the overtures coldly.

Then Chicken knew that he must make one of those desperate, nerve-shattering plunges into speculation that fortune sometimes requires of those who would win her favor. Five cents was his capital, and this he must risk against the chance of winning what lay within the close grasp of the youngster's chubby hand. It was a fearful lottery, Chicken knew. But he must accomplish his end by strategy, since he had a wholesome terror of plundering infants by force. Once, in a park, driven by hunger, he had committed an onslaught upon a bottle of peptonized infant's food in the possession of an occupant of a baby carriage. The outraged infant had so promptly opened its mouth and pressed the button that communicated with the welkin that help arrived, and Chicken did his thirty days in a snug coop. Wherefore he was, as he said, "leary of kids."

Beginning artfully to question the boy concerning his choice of sweets, he gradually drew out the information he wanted. Mamma said he was to ask the drug-store man for ten cents' worth of paregoric in the bottle; he was to keep his hand shut tight over the dollar; he must not stop to talk to any one in the street; he must ask the drug-store man to wrap up the change and put it in the pocket of his trousers. Indeed, they had pockets—two of them! And he liked chocolate creams best.

Chicken went into the store and turned plunger. He invested his entire capital in C. A. N. D. Y. stocks, simply to pave the way to the greater risk following.

He gave the sweets to the youngster, and had the satisfaction of perceiving that confidence was established. After that it was easy to obtain leadership of the expedition, to take the investment by the hand and lead it to a nice drug store he knew of in the same block. There Chicken, with a parental air, passed over the dollar and called for the medicine, while the boy crunched his candy, glad to be relieved of the responsibility of the purchase. And then the successful investor, searching his pockets, found an overcoat button—the extent of his winter trousseau—and, wrapping it carefully, placed the ostensible change in the pocket of confiding juvenility. Setting the youngster's face homeward, and patting him benevolently on the back—for Chicken's heart was as soft as those of his feathered namesakes—the speculator quit the market with a profit of 1,700 per cent. on his invested capital.

Two hours later an Iron Mountain freight engine pulled out of the railroad yards, Texas bound, with a string of empties. In one of the cattle cars, half buried in excelsior, Chicken lay at ease. Beside him in his nest was a quart bottle of very poor whisky and a paper bag of bread and cheese. Mr. Ruggles, in his private car, was on his trip south for the winter season.

For a week that car was trundled southward, shifted, laid over, and manipulated after the manner of rolling stock, but Chicken stuck to it, leaving it only at necessary times to satisfy his hunger and thirst. He knew it must go down to the cattle country, and San Antonio, in the heart of it, was his goal. There the air was salubrious and mild; the people indulgent and long-suffering. The bartenders there would not kick him. If he should eat too long or too often at one place they would swear at him as if by rote and without heat. They swore so drawlingly, and they rarely paused short of their full vocabulary, which was copious, so that Chicken had often gulped a good meal during the process of the vituperative prohibition. The season there was always spring-like; the plazas were pleasant at night, with music and gayety: except during the slight and infrequent cold snaps one could sleep comfortably out of doors in case the interiors should develop inhospitality.

At Texarkana his car was switched to the I. and G. N. Then still southward it trailed until, at length, it crawled across the Colorado bridge at Austin, and lined out, straight as an arrow, for the run to San Antonio.

When the freight halted at that town Chicken was fast asleep. In ten minutes the train was off again for Laredo, the end of the road. Those empty cattle cars were for distribution along the line at points from which the ranches shipped their stock.

When Chicken awoke his car was stationary. Looking out between the slats he saw it was a bright, moonlit night. Scrambling out, he saw his car with three others abandoned on a little siding in a wild and lonesome country. A cattle pen and chute stood on one side of the track. The railroad bisected a vast, dim ocean of prairie, in the midst of which Chicken, with his futile rolling stock, was as completely stranded as was Robinson with his landlocked boat.

A white post stood near the rails. Going up to it, Chicken read the letters at the top, S. A. 90. Laredo was nearly as far to the south. He was almost a hundred miles from any town. Coyotes began to yelp in the mysterious sea around him. Chicken felt lonesome. He had lived in Boston without an education, in Chicago without nerve, in Philadelphia without a sleeping place, in New York without a pull, and in Pittsburgh sober, and yet he had never felt so lonely as now.

Suddenly through the intense silence, he heard the whicker of a horse. The sound came from the side of the track toward the east, and Chicken began to explore timorously in that direction. He stepped high along the mat of curly mesquite grass, for he was afraid of everything there might be in this wilderness—snakes, rats, brigands, centipedes, mirages, cowboys, fandangoes, tarantulas, tamales—he had read of them in the story papers. Rounding a clump of prickly pear that reared high its fantastic and menacing array of rounded heads, he was struck to shivering terror by a snort and a thunderous plunge, as the horse, himself startled, bounded away some fifty yards, and then resumed his grazing. But here was the one thing in the desert that Chicken did not fear. He had been reared on a farm; he had handled horses, understood them, and could ride.

Approaching slowly and speaking soothingly, he followed the animal, which, after its first flight, seemed gentle enough, and secured the end of the twenty-foot lariat that dragged after him in the grass. It required him but a few moments to contrive the rope into an ingenious nose-bridle, after the style of the Mexican *borsal.* In another he was upon the horse's back and off at a splendid lope, giving the animal free choice of direction. "He will take me somewhere," said Chicken to himself.

It would have been a thing of joy, that untrammelled gallop over the moonlit prairie, even to Chicken, who loathed exertion, but that his mood was not for it. His head ached; a growing thirst was upon him; the "somewhere" whither his lucky mount might convey him was full of dismal peradventure.

And now he noted that the horse moved to a definite goal. Where the prairie lay smooth he kept his course straight as an arrow's toward the east. Deflected by hill or arroyo or impracticable spinous brakes, he quickly flowed again into the current, charted by his unerring instinct. At last, upon the side of a gentle rise, he suddenly subsided to a complacent walk. A stone's cast away stood a little mott of coma trees; beneath it a *jacal* such as the Mexicans erect—a one-room house of upright poles daubed with clay and roofed with grass or tule reeds. An experienced eye would have estimated the spot as the headquarters of a small sheep ranch. In the moonlight the ground in the nearby corral showed pulverized to a level smoothness by the hoofs of the sheep. Everywhere was carelessly distributed the paraphernalia of the place—ropes, bridles, saddles, sheep pelts, wool sacks, feed troughs, and camp litter. The barrel of drinking water stood in the end of the two-horse wagon near the door. The harness was piled, promiscuous, upon the wagon tongue, soaking up the dew.

Chicken slipped to earth, and tied the horse to a tree. He halloed again and again, but the house remained quiet. The door stood open, and he entered cautiously. The light was sufficient for him to see that no one was at home. He struck a match and lighted a lamp that stood on a table. The room was that of a bachelor ranchman who was content with the necessaries of life. Chicken rummaged intelligently until he found what he had hardly dared hope for—a small brown jug that still contained something near a quart of his desire.

Half an hour later, Chicken—now a gamecock of hostile aspect—emerged from the house with unsteady steps. He had drawn upon the absent ranchman's equipment to replace his own ragged attire. He wore a suit of coarse brown ducking, the coat being a sort of rakish bolero, jaunty to a degree. Boots he had donned, and spurs that whirred with every lurching step. Buckled around him was a belt full of cartridges with a six-shooter in each of its two holsters.

Prowling about, he found blankets, a saddle and bridle with which he caparisoned his steed. Again mounting, he rode swiftly away, singing a loud and tuneless song.

Bud King's band of desperadoes, outlaws and horse and cattle thieves were in camp at a secluded spot on the bank of the Frio. Their depredations in the Rio Grande country, while no bolder than usual, had been advertised more extensively, and Captain Kinney's company of rangers had been ordered down to look after them. Consequently, Bud King, who was a wise general, instead of cutting out a hot trail for the upholders of the law, as his men wished to do, retired for the time to the prickly fastnesses of the Frio valley.

Though the move was a prudent one, and not incompatible with Bud's well-known courage, it raised dissension among the members of the band. In fact, while they thus lay ingloriously *perdu* in the brush, the question of Bud King's fitness for the leadership was argued, with closed doors, as it were, by his followers. Never before had Bud's skill or efficiency been brought to criticism; but his glory was waning (and such is glory's fate) in the light of a newer star. The sentiment of the band was crystallizing into the opinion that Black Eagle could lead them with more luster, profit, and distinction.

This Black Eagle—sub-titled the "Terror of the Border"—had been a member of the gang about three months.

One night while they were in camp on the San Miguel water-hole a solitary horseman on the regulation fiery steed dashed in among them. The newcomer was of a portentous and devastating aspect. A beak-like nose with a predatory curve projected above a mass of bristling, blue-black whiskers. His eye was cavernous and fierce. He was spurred, sombreroed, booted, garnished with revolvers, abundantly drunk, and very much unafraid. Few people in the country drained by the Rio Bravo would have cared thus to invade alone the camp of Bud King. But this fell bird swooped fearlessly upon them and demanded to be fed.

Hospitality in the prairie country is not limited. Even if your enemy pass your way you must feed him before you shoot him. You must empty your larder into him before you empty your lead. So the stranger of undeclared intentions was set down to a mighty feast.

A talkative bird he was, full of most marvellous loud tales and exploits, and speaking a language at times obscure but never colorless. He was a new sensation to Bud King's men, who rarely encountered new types. They hung, delighted, upon his vainglorious boasting, the spicy strangeness of his lingo, his contemptuous familiarity with life, the world, and remote places, and the extravagant frankness with which he conveyed his sentiments.

To their guest the band of outlaws seemed to be nothing more than a congregation of country bumpkins whom he was "stringing for grub" just as he would have told his stories at the back door of a farmhouse to wheedle a meal. And, indeed, his ignorance was not without excuse, for the "bad man" of the Southwest does not run to extremes. Those brigands might justly have been taken for a little party of peaceable rustics assembled for a fish-fry or pecan gathering. Gentle of manner, slouching of gait, soft-voiced, unpicturesquely clothed; not one of them presented to the eye any witness of the desperate records they had earned.

For two days the glittering stranger within the camp was feasted. Then, by common consent, he was invited to become a member of the band. He consented, presenting for enrollment the prodigious name of "Captain Montressor." This was immediately overruled by the band, and "Piggy" substituted as a compliment to the awful and insatiate appetite of its owner.

Thus did the Texas border receive the most spectacular brigand that ever rode its chaparral.

For the next three months Bud King conducted business as usual, escaping encounters with law officers and being content with reasonable profits. The band ran off some very good companies of horses from the ranges, and a few bunches of fine cattle which they got safely across the Rio Grande and disposed of to fair advantage. Often the band would ride into the little villages and Mexican settlements, terrorizing the inhabitants and plundering for the provisions and ammunition they needed. It was during these bloodless raids that Piggy's ferocious aspect and frightful voice gained him a renown more widespread and glorious than those other gentle-voiced and sad-faced desperadoes could have acquired in a lifetime.

The Mexicans, most apt in nomenclature, first called him The Black Eagle, and used to frighten the babes by threatening them with tales of the dreadful robber who carried off little children in his great beak. Soon the name extended, and Black Eagle, the Terror of the Border, became a recognized factor in exaggerated newspaper reports and ranch gossip.

The country from the Nueces to the Rio Grande was a wild but fertile stretch, given over to the sheep and cattle ranches. Range was free; the inhabitants were few; the law was mainly a letter, and the pirates met with little opposition until the flaunting and garish Piggy gave the band undue advertisement. Then Kinney's ranger company headed for those precincts, and Bud King knew that it meant grim and sudden war or else temporary retirement. Regarding the risk to be unnecessary, he drew off his band to an almost inaccessible spot on the bank of the Frio. Wherefore, as has been said, dissatisfaction arose among the members, and impeachment proceedings against Bud were premeditated, with Black Eagle in high favor for the succession. Bud King was not unaware of the sentiment, and he called aside Cactus Taylor, his trusted lieutenant, to discuss it.

"If the boys," said Bud, "ain't satisfied with me, I'm willin' to step out. They're buckin' against my way of handlin' 'em. And 'specially because I concludes to hit the brush while Sam Kinney is ridin' the line. I saves 'em from bein' shot or sent up on a state contract, and they up and says I'm no good."

"It ain't so much that," explained Cactus, "as it is they're plum locoed about Piggy. They want them whiskers and that nose of his to split the wind at the head of the column."

"There's somethin' mighty seldom about Piggy," declared Bud, musingly. "I never yet see anything on the hoof that he exactly grades up with. He can shore holler a plenty, and he straddles a hoss from where you laid the chunk. But he ain't never been smoked yet. You know, Cactus, we ain't had a row since he's been with us. Piggy's all right for skearin' the greaser kids and layin' waste a cross-roads store. I reckon he's the finest canned oyster buccaneer and cheese pirate that ever was, but how's his appetite for fightin'? I've knowed some citizens you'd think was starvin' for trouble get a bad case of dyspepsy the first dose of lead they had to take."

"He talks all spraddled out," said Cactus, " 'bout the rookuses he's been in. He claims to have saw the elephant and hearn the owl."

"I know," replied Bud, using the cow-puncher's expressive phrase of skepticism, "but it sounds to me!"

This conversation was held one night in camp while the other members of the band—eight in number—were sprawling around the fire, lingering over their supper. When Bud and Cactus ceased talking they heard Piggy's formidable voice holding forth to the others as usual while he was engaged in checking, though never satisfying, his ravening appetite.

"Wat's de use," he was saying, "of chasin' little red cowses and hosses 'round for t'ousands of miles? Dere ain't nuttin' in it. Gallopin' t'rough dese bushes and briers, and gettin' a t'irst dat a brewery couldn't put out, and missin' meals! Say! You know what I'd do if I was main finger of dis bunch? I'd stick up a train. I'd blow de express car and make hard dollars where you guys get wind. Youse makes me tired. Dis sook-cow kind of cheap sport gives me a pain."

Later on, a deputation waited on Bud. They stood on one leg, chewed mesquite twigs and circumlocuted, for they hated to hurt his feelings. Bud foresaw their business, and made it easy for them. Bigger risks and larger profits was what they wanted.

The suggestion of Piggy's about holding up a train had fired their imagination and increased their admiration for the dash and boldness of the instigator. They were such simple, artless, and custom-bound bush-rangers that they had never before thought of extending their habits beyond the running off of livestock and the shooting of such of their acquaintances as ventured to interfere.

Bud acted "on the level," agreeing to take a subordinate place in the gang until Black Eagle should have been given a trial as leader.

After a great deal of consultation, studying of timetables and discussion of the country's topography, the time and place for carrying out their new enterprise was decided upon. At that time there was a feedstuff famine in Mexico and a cattle famine in certain parts of the United States, and there was a brisk international trade. Much money was being shipped along the railroads that connected the two republics. It was agreed that the most promising place for the contemplated robbery was at Espina, a little station on the I. and G. N., about forty miles north of Laredo. The train stopped there one minute; the country around was wild and unsettled; the station consisted of but one house in which the agent lived.

Black Eagle's band set out, riding by night. Arriving in the vicinity of Espina they rested their horses all day in a thicket a few miles distant.

The train was due at Espina at 10:30 P.M. They could rob the train and be well over the Mexican border with their booty by daylight the next morning.

To do Black Eagle justice, he exhibited no signs of flinching from the responsible honors that had been conferred upon him.

He assigned his men to their respective posts with discretion, and coached them carefully as to their duties. On each side of the track four of the band were to lie concealed in the chaparral. Gotch-Ear Rodgers was to stick up the station agent. Bronco Charlie was to remain with the horses, holding them in readiness. At a spot where it was calculated the engine would be when the train stopped, Bud King was to lie hidden on one side, and Black Eagle himself on the other. The two would get the drop on the engineer and fireman, force them to descend and proceed to the rear. Then the express car would be looted, and the escape made. No one was to move until Black Eagle gave the signal by firing his revolver. The plan was perfect.

At ten minutes to train time every man was at his post, effectually concealed by the thick chaparral that grew almost to the rails. The night was dark and lowering, with a fine drizzle falling from the flying gulf clouds. Black Eagle crouched behind a bush within five yards of the track. Two six-shooters were belted around him. Occasionally he drew a large black bottle from his pocket and raised it to his mouth.

A star appeared far down the track which soon waxed into the headlight of the approaching train. It came on with an increasing roar; the engine bore down upon the ambushing desperadoes with a glare and a shriek like some avenging monster come to deliver them to justice. Black Eagle flattened himself upon the ground. The engine, contrary to their calculations, instead of stopping between him and Bud King's place of concealment, passed fully forty yards further before it came to a stand.

The bandit leader rose to his feet and peered around the bush. His men all lay quiet, awaiting the signal. Immediately opposite Black Eagle was a thing that drew his attention. Instead of being a regular passenger train it was a mixed one. Before him stood a box car, the door of which, by some means, had been left slightly open. Black Eagle went up to it and pushed the door farther open. An odor came forth—a damp, rancid, familiar, musty, intoxicating, beloved odor stirring strongly at old memories of happy days and travels. Black Eagle sniffed at the witching smell as the returned wanderer smells of the rose that twines his boyhood's cottage home. Nostalgia seized him. He put his hand inside. Excelsior—dry, springy, curly, soft, enticing, covered the floor. Outside the drizzle had turned to a chilling rain.

The train bell clanged. The bandit chief unbuckled his belt and cast it, with its revolvers, upon the ground. His spurs followed quickly, and his broad sombrero. Black Eagle was moulting. The train started with a rattling jerk. The ex-Terror of the Border scrambled into the box car and closed the door. Stretched luxuriously upon the excelsior, with the black bottle clasped closely to his breast, his eyes closed, and a foolish, happy smile upon his terrible features Chicken Ruggles started upon his return trip.

Undisturbed, with the band of desperate bandits lying motionless, awaiting the signal to attack, the train pulled out from Espina. As its speed increased, and the black masses of chaparral went whizzing past on either side, the express messenger, lighting his pipe, looked through his window and remarked, feelingly:

"What a jim-dandy place for a hold-up!"

THE TWO-GUN MAN
BY STEWART EDWARD WHITE
(Under a Texas Moon)

Stewart Edward White (1873–1946) has been acclaimed as the first author to write of the West on its own terms from its own point of view; his body of work, more fully than that of any other writer, represents all phases of pioneer America—Indian fighting, cattle ranching, logging, early exploration, gold rushes, land booms, and the exploits of mountain men, trappers, outlaws, and lawmen. A number of films have been made from his novels and stories, all silents except for Under a Texas Moon *and* Mystery Ranch *(1932); the latter title is based on a long, tense novelette entitled "The Killer." The most notable of the silents is* The Westerners *(1919), which was developed from White's first novel of the same title, published in 1901.*

I THE CATTLE RUSTLERS

Buck Johnson was American born, but with a black beard and a dignity of manner that had earned him the title of Señor. He had drifted into southeastern Arizona in the days of Cochise and Victorio and Geronimo. He had persisted, and so in time had come to control the water—and hence the grazing—of nearly all the Soda Springs Valley. His troubles were many, and his difficulties great. There were the ordinary problems of lean and dry years. There were also the extraordinary problems of devastating Apaches; rivals for early and ill-defined range rights—and cattle rustlers.

Señor Buck Johnson was a man of capacity, courage, directness of method, and perseverance. Especially the latter. Therefore he had survived to see the Apaches subdued, the range rights adjusted, his cattle increased to thousands, grazing the area of a principality. Now, all the energy and fire of his frontiersman's nature he had turned to wiping out the third uncertainty of an uncertain business. He found it a task of some magnitude.

For Señor Buck Johnson lived just north of that terra incognita filled with the mystery of a double chance of death from man or the flaming desert known as the Mexican border. There, by natural gravitation, gathered all the desperate characters of three States and two republics. He who rode into it took good care that no one should ride behind him, lived warily, slept light, and breathed deep when once he had again sighted the familiar peaks of Cochise's Stronghold. No one professed knowledge of those who dwelt therein. They moved, mysterious as the desert illusions that compassed them about. As you rode, the ranges of mountains visibly changed form, the monstrous, snaky, sealike growths of the cactus clutched at your stirrup, mock lakes sparkled and dissolved in the middle distance, the sun beat hot and merciless, the powdered dry alkali beat hotly and mercilessly back—and strange, grim men, swarthy, bearded, heavily armed, with red-rimmed unshifting eyes, rode silently out of the mists of illusion to look on you steadily, and then to ride silently back into the desert haze. They might be only the herders of the gaunt cattle, or again they might belong to the Lost Legion that peopled the country. All you could know was that of the men who entered in, but few returned.

Directly north of this unknown land you encountered parallel fences running across the country. They enclosed nothing, but offered a check to the cattle drifting toward the clutch of the renegades, and an obstacle to swift, dashing forays.

Of cattle-rustling there are various forms. The boldest consists quite simply of running off a bunch of stock, hustling it over the Mexican line, and there selling it to some of the big Sonora ranch owners. Generally this sort means war. Also are there subtler means, grading in skill from the rebranding through a wet blanket, through the crafty refashioning of a brand to the various methods of separating the cow from her unbranded calf. In the course of his task Señor Buck Johnson would have to do with them all, but at present he existed in a state of warfare, fighting an enemy who stole as the Indians used to steal.

Already he had fought two pitched battles, and had won them both. His cattle increased, and he became rich. Nevertheless he knew that constantly his resources were being drained. Time and again he and his new Texas foreman, Jed Parker, had followed the trail of a stampeded bunch of twenty or thirty, followed them on down through the Soda Springs Valley to the cut drift fences, there to abandon them. For, as yet, an armed force would be needed to penetrate the borderland. Once he and his men had experienced the glory of a night pursuit. Then, at the drift fences, he had fought one of his battles. But it was impossible adequately to patrol all parts of a range bigger than some Eastern States.

Buck Johnson did his best, but it was like stopping with sand the innumerable little leaks of a dam. Did his riders watch toward the Chiricahuas, then a score of beef steers disappeared from Grant's Pass forty miles away. Pursuit here meant leaving cattle unguarded there. It was useless, and the Señor soon perceived that sooner or later he must strike in offence.

For this purpose he began slowly to strengthen the forces of his riders. Men were coming in from Texas. They were good men, addicted to the grass-rope, the double cinch, and the ox-bow stirrup. Señor Johnson wanted men who could shoot, and he got them.

"Jed," said Señor Johnson to his foreman, "the next son of a gun that rustles any of our cows is sure loading himself full of trouble. We'll hit his trail and will stay with it, and we'll reach his cattle-rustling conscience with a rope."

So it came about that a little army crossed the drift fences and entered the border country. Two days later it came out, and mighty pleased to be able to do so. The rope had not been used.

The reason for the defeat was quite simple. The thief had run his cattle through the lava beds where the trail at once became difficult to follow. This delayed the pursuing party; they ran out of water, and, as there was among them not one man well enough acquainted with the country to know where to find more, they had to return.

"No use, Buck," said Jed. "We'd any of us come in on a gun play, but we can't buck the desert. We'll have to get someone who knows the country."

"That's all right—but where?" queried Johnson.

"There's Pereza," suggested Parker. "It's the only town down near that country."

"Might get someone there," agreed the Señor.

Next day he rode away in search of a guide. The third evening he was back again, much discouraged.

"The country's no good," he explained. "The regular inhabitants 're a set of Mexican bums and old soaks. The cowmen's all from north and don't know nothing more than we do. I found lots who claimed to know that country, but when I told 'em what I wanted they shied like a colt. I couldn't hire 'em, for no money, to go down in that country. They ain't got the nerve. I took two days to her, too, and rode out to a ranch where they said a man lived who knew all about it down there. Nary riffle. Man looked all right, but his tail went down like the rest when I told him what we wanted. Seemed plumb scairt to death. Says he lives too close to the gang. Says they'd wipe him out sure if he done it. Seemed plumb *scairt*." Buck Johnson grinned. "I told him so and he got hosstyle right off. Didn't seem no ways scairt of me. I don't know what's the matter with that outfit down there. They're plumb terrorised."

That night a bunch of steers was stolen from the very corrals of the home ranch. The home ranch was far north, near Fort Sherman itself, and so had always been considered immune from attack. Consequently these steers were very fine ones.

For the first time Buck Johnson lost his head and his dignity. He ordered the horses.

"I'm going to follow that —— —— into Sonora," he shouted to Jed Parker. "This thing's got to stop!"

"You can't make her, Buck," objected the foreman. "You'll get held up by the desert, and, if that don't finish you, they'll tangle you up in all those little mountains down there, and ambush you, and massacre you. You know it damn well."

"I don't give a ——," exploded Señor Johnson, "if they do. No man can slap my face and not get a run for it."

Jed Parker communed with himself.

"Señor," said he, at last, "it's no good; you can't do it. You got to have a guide. You wait three days and I'll get you one."

"You can't do it," insisted the Señor. "I tried every man in the district."

"Will you wait three days?" repeated the foreman.

Johnson pulled loose his latigo. His first anger had cooled.

"All right," he agreed, "and you can say for me that I'll pay five thousand dollars in gold and give all the men and horses he needs to the man who has the nerve to get back that bunch of cattle, and bring in the man who rustled them. I'll sure make this a test case."

So Jed Parker set out to discover his man with nerve.

II THE MAN WITH NERVE

At about ten o'clock of the Fourth of July a rider topped the summit of the last swell of land, and loped his animal down into the single street of Pereza. The buildings on either side were flat-roofed and coated with plaster. Over the sidewalks extended wooden awnings, beneath which opened very wide doors into the coolness of saloons. Each of these places ran a bar, and also games of roulette, faro, craps, and stud poker. Even this early in the morning every game was patronised.

The day was already hot with the dry, breathless, but exhilarating, heat of the desert. A throng of men idling at the edge of the sidewalks, jostling up and down their centre, or eddying into the places of amusement, acknowledged the power of summer by loosening their collars, carrying their coats on their arms. They were as yet busily engaged in recognising acquaintances. Later they would drink freely and gamble, and perhaps fight. Toward all but those whom they recognised they preserved an attitude of potential suspicion, for here were gathered the "bad men" of the border countries. A certain jealousy or touchy egotism lest the other man be considered quicker on the trigger, bolder, more aggressive than himself, kept each strung to tension. An occasional shot attracted little notice. Men in the cow-countries shoot as casually as we strike matches, and some subtle instinct told them that the reports were harmless.

As the rider entered the one street, however, a more definite cause of excitement drew the loose population toward the centre of the road. Immediately their mass blotted out what had interested them. Curiosity attracted the saunterers; then in turn the frequenters of the bars and gambling games. In a very few moments the barkeepers, gamblers, and look-out men, held aloof only by the necessities of their calling, alone of all the population of Pereza were not included in the newly-formed ring.

The stranger pushed his horse resolutely to the outer edge of the crowd where, from his point of vantage, he could easily overlook their heads. He was a quiet-appearing young fellow, rather neatly dressed in the border costume, rode a "centre fire," or single-cinch, saddle, and wore no chaps. He was what is known as a "two-gun man": that is to say, he wore a heavy Colt's revolver on either hip. The fact that the lower ends of his holsters were tied down, in order to facilitate the easy withdrawal of the revolvers, seemed to indicate that he expected to use them. He had furthermore a quiet grey eye, with the glint of steel that bore out the inference of the tied holsters.

The newcomer dropped his reins on his pony's neck, eased himself to an attitude of attention, and looked down gravely on what was taking place.

He saw over the heads of the bystanders a tall, muscular, wild-eyed man, hatless, his hair rumpled into staring confusion, his right sleeve rolled to his shoulder, a wicked-looking nine-inch knife in his hand, and a red bandana handkerchief hanging by one corner from his teeth.

"What's biting the locoed stranger?" the young man inquired of his neighbour.

The other frowned at him darkly.

"Dares anyone to take the other end of that handkerchief in his teeth, and fight it out without letting go."

"Nice joyful proposition," commented the young man.

He settled himself to closer attention. The wild-eyed man was talking rapidly. What he said cannot be printed here. Mainly was it derogatory of the southern countries. Shortly it became boastful of the northern, and then of the man who uttered it. He swaggered up and down, becoming always the more insolent as his challenge remained untaken.

"Why don't you take him up?" inquired the young man, after a moment.

"Not me!" negatived the other vigorously. "I'll go yore little old gunfight to a finish, but I don't want any cold steel in mine. Ugh! it gives me the shivers. It's a reg'lar Mexican trick! With a gun it's down and out, but this knife work is too slow and searchin'."

The newcomer said nothing, but fixed his eye again on the raging man with the knife.

"Don't you reckon he's bluffing?" he inquired.

"Not any!" denied the other with emphasis. "He's jest drunk enough to be crazy mad."

The newcomer shrugged his shoulders and cast his glance searchingly over the fringe of the crowd. It rested on a Mexican.

"Hi, Tony! come here," he called.

The Mexican approached, flashing his white teeth.

"Here," said the stranger, "lend me your knife a minute."

The Mexican, anticipating sport of his own peculiar kind, obeyed with alacrity.

"You fellows make me tired," observed the stranger, dismounting. "He's got the whole townful of you bluffed to a standstill. Damn if I don't try his little game."

He hung his coat on his saddle, shouldered his way through the press, which parted for him readily, and picked up the other corner of the handkerchief.

"Now, you mangy son of a gun," said he.

III THE AGREEMENT

Jed Parker straightened his back, rolled up the bandana handkerchief, and thrust it into his pocket, hit flat with his hand the touselled mass of his hair, and thrust the long hunting knife into its sheath.

"You're the man I want," said he.

Instantly the two-gun man had jerked loose his weapons and was covering the foreman.

"*Am* I!" he snarled.

"Not jest that way," explained Parker. "My gun is on my hoss, and you can have this old toadsticker if you want it. I been looking for you and took this way of finding you. Now, let's go talk."

The stranger looked him in the eye for nearly a half minute without lowering his revolvers.

"I go with you," said he briefly, at last.

But the crowd, missing the purport, and in fact the very occurrence of this colloquy, did not understand. It thought the bluff had been called, and naturally, finding harmless what had intimidated it, gave way to an exasperated impulse to get even.

"You — — — bluffer!" shouted a voice, "don't you think you can run any such ranikaboo here!"

Jed Parker turned humorously to his companion.

"Do we get that talk?" he inquired gently.

For answer the two-gun man turned and walked steadily in the direction of the man who had shouted. The latter's hand strayed uncertainly toward his own weapon, but the movement paused when the stranger's clear, steel eye rested on it.

"This gentleman," pointed out the two-gun man softly, "is an old friend of mine. Don't you get to calling of him names."

His eye swept the bystanders calmly.

"Come on, Jack," said he, addressing Parker.

On the outskirts he encountered the Mexican from whom he had borrowed the knife.

"Here, Tony," said he with a slight laugh, "here's a *peso*. You'll find your knife back there where I had to drop her."

He entered a saloon, nodded to the proprietor, and led the way through it to a box-like room containing a board table and two chairs.

"Make good," he commanded briefly.

"I'm looking for a man with nerve," explained Parker, with equal succinctness. "You're the man."

"Well?"

"Do you know the country south of here?"

The stranger's eyes narrowed.

"Proceed," said he.

"I'm foreman of the Lazy Y of Soda Springs Valley range," explained Parker. "I'm looking for a man with sand enough and *sabe* of the country enough to lead a posse after cattle-rustlers into the border country."

"I live in this country," admitted the stranger.

"So do plenty of others, but their eyes stick out like two raw oysters when you mention the border country. Will you tackle it?"

"What's the proposition?"

"Come and see the old man. He'll put it to you."

They mounted their horses and rode the rest of the day. The desert compassed them about, marvellously changing shape and colour, and every character, with all the noiselessness of phantasmagoria. At evening the desert stars shone steady and unwinking, like the flames of candles. By moonrise they came to the home ranch.

The buildings and corrals lay dark and silent against the moonlight that made of the plain a sea of mist. The two men unsaddled their horses and turned them loose in the wire-fenced "pasture," the necessary noises of their movements sounding sharp and clear against the velvet hush of the night. After a moment they walked stiffly past the sheds and cook shanty, past the men's bunk houses, and the tall windmill silhouetted against the sky, to the main building of the home ranch under its great cottonwoods. There a light still burned, for this was the third day, and Buck Johnson awaited his foreman.

Jed Parker pushed in without ceremony.

"Here's your man, Buck," said he.

The stranger had stepped inside and carefully closed the door behind him. The lamplight threw into relief the bold, free lines of his face, the details of his costume powdered thick with alkali, the shiny butts of the two guns in their open holsters tied at the bottom. Equally it defined the resolute countenance of Buck Johnson turned up in inquiry. The two men examined each other—and liked each other at once.

"How are you," greeted the cattleman.

"Good-evening," responded the stranger.

"Sit down," invited Buck Johnson.

The stranger perched gingerly on the edge of a chair, with an appearance less of embarrassment than of habitual alertness.

"You'll take the job?" inquired the Señor.

"I haven't heard what it is," replied the stranger.

"Parker here——?"

"Said you'd explain."

"Very well," said Buck Johnson. He paused a moment, collecting his thoughts. "There's too much cattle-rustling here. I'm going to stop it. I've got good men here ready to take the job, but no one who knows the country south. Three days ago I had a bunch of cattle stolen right here from the home-ranch corrals, and by one man, at that. It wasn't much of a bunch—about twenty head—but I'm going to make a starter right here, and now. I'm going to get that bunch back, and the man who stole them, if I have to go to hell to do it. And I'm going to do the same with every case of rustling that comes up from now on. I don't care if it's only one cow, I'm going to get it back—every trip. Now, I want to know if you'll lead a posse down into the south country and bring out that last bunch, and the man who rustled them?"

"I don't know——" hesitated the stranger.

"I offer you five thousand dollars in gold if you'll bring back those cows and the man who stole 'em," repeated Buck Johnson. "And I'll give you all the horses and men you think you need."

"I'll do it," replied the two-gun man promptly.

"Good!" cried Buck Johnson, "and you better start to-morrow."

"I shall start to-night—right now."

"Better yet. How many men do you want, and grub for how long?"

"I'll play her a lone hand."

"Alone!" exclaimed Johnson, his confidence visibly cooling. "Alone! Do you think you can make her?"

"I'll be back with those cattle in not more than ten days."

"And the man," supplemented the Señor.

"And the man. What's more, I want that money here when I come in. I don't aim to stay in this country over night."

A grin overspread Buck Johnson's countenance. He understood.

"Climate not healthy for you?" he hazarded. "I guess you'd be safe enough all right with us. But suit yourself. The money will be here."

"That's agreed?" insisted the two-gun man.

"Sure."

"I want a fresh horse—I'll leave mine—he's a good one. I want a little grub."

"All right. Parker'll fit you out."

The stranger rose.

"I'll see you in about ten days."

"Good luck," Señor Buck Johnson wished him.

IV THE ACCOMPLISHMENT

The next morning Buck Johnson took a trip down into the "pasture" of five hundred wire-fenced acres.

"He means business," he confided to Jed Parker, on his return. "That cavallo of his is a heap sight better than the Shorty horse we let him take. Jed, you found your man with nerve, all right. How did you do it?"

The two settled down to wait, if not with confidence, at least with interest. Sometimes, remembering the desperate character of the outlaws, their fierce distrust of any intruder, the wildness of the country, Buck Johnson and his foreman inclined to the belief that the stranger had undertaken a task beyond the powers of any one man. Again, remembering the stranger's cool grey eye, the poise of his demeanour, the quickness of his movements, and the two guns with tied holsters to permit of easy withdrawal, they were almost persuaded that he might win.

"He's one of those long-chance fellows," surmised Jed. "He likes excitement. I see that by the way he takes up with my knife play. He'd rather leave his hide on the fence than stay in the corral."

"Well, he's all right," replied Señor Buck Johnson, "and if he ever gets back, which same I'm some doubtful of, his dinero 'll be here for him."

In pursuance of this he rode in to Willets, where shortly the overland train brought him from Tucson the five thousand dollars in double eagles.

In the meantime the regular life of the ranch went on. Each morning Sang, the Chinese cook, rang the great bell, summoning the men. They ate, and then caught up the saddle horses for the day, turning those not wanted from the corral into the pasture. Shortly they jingled away in different directions, two by two, on the slow Spanish trot of the cow-puncher. All day long thus they would ride, without food or water for man or beast, looking the range, identifying the stock, branding the young calves, examining generally into the state of affairs, gazing always with grave eyes on the magnificent, flaming, changing, beautiful, dreadful desert of the Arizona plains. At evening, when the coloured atmosphere, catching the last glow, threw across the Chiricahuas its veil of mystery, they jingled in again, two by two, untired, unhasting, the glory of the desert in their deep-set, steady eyes.

And all day long, while they were absent, the cattle, too, made their pilgrimage, straggling in singly, in pairs, in bunches, in long files, leisurely, ruminantly, without haste. There, at the long troughs filled by the windmill or the blindfolded pump mule, they drank, then filed away again into the mists of the desert. And Señor Buck Johnson, or his foreman, Parker, examined them for their condition, noting the increase, remarking the strays from another range. Later, perhaps, they, too, rode abroad. The same thing happened at nine other ranches from five to ten miles apart, where dwelt other fierce, silent men all under the authority of Buck Johnson.

And when night fell, and the topaz and violet and saffron and amethyst and mauve and lilac had faded suddenly from the Chiricahuas, like a veil that has been rent, and the ramparts had become slate-grey and then black—the soft-breathed night wandered here and there over the desert, and the land fell under an enchantment even stranger than the day's.

So the days went by, wonderful, fashioning the ways and the characters of men. Seven passed. Buck Johnson and his foreman began to look for the stranger. Eight, they began to speculate. Nine, they doubted. On the tenth they gave him up—and he came.

They knew him first by the soft lowing of cattle. Jed Parker, dazzled by the lamp, peered out from the door, and made him out dimly turning the animals into the corral. A moment later his pony's hoofs impacted softly on the baked earth, he dropped from the saddle and entered the room.

"I'm late," said he briefly, glancing at the clock, which indicated ten; "but I'm here."

His manner was quick and sharp, almost breathless, as though he had been running.

"Your cattle are in the corral: all of them. Have you the money?"

"I have the money here," replied Buck Johnson, laying his hand against a drawer, "and it's ready for you when you've earned it. I don't care so much for the cattle. What I wanted is the man who stole them. Did you bring him?"

"Yes, I brought him," said the stranger. "Let's see that money."

Buck Johnson threw open the drawer, and drew from it the heavy canvas sack.

"It's here. Now bring in your prisoner."

The two-gun man seemed suddenly to loom large in the doorway. The muzzles of his revolvers covered the two before him. His speech came short and sharp.

"I told you I'd bring back the cows and the one who rustled them," he snapped. "I've never lied to a man yet. Your stock is in the corral. I'll trouble you for that five thousand. I'm the man who stole your cattle!"

BACK TO GOD'S COUNTRY
BY JAMES OLIVER CURWOOD
(Back to God's Country)

Like Jack London and Rex Beach, James Oliver Curwood (1879–1927) wrote often and extremely well of Alaska and the Canadian Northwest; "Back to God's Country" is among the best of his shorter works of adventure set in the vast reaches of that part of the world. Literally scores of silent and sound films have been adapted from his novels and short stories, among the best known of which are The Valley of Silent Men *(1922), based on the novel of the same title;* Northern Frontier *(1935), adapted from the short story "Four Minutes Late";* Call of the Yukon *(1938), taken from the novel* Swift Lightning; *and* The River's End *(two versions, 1930 and 1940), from the novel of the same title. Both screen versions of* River's End *are excellent; the earlier stars Charles Bickford and was directed by Michael Curtiz, the latter features Dennis Morgan and was directed by Ray Enright.*

When Shan Tung, the long-cued Chinaman from Vancouver, started up the Frazer River in the old days when the Telegraph Trail and the headwaters of the Peace were the Meccas of half the gold-hunting population of British Columbia, he did not foresee tragedy ahead of him. He was a clever man, was Shan Tung, a cha-sukeed, a very devil in the collecting of gold, and far-seeing. But he could not look forty years into the future, and when Shan Tung set off into the north, that winter, he was in reality touching fire to the end of a fuse that was to burn through four decades before the explosion came.

With Shan Tung went Tao, a Great Dane. The Chinaman had picked him up somewhere on the coast and had trained him as one trains a horse. Tao was the biggest dog ever seen about the Height of Land, the most powerful, and at times the most terrible. Of two things Shan Tung was enormously proud in his silent and mysterious oriental way—of Tao, the dog, and of his long, shining cue which fell to the crook of his knees when he let it down. It had been the longest cue in Vancouver, and therefore it was the longest cue in British Columbia. The cue and the dog formed the combination which set the forty-year fuse of romance and tragedy burning.

Shan Tung started for the El Dorados early in the winter, and Tao alone pulled his sledge and outfit. It was no more than an ordinary task for the monstrous Great Dane, and Shan Tung subserviently but with hidden triumph passed outfit after outfit exhausted by the way. He had reached Copper Creek Camp, which was boiling and frothing with the excitement of gold-maddened men, and was congratulating himself that he would soon be at the camps west of the Peace, when the thing happened. A drunken Irishman, filled with a grim and unfortunate sense of humor, spotted Shan Tung's wonderful cue and coveted it. Wherefore there followed a bit of excitement in which Shan Tung passed into his empyrean home with a bullet through his heart, and the drunken Irishman was strung up for his misdeed fifteen minutes later. Tao, the Great Dane, was taken by the leader of the men who pulled on the rope.

Tao's new master was a "drifter," and as he drifted, his face was always set to the north, until at last a new humor struck him and he turned eastward to the Mackenzie. As the seasons passed, Tao found mates along the way and left a string of his progeny behind him, and he had new masters, one after another, until he was grown old and his muzzle was turning gray. And never did one of these masters turn south with him. Always it was north, north with the white man first, north with the Cree, and then with the Chippewayan, until in the end the dog born in a Vancouver kennel died in an Eskimo igloo on the Great Bear. But the breed of the Great Dane lived on. Here and there, as the years passed, one would find among the Eskimo tracedogs, a grizzled-haired, powerful-jawed giant that was alien to the arctic stock, and in these occasional aliens ran the blood of Tao, the Dane.

Forty years, more or less, after Shan Tung lost his life and his cue at Copper Creek Camp, there was born on a firth of Coronation Gulf a dog who was named Wapi, which means "the Walrus." Wapi, at full growth, was a throwback of more than forty dog generations. He was nearly as large as his forefather, Tao. His fangs were an inch in length, his great jaws could crack the thigh-bone of a caribou, and from the beginning the hands of men and the fangs of beasts were against him. Almost from the day of his birth until this winter of his fourth year, life for Wapi had been an unceasing fight for existence. He was maya-tisew—bad with the badness of a devil. His reputation had gone from master to master and from igloo to igloo; women and children were afraid of him, and men always spoke to him with the club or the lash in their hands. He was hated and feared, and yet because he could run down a barren-land caribou and kill it within a mile, and would hold a big white bear at bay until the hunters came, he was not sacrificed to this hate and fear. A hundred whips and clubs and a hundred pairs of hands were against him between Cape Perry and the crown of Franklin Bay—and the fangs of twice as many dogs.

The dogs were responsible. Quick-tempered, clannish with the savage brotherhood of the wolves, treacherous, jealous of leadership, and with the older instincts of the dog dead within them, their merciless feud with what they regarded as an interloper of another breed put the devil heart in Wapi. In all the gray and desolate sweep of his world he had no friend. The heritage of Tao, his forefather, had fallen upon him, and he was an alien in a land of strangers. As the dogs and the men and women and children hated him, so he hated them. He hated the sight and smell of the round-faced, blear-eyed creatures who were his master, yet he obeyed them, sullenly, watchfully, with his lips wrinkled warningly over fangs which had twice torn out the life of white bears. Twenty times he had killed other dogs. He had fought them singly, and in pairs, and in packs. His giant body bore the scars of a hundred wounds. He had been clubbed until a part of his body was deformed and he traveled with a limp. He kept to himself even in the mating season. And all this because Wapi, the Walrus, forty years removed from the Great Dane of Vancouver, was a white man's dog.

Stirring restlessly within him, sometimes coming to him in dreams and sometimes in a great and unfulfilled yearning, Wapi felt vaguely the strange call of his forefathers. It was impossible for him to understand. It was impossible for him to know what it meant. And yet he did know that somewhere there was something for which he was seeking and which he never found. The desire and the questing came to him most compellingly in the long winter filled with its eternal starlight, when the maddening yap, yap, yap of the little white foxes, the barking of the dogs, and the Eskimo chatter oppressed him like the voices of haunting ghosts. In these long months, filled with the horror of the arctic night, the spirit of Tao whispered within him that somewhere there was light and sun, that somewhere there was warmth and flowers, and running streams, and voices he could understand, and things he could love. And then Wapi would whine, and perhaps the whine would bring him the blow of a club, or the lash of a whip, or an Eskimo threat, or the menace of an Eskimo dog's snarl. Of the latter Wapi was unafraid. With a snap of his jaws, he could break the back of any other dog on Franklin Bay.

Such was Wapi, the Walrus, when for two sacks of flour, some tobacco, and a bale of cloth he became the property of Blake, the uta-wawe-yinew, the trader in seals, whalebone—and women. On this day Wapi's soul took its flight back through the space of forty years. For Blake was white, which is to say that at one time or another he had been white. His skin and his appearance did not betray how black he had turned inside and Wapi's brute soul cried out to him, telling him how he had waited and watched for this master he knew would come, how he would fight for him, how he wanted to lie down and put his great head on the white man's feet in token of his fealty. But Wapi's bloodshot eyes and battle-scarred face failed to reveal what was in him, and Blake—following the instructions of those who should know—ruled him from the beginning with a club that was more brutal than the club of the Eskimo.

For three months Wapi had been the property of Blake, and it was now the dead of a long and sunless arctic night. Blake's cabin, built of ship timber and veneered with blocks of ice, was built in the face of a deep pit that sheltered it from wind and storm. To this cabin came the Nanatalmutes from the east, and the Kogmollocks from the west, bartering their furs and whalebone and seal-oil for the things Blake gave in exchange, and adding women to their wares whenever Blake announced a demand. The demand had been excellent this winter. Over in Darnley Bay, thirty miles across the headland, was the whaler *Harpoon* frozen up for the winter with a crew of thirty men, and straight out from the face of his igloo cabin, less than a mile away, was the *Flying Moon* with a crew of twenty more. It was Blake's business to wait and watch like a hawk for such opportunities as there, and tonight—his watch pointed to the hour of twelve, midnight—he was sitting in the light of a sputtering seal-oil lamp adding up figures which told him that his winter, only half gone, had already been an enormously profitable one.

"If the Mounted Police over at Herschel only knew," he chuckled. "Uppy, if they did, they'd have an outfit after us in twenty-four hours."

Oopi, his Eskimo right-hand man, had learned to understand English, and he nodded, his moon-face split by a wide and enigmatic grin. In his way, "Uppy" was as clever as Shan Tung had been in his.

And Blake added, "We've sold every fur and every pound of bone and oil, and we've forty Upisk wives to our credit at fifty dollars apiece."

Uppy's grin became larger, and his throat was filled with an exultant rattle. In the matter of the Upisk wives he knew that he stood ace-high.

"Never," said Blake, "has our wife-by-the-month business been so good. If it wasn't for Captain Rydal and his love-affair, we'd take a vacation and go hunting."

He turned, facing the Eskimo, and the yellow flame of the lamp lit up his face. It was the face of a remarkable man. A black beard concealed much of its cruelty and its cunning, a beard as carefully Vandycked as though Blake sat in a professional chair two thousand miles south, but the beard could not hide the almost inhuman hardness of the eyes. There was a glittering light in them as he looked at the Eskimo. "Did you see her today, Uppy? Of course you did. My Gawd, if a woman could ever tempt me, she could! And Rydal is going to have her. Unless I miss my guess, there's going to be money in it for us—a lot of it. The funny part of it is, Rydal's got to get rid of her husband. And how's he going to do it, Uppy? Eh? Answer me that. How's he going to do it?"

In a hole he had dug for himself in the drifted snow under a huge scarp of ice a hundred yards from the igloo cabin lay Wapi. His bed was red with the stain of blood, and a trail of blood led from the cabin to the place where he had hidden himself. Not many hours ago, when by God's sun it should have been day, he had turned at last on a teasing, snarling, back-biting little kiskanuk of a dog and had killed it. And Blake and Uppy had beaten him until he was almost dead.

It was not of the beating that Wapi was thinking as he lay in his wallow. He was thinking of the fur-clad figure that had come between Blake's club and his body, of the moment when for the first time in his life he had seen the face of a white woman. She had stopped Blake's club. He had heard her voice. She had bent over him, and she would have put her hand on him if his master had not dragged her back with a cry of warning. She had gone into the cabin then, and he had dragged himself away.

Since then a new and thrilling flame had burned in him. For a time his senses had been dazed by his punishment, but now every instinct in him was like a living wire. Slowly he pulled himself from his retreat and sat down on his haunches. His gray muzzle was pointed to the sky. The same stars were there, burning in cold, white points of flame as they had burned week after week in the maddening monotony of the long nights near the pole. They were like a million pitiless eyes, never blinking, always watching, things of life and fire, and yet dead. And at those eyes, the little white foxes yapped so incessantly that the sound of it drove men mad. They were yapping now. They were never still. And with their yapping came the droning, hissing monotone of the aurora, like the song of a vast piece of mechanism in the still farther north. Toward this Wapi turned his bruised and beaten head. Out there, just beyond the ghostly pale of vision, was the ship. Fifty times he had slunk out and around it, cautiously as the foxes themselves. He had caught its smells and its sounds; he had come near enough to hear the voices of men, and those voices were like the voice of Blake, his master. Therefore, he had never gone nearer.

There was a change in him now. His big pads fell noiselessly as he slunk back to the cabin and sniffed for a scent in the snow. He found it. It was the trail of the white woman. His blood tingled again, as it had tingled when her face bent over him and her hand reached out, and in his soul there rose up the ghost of Tao to whip him on. He followed the woman's footprints slowly, stopping now and then to listen, and each moment the spirit in him grew more insistent, and he whined up at the stars. At last he saw the ship, a wraithlike thing in its piled-up bed of ice, and he stopped. This was his deadline. He had never gone nearer. But tonight—if any one period could be called night—he went on.

It was the hour of sleep, and there was no sound aboard. The foxes, never tiring of their infuriating sport, were yapping at the ship. They barked faster and louder when they caught the scent of Wapi, and as he approached, they drifted farther away. The scent of the woman's trail led up the wide bridge of ice, and Wapi followed this as he would have followed a road, until he found himself all at once on the deck of the *Flying Moon*. For a space he was startled. His long fangs bared themselves at the shadows cast by the stars. Then he saw ahead of him a narrow ribbon of yellow light. Toward this Wapi sniffed out, step by step, the footprints of the woman. When he stopped again, his muzzle was at the narrow crack through which came the glimmer of light.

It was the door of a deck-house veneered like an igloo with snow and ice to protect it from cold and wind. It was, perhaps, half an inch ajar, and through that aperture Wapi drank the warm, sweet perfume of the woman. With it he caught also the smell of a man. But in him the woman scent submerged all else. Overwhelmed by it, he stood trembling, not daring to move, every inch of him thrilled by a vast and mysterious yearning. He was no longer Wapi, the Walrus; Wapi, the Killer. Tao was there. And it may be that the spirit of Shan Tung was there. For after forty years the change had come, and Wapi, as he stood at the woman's door, was just dog,—a white man's dog— again the dog of the Vancouver kennel—the dog of a white man's world.

He thrust open the door with his nose. He slunk in, so silently that he was not heard. The cabin was lighted. In a bed lay a white-faced, hollow-cheeked man—awake. On a low stool at his side sat a woman. The light of the lamp hanging from above warmed with gold fires the thick and radiant mass of her hair. She was leaning over the sick man. One slim, white hand was stroking his face gently, and she was speaking to him in a voice so sweet and soft that it stirred like wonderful music in Wapi's warped and beaten soul. And then, with a great sigh, he flopped down, an abject slave, on the edge of her dress.

With a startled cry the woman turned. For a moment she stared at the great beast wide-eyed, then there came slowly into her face recognition and understanding. "Why, it's the dog Blake whipped so terribly," she gasped. "Peter, it's—it's Wapi!"

For the first time Wapi felt the caress of a woman's hand, soft, gentle, pitying, and out of him there came a wimpering sound that was almost a sob.

"It's the dog—he whipped," she repeated, and, then, if Wapi could have understood, he would have noted the tense pallor of her lovely face and the look of a great fear that was away back in the staring blue depths of her eyes.

From his pillow Peter Keith had seen the look of fear and the paleness of her cheeks, but he was a long way from guessing the truth. Yet he thought he knew. For days—yes, for weeks—there had been that growing fear in her eyes. He had seen her mighty fight to hide it from him. And he thought he understood.

"I know it has been a terrible winter for you, dear," he had said to her many times. "But you mustn't worry so much about me. I'll be on my feet again—soon." He had always emphasized that. "I'll be on my feet again soon!"

Once, in the breaking terror of her heart, she had almost told him the truth. Afterward she had thanked God for giving her the strength to keep it back. It was day—for they spoke in terms of day and night—when Rydal, half drunk, had dragged her into his cabin, and she had fought him until her hair was down about her in tangled confusion—and she had told Peter that it was the wind. After that, instead of evading him, she had played Rydal with her wits, while praying to God for help. It was impossible to tell Peter. He had aged steadily and terribly in the last two weeks. His eyes were sunken into deep pits. His blond hair was turning gray over the temples. His cheeks were hollowed, and there was a different sort of luster in his eyes. He looked fifty instead of thirty-five. Her heart bled in its agony. She loved Peter with a wonderful love.

The truth! If she told him that! She could see Peter rising up out of his bed like a ghost. It would kill him. If he could have seen Rydal—only an hour before—stopping her out on the deck, taking her in his arms, and kissing her until his drunken breath and his beard sickened her! And if he could have heard what Rydal had said! She shuddered. And suddenly she dropped down on her knees beside Wapi and took his great head in her arms, unafraid of him—and glad that he had come.

Then she turned to Peter. "I'm going ashore to see Blake again—now," she said. "Wapi will go with me, and I won't be afraid. I insist that I am right, so please don't object any more, Peter dear."

She bent over and kissed him, and then in spite of his protest, put on her fur coat and hood, and stood for a moment smiling down at him. The fear was gone out of her eyes now. It was impossible for him not to smile at her loveliness. He had always been proud of that. He reached up a thin hand and plucked tenderly at the shining little tendrils of gold that crept out from under her hood.

"I wish you wouldn't, dear," he pleaded.

How pathetically white, and thin, and weak he was! She kissed him again and turned quickly to hide the mist in her eyes. At the door she blew him a kiss from the tip of her big fur mitten, and as she went out she heard him say in the thin, strange voice that was so unlike the old Peter:

"Don't be long, Dolores."

She stood silently for a few moments to make sure that no one would see her. Then she moved swiftly to the ice bridge and out into the star-lighted ghostliness of the night. Wapi followed close behind her, and dropping a hand to her side she called softly to him. In an instant Wapi's muzzle was against her mitten, and his great body quivered with joy at her direct speech to him. She saw the response in his red eyes and stopped to stroke him with both mittened hands, and over and over again she spoke his name. "Wapi—Wapi—Wapi." He whined. She could feel him under her touch as if alive with an electrical force. Her eyes shone. In the white starlight there was a new emotion in her face. She had found a friend, the one friend she and Peter had, and it made her braver.

At no time had she actually been afraid—for herself. It was for Peter. And she was not afraid now. Her cheeks flushed with exertion and her breath came quickly as she neared Blake's cabin. Twice she had made excuses to go ashore—just because she was curious, she had said—and she believed that she had measured up Blake pretty well. It was a case in which her woman's intuition had failed her miserably. She was amazed that such a man had marooned himself voluntarily on the arctic coast. She did not, of course, understand his business—entirely. She thought him simply a trader. And he was unlike any man aboard ship. By his carefully clipped beard, his calm, cold manner of speech, and the unusual correctness with which he used his words she was convinced that at some time or another he had been part of what she mentally thought of as "an entirely different environment." She was right. There was a time when London and New York would have given much to lay their hands on the man who now called himself Blake.

Dolores, excited by the conviction that Blake would help her when he heard her story, still did not lose her caution. Rydal had given her another twenty-four hours, and that was all. In those twenty-four hours she must fight out their salvation, her own and Peter's. If Blake should fail——

Fifty paces from his cabin she stopped, slipped the big fur mitten from her right hand and unbuttoned her coat so that she could quickly and easily reach an inside pocket in which was Peter's revolver. She smiled just a bit grimly, as her fingers touched the cold steel. It was to be her last resort. And she was thinking in that flash of the days "back home" when she was counted the best revolver shot at the Piping Rock. She could beat Peter, and Peter was good. Her fingers twined a bit fondly about the pearl-handled thing in her pocket. The last resort—and from the first it had given her courage to keep the truth from Peter!

She knocked at the heavy door of the igloo cabin. Blake was still up, and when he opened it, he stared at her in wide-eyed amazement. Wapi hung outside when Dolores entered, and the door closed.

"I know you think it strange for me to come at this hour," she apologized, "but in this terrible gloom I've lost all count of hours. They have no significance for me any more. And I wanted to see you—alone."

She emphasized the word. And as she spoke, she loosened her coat and threw back her hood, so that the glow of the lamp lit up the ruffled mass of gold the hood had covered. She sat down without waiting for an invitation, and Blake sat down opposite her with a narrow table between them. Her face was flushed with cold and wind as she looked at him. Her eyes were blue with the blue of a steady flame, and they met his own squarely. She was not nervous. Nor was she afraid.

"Perhaps you can guess—why I have come?" she asked.

He was appraising her almost startling beauty with the lamp glow flooding down on her. For a moment he hesitated; then he nodded, looking at her steadily. "Yes, I think I know," he said quietly. "It's Captain Rydal. In fact, I'm quite positive. It's an unusual situation, you know. Have I guessed correctly?"

She nodded, drawing in her breath quickly and leaning a little toward him, wondering how much he knew and how he had come by it.

"A very unusual situation," he repeated. "There's nothing in the world that makes beasts out of men—most men—more quickly than an arctic night, Mrs. Keith. And they're all beasts out there—now—all except your husband, and he is contented because he possesses the one white woman aboard ship. It's putting it brutally plain, but it's the truth, isn't it? For the time being they're beasts, every man of the twenty, and you—pardon me!—are very beautiful. Rydal wants you, and the fact that your husband is dying——"

"He is not dying," she interrupted him fiercely. "He shall not die! If he did——"

"Do you love him?" There was no insult in Blake's quiet voice. He asked the question as if much depended on the answer, as if he must assure himself of that fact.

"Love him—my Peter? Yes!"

She leaned forward eagerly, gripping her hands in front of him on the table. She spoke swiftly, as if she must convince him before he asked her another question. Blake's eyes did not change. They had not changed for an instant. They were hard, and cold, and searching, unwarmed by her beauty, by the luster of her shining hair, by the touch of her breath as it came to him over the table.

"I have gone everywhere with him—everywhere," she began. "Peter writes books, you know, and we have gone into all sorts of places. We love it—both of us—this adventuring. We have been all through the country down there," she swept a hand to the south, "on dog sledges, in canoes, with snowshoes, and pack-trains. Then we hit on the idea of coming north on a whaler. You know, of course, Captain Rydal planned to return this autumn. The crew was rough, but we expected that. We expected to put up with a lot. But even before the ice shut us in, before this terrible night came, Rydal insulted me. I didn't dare tell Peter. I thought I could handle Rydal, that I could keep him in his place, and I knew that if I told Peter, he would kill the beast. And then the ice—and this night——" She choked.

Blake's eyes, gimleting to her soul, were shot with a sudden fire as he, too, leaned a little over the table. But his voice was unemotional as rock. It merely stated a fact. "That's why Captain Rydal allowed himself to be frozen in," he said. "He had plenty of time to get into the open channels, Mrs. Keith. But he wanted you. And to get you he knew he would have to lay over. And if he laid over, he knew that he would get you, for many things may happen in an arctic night. It shows the depth of the man's feelings, doesn't it? He is sacrificing a great deal to possess you, losing a great deal of time, and money, and all that. And when your husband dies———"

Her clenched little fist struck the table. "He won't die, I tell you! Why do you say that?"

"Because—Rydal says he is going to die."

"Rydal—lies. Peter had a fall, and it hurt his spine so that his legs are paralyzed. But I know what it is. If he could get away from that ship and could have a doctor, he would be well again in two or three months."

"But Rydal says he is going to die."

There was no mistaking the significance of Blake's words this time. Her eyes filled with sudden horror. Then they flashed with the blue fire again. "So —he has told you? Well, he told me the same thing today. He didn't intend to, of course. But he was half mad, and he had been drinking. He has given me twenty-four hours."

"In which to—surrender?"

There was no need to reply.

For the first time Blake smiled. There was something in that smile that made her flesh creep. "Twenty-four hours is a short time," he said, "and in this matter, Mrs. Keith, I think that you will find Captain Rydal a man of his word. No need to ask you why you don't appeal to the crew! Useless! But you have hope that I can help you? Is that it?"

Her heart throbbed. "That is why I have come to you, Mr. Blake. You told me today that Fort Confidence is only a hundred and fifty miles away and that a Northwest Mounted Police garrison is there this winter—with a doctor. Will you help me?"

"A hundred and fifty miles, in this country, at this time of the year, is a long distance, Mrs. Keith," reflected Blake, looking into her eyes with a steadiness that at any other time would have been embarrassing. "It means the McFarlane, the Lacs Delesse, and the Arctic Barren. For a hundred miles there isn't a stick of timber. If a storm came—no man or dog could live. It is different from the coast. Here there is shelter everywhere." He spoke slowly, and he was thinking swiftly. "It would take five days at thirty miles a day. And the chances are that your husband would not stand it. One hundred and twenty hours at fifty degrees below zero, and no fire until the fourth day. He would die."

"It would be better—for if we stay———" she stopped, unclenching her hands slowly.

"What?" he asked.

"I shall kill Captain Rydal," she declared. "It is the only thing I can do. Will you force me to do that, or will you help me? You have sledges and many dogs, and we will pay. And I have judged you to be—a man."

He rose from the table, and for a moment his face was turned from her. "You probably do not understand my position, Mrs. Keith," he said, pacing slowly back and forth and chuckling inwardly at the shock he was about to give her. "You see, my livelihood depends on such men as Captain Rydal. I have already done a big business with him in bone, oil, pelts—and Eskimo women."

Without looking at her he heard the horrified intake of her breath. It gave him a pleasing sort of thrill, and he turned, smiling, to look into her dead-white face. Her eyes had changed. There was no longer hope or entreaty in them. They were simply pools of blue flame. And she, too, rose to her feet.

"Then—I can expect—no help—from you."

"I didn't say that, Mrs. Keith. It shocks you to know that I am responsible. But up here, you must understand the code of ethics is a great deal different from yours. We figure that what I have done for Rydal and his crew keeps sane men from going mad during the long months of darkness. But that doesn't mean I'm not going to help you—and Peter. I think I shall. But you must give me a little time in which to consider the matter—say an hour or so. I understand that whatever is to be done must be done quickly. If I make up my mind to take you to Fort Confidence, we shall start within two or three hours. I shall bring you word aboard ship. So you might return and prepare yourself and Peter for a probable emergency."

She went out dumbly into the night, Blake seeing her to the door and closing it after her. He was courteous in his icy way but did not offer to escort her back to the ship. She was glad. Her heart was choking her with hope and fear. She had measured him differently this time. And she was afraid. She had caught a glimpse that had taken her beyond the man, to the monster. It made her shudder. And yet what did it matter, if Blake helped them?

She had forgotten Wapi. Now she found him again close at her side, and she dropped a hand to his big head as she hurried back through the pallid gloom. She spoke to him, crying out with sobbing breath what she had not dared to reveal to Blake. For Wapi the long night had ceased to be a hell of ghastly emptiness, and to her voice and the touch of her hand he responded with a whine that was the whine of a white man's dog. They had traveled two-thirds of the distance to the ship when he stopped in his tracks and sniffed the wind that was coming from shore. A second time he did this, and a third, and the third time Dolores turned with him and faced the direction from which they had come. A low growl rose in Wapi's throat, a snarl of menace with a note of warning in it.

"What is it, Wapi?" whispered Dolores. She heard his long fangs click, and under her hand she felt his body grow tense. "What is it?" she repeated.

A thrill, a suspicion, shot into her heart as they went on. A fourth time Wapi faced the shore and growled before they reached the ship. Like shadows they went up over the ice bridge. Dolores did not enter the cabin but drew Wapi behind it so they could not be seen. Ten minutes, fifteen, and suddenly she caught her breath and fell down on her knees beside Wapi, putting her arms about his gaunt shoulders. "Be quiet," she whispered. "Be quiet."

Up out of the night came a dark and grotesque shadow. It paused below the bridge, then it came on silently and passed almost without sound toward the captain's quarters. It was Blake. Dolores' heart was choking her. Her arms clutched Wapi, whispering for him to be quiet, to be quiet. Blake disappeared, and she rose to her feet. She had come of fighting stock. Peter was proud of that. "You slim wonderful little thing!" he had said to her more than once. "You've a heart in that pretty body of yours like the general's!" The general was her father, and a fighter. She thought of Peter's words now, and the fighting blood leaped through her veins. It was for Peter more than herself that she was going to fight now.

She made Wapi understand that he must remain where he was. Then she followed after Blake, followed until her ears were close to the door behind which she could already hear Blake and Rydal talking.

Ten minutes later she returned to Wapi. Under her hood her face was as white as the whitest star in the sky. She stood for many minutes close to the dog, gathering her courage, marshaling her strength, preparing herself to face Peter. He must not suspect until the last moment. She thanked God that Wapi had caught the taint of Blake in the air, and she was conscious of offering a prayer that God might help her and Peter.

Peter gave a cry of pleasure when the door opened and Dolores entered. He saw Wapi crowding in, and laughed. "Pals already! I guess I needn't have been afraid for you. What a giant of a dog!"

The instant she appeared, Dolores forced upon herself an appearance of joyous excitement. She flung off her coat and ran to Peter, hugging his head against her as she told him swiftly what they were going to do. Fort Confidence was only one hundred and fifty miles away, and a garrison of police and a doctor were there. Five days on a sledge! That was all. And she had persuaded Blake, the trader, to help them. They would start now, as soon as she got him ready and Blake came. She must hurry. And she was wildly and gloriously happy, she told him. In a little while they would be at least on the outer edge of this horrible night, and he would be in a doctor's hands.

She was holding Peter's head so that he could not see her face, and by the time she jumped up and he did see it, there was nothing in it to betray the truth or the fact that she was acting a lie. First she began to dress Peter for the trail. Every instant gave her more courage. This helpless, sunken-cheeked man with the hair graying over his temples was Peter, her Peter, the Peter who had watched over her, and sheltered her, and fought for her ever since she had known him, and now had come her chance to fight for him. The thought filled her with a wonderful exultation. It flushed her cheeks, and put a glory into her eyes, and made her voice tremble. How wonderful it was to love a man as she loved Peter! It was impossible for her to see the contrast they made—Peter with his scrubby beard, his sunken cheeks, his emaciation, and she with her radiant, golden beauty. She was ablaze with the desire to fight. And how proud of her Peter would be when it was all over!

She finished dressing him and began putting things in their big dunnage sack. Her lips tightened as she made this preparation. Finally she came to a box of revolver cartridges and emptied them into one of the pockets of her under-jacket. Wapi, flattened out near the door, watched every movement she made.

When the dunnage sack was filled, she returned to Peter. "Won't it be a joke on Captain Rydal!" she exulted. "You see, we aren't going to let him know anything about it." She appeared not to observe Peter's surprise. "You know how I hate him, Peter dear," she went on. "He is a beast. But Mr. Blake has done a great deal of trading with him, and he doesn't want Captain Rydal to know the part he is taking in getting us away. Not that Rydal would miss us, you know! I don't think he cares very much whether you live or die, Peter, and that's why I hate him. But we must humor Mr. Blake. He doesn't want him to know."

"Odd," mused Peter. "It's sort of—sneaking away."

His eyes had in them a searching question which Dolores tried not to see and which she was glad he did not put into words. If she could only fool him another hour—just one more hour.

It was less than that—half an hour after she had finished the dunnage sack —when they heard footsteps crunching outside and then a knock at the door. Wapi answered with a snarl, and when Dolores opened the door and Blake entered, his eyes fell first of all on the dog.

"Attached himself, eh?" he greeted, turning his quiet, unemotional smile on Peter. "First white woman he has ever seen, and I guess the case is hopeless. Mrs. Keith may have him."

He turned to her. "Are you ready?"

She nodded and pointed to the dunnage sack. Then she put on her fur coat and hood and helped Peter sit up on the edge of the bed while Blake opened the door again and made a low signal. Instantly Uppy and another Eskimo came in. Blake led with the sack, and the two Eskimos carried Peter. Dolores followed last, with the fingers of one little hand gripped about the revolver in her pocket. Wapi hugged so close to her that she could feel his body.

On the ice was a sledge without dogs. Peter was bundled on this, and the Eskimos pulled him. Blake was still in the lead. Twenty minutes after leaving the ship they pulled up beside his cabin.

There were two teams ready for the trail, one of six dogs, and another of five, each watched over by an Eskimo. The visor of Dolores' hood kept Blake from seeing how sharply she took in the situation. Under it her eyes were ablaze. Her bare hand gripped her revolver, and if Peter could have heard the beating of her heart, he would have gasped. But she was cool, for all that. Swiftly and accurately she appraised Blake's preparations. She observed that in the six-dog team, in spite of its numerical superiority, the animals were more powerful than those in the five-dog team. The Eskimos placed Peter on the six-dog sledge, and Dolores helped to wrap him up warmly in the bearskins. Their dunnage sack was tied on at Peter's feet. Not until then did she seem to notice the five-dog sledge. She smiled at Blake. "We must be sure that in our excitement we haven't forgotten something," she said, going over what was on the sledge. "This is a tent, and here are plenty of warm bearskins—and—and—" She looked up at Blake, who was watching her silently. "If there is no timber for so long, Mr. Blake, shouldn't we have a big bundle of kindling? And surely we should have meat for the dogs!"

Blake stared at her and then turned sharply on Uppy with a rattle of Eskimo. Uppy and one of the companions made their exit instantly and in great haste.

"The fools!" he apologized. "One has to watch them like children, Mrs. Keith. Pardon me while I help them."

She waited until he followed Uppy into the cabin. Then, with the remaining Eskimo staring at her in wonderment, she carried an extra bearskin, the small tent, and a narwhal grub-sack to Peter's sledge. It was another five minutes before Blake and the two Eskimos reappeared with a bag of fish and a big bundle of ship-timber kindlings. Dolores stood with a mittened hand on Peter's shoulder, and bending down, she whispered:

"Peter, if you love me, don't mind what I'm going to say now. Don't move, for everything is going to be all right, and if you should try to get up or roll off the sledge, it would be so much harder for me. I haven't even told you why we're going to Fort Confidence. Now you'll know!"

She straightened up to face Blake. She had chosen her position, and Blake was standing clear and unshadowed in the starlight half a dozen paces from her. She had thrust her hood back a little, inspired by her feminine instinct to let him see her contempt for him.

"You beast!"

The words hissed hot and furious from her lips, and in that same instant Blake found himself staring straight into the unquivering muzzle of her revolver.

"You beast!" she repeated. "I ought to kill you. I ought to shoot you down where you stand, for you are a cur and a coward. I know what you have planned. I followed you when you went to Rydal's cabin a little while ago, and I heard everything that passed between you. Listen, Peter, and I'll tell you what these brutes were going to do with us. You were to go with the six-dog team and I with the five, and out on the barrens we were to become separated, you to go on and be killed when you were a proper distance away, and I to be brought back—to Rydal. Do you understand, Peter dear? Isn't it splendid that we should have forced on us like this such wonderful material for a story!"

She was gloriously unafraid now. A paean of triumph rang in her voice, triumph, contempt, and utter fearlessness. Her mittened hand pressed on Peter's shoulder, and before the weapon in her other hand Blake stood as if turned into stone.

"You don't know," she said, speaking to him directly, "how near I am to killing you. I think I shall shoot unless you have the meat and kindlings put on Peter's sledge immediately and give Uppy instructions—in English—to drive us to Fort Confidence. Peter and I will both go with the six-dog sledge. Give the instructions quickly, Mr. Blake!"

Blake, recovering from the shock she had given him, flashed back at her his cool and cynical smile. In spite of being caught in an unpleasant lie, he admired this golden-haired, blue-eyed slip of a woman for the colossal bluff she was playing. "Personally, I'm sorry," he said, "but I couldn't help it. Rydal——"

"I am sure, unless you give the instructions quickly, that I shall shoot," she interrupted him. Her voice was so quiet that Peter was amazed.

"I'm sorry, Mrs. Keith. But——"

A flash of fire blinded him, and with the flash Blake staggered back with a cry of pain and stood swaying unsteadily in the starlight, clutching with one hand at an arm which hung limp and useless at his side.

"That time, I broke your arm," said Dolores, with scarcely more excitement than if she had made a bull's-eye on the Piping Rock range. "If I fire again, I am quite positive that I shall kill you!"

The Eskimos had not moved. They were like three lifeless, staring gargoyles. For another second or two Blake stood clutching at his arm. Then he said,

"Uppy, put the dog meat and the kindlings on the big sledge—and drive like hell for Fort Confidence!" And then, before she could stop him, he followed up his words swiftly and furiously in Eskimo.

"Stop!"

She almost shrieked the one word of warning, and with it a second shot burned its way through the flesh of Blake's shoulder and he went down. The revolver turned on Uppy, and instantly he was electrified into life. Thirty seconds later, at the head of the team, he was leading the way out into the chaotic gloom of the night. Hovering over Peter, riding with her hand on the gee-bar of the sledge, Dolores looked back to see Blake staggering to his feet. He shouted after them, and what he said was in Uppy's tongue. And this time she could not stop him.

She had forgotten Wapi. But as the night swallowed them up, she still looked back, and through the gloom she saw a shadow coming swiftly. In a few moments Wapi was running at the tail of the sledge. Then she leaned over Peter and encircled his shoulders with her furry arms.

"We're off!" she cried, a breaking note of gladness in her voice. "We're off! And, Peter dear, wasn't it perfectly thrilling!"

A few minutes later she called upon Uppy to stop the team. Then she faced him, close to Peter, with the revolver in her hand.

"Uppy," she demanded, speaking slowly and distinctly, "what was it Blake said to you?"

For a moment Uppy made as if to feign stupidity. The revolver covered a spot half-way between his narrow-slit eyes.

"I shall shoot——"

Uppy gave a choking gasp. "He said—no take trail For' Con'dence—go wrong—he come soon get you."

"Yes, he said just that." She picked her words even more slowly. "Uppy, listen to me. If you let them come up with us—unless you get us to Fort Confidence—I will kill you. Do you understand?"

She poked her revolver a foot nearer, and Uppy nodded emphatically. She smiled. It was almost funny to see Uppy's understanding liven up at the point of the gun, and she felt a thrill that tingled to her finger-tips. The little devils of adventure were wide-awake in her, and, smiling at Uppy, she told him to hold up the end of his driving whip. He obeyed. The revolver flashed, and a muffled yell came from him as he felt the shock of the bullet as it struck fairly against the butt of his whip. In the same instant there came a snarling deep-throated growl from Wapi. From the sledge Peter gave a cry of warning. Uppy shrank back, and Dolores cried out sharply and put herself swiftly between Wapi and the Eskimo. The huge dog, ready to spring, slunk back to the end of the sledge at the command of her voice. She patted his big head before she got on the sledge behind Peter.

There was no indecision in the manner of Uppy's going now. He struck out swift and straight for the pale constellation of stars that hung over Fort Confidence. It was splendid traveling. The surface of the arctic plain was frozen solid. What little wind there was came from behind them, and the dogs were big and fresh. Uppy ran briskly, snapping the lash of his whip and la-looing to the dogs in the manner of the Eskimo driver. Dolores did not wait for Peter's demand for a further explanation of their running away and her remarkable words to Blake. She told him. She omitted, for the sake of Peter's peace of mind, the physical insults she had suffered at Captain Rydal's hands. She did not tell him that Rydal had forced her into his arms a few hours before and kissed her. What she did reveal made Peter's arms and shoulders grow tense and he groaned in his helplessness.

"If you'd only told me!" he protested.

Dolores laughed triumphantly, with her arm about his shoulder. "I knew my dear old Peter too well for that," she exulted. "If I had told you, what a pretty mess we'd be in now, Peter! You would have insisted on calling Captain Rydal into our cabin and shooting him from the bed—and then where would we have been? Don't you think I'm handling it pretty well, Peter dear?"

Peter's reply was smothered against her hooded cheek.

He began to question her more directly now, and with his ability to grasp at the significance of things he pointed out quickly the tremendous hazard of their position. There were many more dogs and other sledges at Blake's place, and it was utterly inconceivable that Blake and Captain Rydal would permit them to reach Fort Confidence without making every effort in their power to stop them. Once they succeeded in placing certain facts in the hands of the Mounted Police, both Rydal and Blake would be done for. He impressed this uncomfortable truth on Dolores and suggested that if she could have smuggled a rifle along in the dunnage sack it would have helped matters considerably. For Rydal and Blake would not hesitate at shooting. For them it must be either capture or kill—death for him, anyway, for he was the one factor not wanted in the equation. He summed up their chances and their danger calmly and pointedly, as he always looked at troubling things. And Dolores felt her heart sinking within her. After all, she had not handled the situation any too well. She almost wished she had killed Rydal herself and called it self-defense. At least she had been criminally negligent in not smuggling along a rifle.

"But we'll beat them out," she argued hopefully. "We've got a splendid team, Peter, and I'll take off my coat and run behind the sledge as much as I can. Uppy won't dare play a trick on us now, for he knows that if I should miss him, Wapi would tear the life out of him at a word from me. We'll win out, Peter dear. See if we don't!"

Peter hugged his thoughts to himself. He did not tell her that Blake and Rydal would pursue with a ten- or twelve-dog team, and that there was almost no chance at all of a straight get-away. Instead, he pulled her head down and kissed her.

To Wapi there had come at last a response to the great yearning that was in him. Instinct, summer and winter, had drawn him south, had turned him always in that direction, filled with the uneasiness of the mysterious something that was calling to him through the years of forty generations of his kind. And now he was going south. He sensed the fact that this journey would not end at the edge of the Arctic plain and that he was not to hunt caribou or bear. His mental formulae necessitated no process of reasoning. They were simple and to the point. His world had suddenly divided itself into two parts; one contained the woman, and the other his old masters and slavery. And the woman stood against these masters. They were her enemies as well as his own. Experience had taught him the power and the significance of firearms, just as it had made him understand the uses for which spears, and harpoons, and whips were made. He had seen the woman shoot Blake, and he had seen her ready to shoot at Uppy. Therefore he understood that they were enemies and that all associated with them were enemies. At a word from her he was ready to spring ahead and tear the life out of the Eskimo driver and even out of the dogs that were pulling the sledge. It did not take him long to comprehend that the man on the sledge was a part of the woman.

He hung well back, twenty or thirty paces behind the sledge, and unless Peter or the woman called to him, or the sledge stopped for some reason, he seldom came nearer.

It took only a word from Dolores to bring him to her side.

Hour after hour the journey continued. The plain was level as a floor, and at intervals Dolores would run in the trail that the load might be lightened and the dogs might make better time. It was then that Peter watched Uppy with the revolver, and it was also in these intervals—running close beside the woman—that the blood in Wapi's veins was fired with a riotous joy.

For three hours there was almost no slackening in Uppy's speed. The fourth and fifth were slower. In the sixth and seventh the pace began to tell. And the plain was no longer hard and level, swept like a floor by the polar winds. Rolling undulations grew into ridges of snow and ice; in places the dogs dragged the sledge over thin crusts that broke under the runners; fields of drift snow, fine as shot, lay in their way; and in the eighth hour Uppy stopped the lagging dogs and held up his two hands in the mute signal of the Eskimo that they could go no farther without a rest.

Wapi dropped on his belly and watched. His eyes followed Uppy suspiciously as he strung up the tent on its whalebone supports to keep the bite of the wind from the sledge on which Dolores sat at Peter's feet. Then Uppy built a fire of kindlings, and scraped up a pot of ice for tea-water. After that, while the water was heating, he gave each of the trace dogs a frozen fish. Dolores herself picked out one of the largest and tossed it to Wapi. Then she sat down again and began to talk to Peter, bundled up in his furs. After a time they ate, and drank hot tea, and after he had devoured a chunk of raw meat the size of his two fists, Uppy rolled himself in his sleeping bag near the dogs. A little at a time Wapi dragged himself nearer until his head lay on Dolores' coat. After that there was a long silence broken only by the low voices of the woman and the man, and the heavy breathing of the tired dogs. Wapi himself dozed off, but never for long. Then Dolores nodded, and her head drooped until it found a pillow on Peter's shoulder. Gently Peter drew a bearskin about her, and for a long time sat wide-awake, guarding Uppy and baring his ears at intervals to listen. A dozen times he saw Wapi's bloodshot eyes looking at him, and twice he put out a hand to the dog's head and spoke to him in a whisper.

Even Peter's eyes were filmed by a growing drowsiness when Wapi drew silently away and slunk suspiciously into the night. There was no yapping foxes here, forty miles from the coast. An almost appalling silence hung under the white stars, a silence broken only by the low and distant moaning the wind always makes on the barrens. Wapi listened to it, and he sniffed with his gray muzzle turned to the north. And then he whined. Had Dolores or Peter seen him or heard the note in his throat, they, too, would have stared back over the trail they had traveled. For something was coming to Wapi. Faint, elusive, and indefinable breath in the air, he smelled it in one moment, and the next it was gone. For many minutes he stood undecided, and then he returned to the sledge, his spine bristling and a growl in his throat.

Wide-eyed and staring, Peter was looking back. "What is it, Wapi?"

His voice aroused Dolores. She sat up with a start. The growl had grown into a snarl in Wapi's throat.

"I think they are coming," said Peter calmly. "You'd better rouse Uppy. He hasn't moved in the last two hours."

Something that was like a sob came from Dolores' lips as she stood up. "They're not coming," she whispered. "They've stopped—and they're building a fire!"

Not more than a third of a mile away a point of yellow flame flared up in the night.

"Give me the revolver, Peter."

Peter gave it to her without a word. She went to Uppy, and at the touch of her foot he was out of his sleeping-bag, his moon-face staring at her. She pointed back to the fire. Her face was dead white. The revolver was pointed straight at Uppy's heart.

"If they come up with us, Uppy—you die!"

The Eskimo's narrow eyes widened. There was murder in this white woman's face, in the steadiness of her hand, and in her voice. If they came up with them—he would die! Swiftly he gathered up his sleeping-bag and placed it on the sledge. Then he roused the dogs, tangled in their traces. They rose to their feet, sleepy and ill-humored. One of them snapped at his hand. Another snarled viciously as he untwisted a trace. Then one of the yawning brutes caught the new smell in the air, the smell that Wapi had gathered when it was a mile farther off. He sniffed. He sat back on his haunches and sent forth a yelping howl to his comrades in the other team. In ten seconds the other five were howling with him, and scarcely had the tumult burst from their throats when there came a response from the fire half a mile away.

"My God!" gasped Peter, under his breath.

Dolores sprang to the gee-bar, and Uppy lashed his long whip until it cracked like a repeating rifle over the pack. The dogs responded and sped through the night. Behind them the pandemonium of dog voices in the other camp had ceased. Men had leaped into life. Fifteen dogs were straightening in the tandem trace of a single sledge.

Dolores laughed, a sobbing, broken laugh, that in itself was a cry of despair. "Peter, if they come up with us, what shall we do?"

"If they overtake us," said Peter, "give me the revolver. It is fully loaded?"

"I have cartridges——"

For the first time she remembered that she had not filled the three empty chambers. Crooking her arm under the gee-bar, she fumbled in her pocket.

The dogs, refreshed by their sleep and urged by Uppy's whip, were tearing off the first mile at a great speed. The trail ahead of them was level and hard again. Uppy knew they were on the edge of the big barren of the Lacs Delesse, and he cracked his whip just as the off runner of the sledge struck a hidden snow-blister. There was a sudden lurch, and in a vicious up-shoot of the gee-bar the revolver was knocked from Dolores' hand—and was gone. A shriek rose to her lips, but she stifled it before it was given voice. Until this minute she had not felt the terror of utter hopelessness upon her. Now it made her faint. The revolver had not only given her hope, but also a steadfast faith in herself. From the beginning she had made up her mind how she would use it in the end, even though a few moments before she had asked Peter what they would do.

Crumpled down on the sledge, she clung to Peter, and suddenly the inspiration came to her not to let him know what had happened. Her arms tightened about his shoulders, and she looked ahead over the backs of the wolfish pack, shivering as she thought of what Uppy would do could he guess her loss. But he was running now for his life, driven on by his fear of her unerring marksmanship—and Wapi. She looked over her shoulder. Wapi was there, a huge gray shadow twenty paces behind. And she thought she heard a shout!

Peter was speaking to her. "Blake's dogs are tired," he was saying. "They were just about to camp, and ours have had a rest. Perhaps——"

"We shall beat them!" she interrupted him. "See how fast we are going, Peter! It is splendid!"

A rifle-shot sounded behind them. It was not far away, and involuntarily she clutched him tighter. Peter reached up a hand.

"Give me the revolver, Dolores."

"No," she protested. "They are not going to overtake us."

"You must give me the revolver," he insisted.

"Peter, I can't. You understand. I can't. I must keep the revolver."

She looked back again. There was no doubt now. Their pursuers were drawing nearer. She heard a voice, the la-looing of running Eskimos, a faint shout which she knew was a white man's shout—and another rifle shot. Wapi was running nearer. He was almost at the tail of the sledge, and his red eyes were fixed on her as he ran.

"Wapi!" she cried. "Wapi!"

His jaws dropped agape. She could hear his panting response to her voice. A third shot—over their heads sped a strange droning sound.

"Wapi," she almost screamed, "go back! Sick 'em, Wapi—sick 'em—sick 'em—sick 'em!" She flung out her arms, driving him back, repeating the words over and over again. She leaned over the edge of the sledge, clinging to the gee-bar. "Go back, Wapi! Sick 'em—sick 'em—sick 'em!"

As if in response to her wild exhortation, there came a sudden yelping outcry from the team behind. It was close upon them now. Another ten minutes.

And then she saw that Wapi was dropping behind. Quickly he was swallowed up in the starlit chaos of the night.

"Peter," she cried, sobbingly. "Peter!"

Listening to the retreating sound of the sledge, Wapi stood a silent shadow in the trail. Then he turned and faced the north. He heard the other sound now, and ahead of it the wind brought him a smell, the smell of things he hated. For many years something had been fighting itself toward understanding within him, and the yelping of dogs and the taint in the air of creatures who had been his slave-masters narrowed his instinct to the one vital point. Again it was not a process of reason but the cumulative effect of things that had happened and were happening. He had scented menace when first he had given warning of the nearness of pursuers, and this menace was no longer an elusive and unseizable thing that had merely stirred the fires of his hatred. It was now a near and physical fact. He had tried to run away from it—with the woman—but it had followed and was overtaking him, and the yelping dogs were challenging him to fight as they had challenged him from the day he was old enough to take his own part. And now he had something to fight for. His intelligence gripped the fact that one sledge was running away from the other, and that the sledge which was running away was his sledge—and that for his sledge he must fight.

He waited, almost squarely in the trail. There was no longer the slinking, club-driven attitude of a creature at bay in the manner in which he stood in the path of his enemies. He had risen out of his serfdom. The stinging slash of the whip and his dread of it were gone. Standing there in the starlight with his magnificent head thrown up and the muscles of his huge body like corded steel, the passing spirit of Shan Tung would have taken him for Tao, the Great Dane. He was not excited—and yet he was filled with a mighty desire —more than that, a tremendous purpose. The yelping excitement of the oncoming Eskimo dogs no longer urged him to turn aside to avoid their insolent bluster, as he would have turned aside yesterday or the day before. The voices of his old masters no longer sent him slinking out of their way, a growl in his throat and his body sagging with humiliation and the rage of his slavery. He stood like a rock, his broad chest facing them squarely, and when he saw the shadows of them racing up out of the star-mist an eighth of a mile away, it was not a growl but a whine that rose in his throat, a whine of low and repressed eagerness, of a great yearning about to be fulfilled. Two hundred yards—a hundred—eighty—not until the dogs were less than fifty from him did he move. And then, like a rock hurled by a mighty force, he was at them.

He met the onrushing weight of the pack breast to breast. There was no warning. Neither men nor dogs had seen the waiting shadow. The crash sent the lead-dog back with Wapi's great fangs in his throat, and in an instant the fourteen dogs behind had piled over them, tangled in their traces, yelping and snarling and biting, while over them round-faced, hooded men shouted shrilly and struck with their whips, and from the sledge a white man sprang with a rifle in his hands. It was Rydal.

Under the mass of dogs Wapi, the Walrus, heard nothing of the shouts of men. He was fighting. He was fighting as he had never fought before in all the days of his life. The fierce little Eskimo dogs had smelled him, and they knew their enemy. The lead-dog was dead. A second Wapi had disemboweled with a single slash of his inch-long fangs. He was buried now. But his jaws met flesh and bone, and out of the squirming mass there rose fearful cries of agony that mingled hideously with the bawling of men and the snarling and yelping of beasts that had not yet felt Wapi's fangs. Three and four at a time they were at him. He felt the wolfish slash of their teeth in his flesh. In him the sense of pain was gone. His jaws closed on a foreleg, and it snapped like a stick. His teeth sank like ivory knives into the groin of a brute that had torn a hole in his side, and a smothered death-howl rose out of the heap. A fang pierced his eye. Even then no cry came from Wapi, the Walrus. He heaved upward with his giant body. He found another throat, and it was then that he rose above the pack, shaking the life from his victim as a terrier would have shaken a rat. For the first time the Eskimos saw him, and out of their superstitious souls strange cries found utterance as they sprang back and shrieked out to Rydal that it was a devil and not a beast that had waited for them in the trail. Rydal threw up his rifle. The shot came. It burned a crease in Wapi's shoulder and tore a hole as big as a man's fist in the breast of a dog about to spring upon him from behind. Again he was down, and Rydal dropped his rifle, and snatched a whip from the hand of an Eskimo. Shouting and cursing, he lashed the pack, and in a moment he saw a huge, open-jawed shadow rise up on the far side and start off into the open starlight. He sprang back to his rifle. Twice he fired at the retreating shadow before it disappeared. And the Eskimo dogs made no movement to follow. Five of the fifteen were dead. The remaining ten, torn and bleeding—three of them with legs that dragged in the bloody snow—gathered in a whipped and whimpering group. And the Eskimos, shivering in their fear of this devil that had entered into the body of Wapi, the Walrus, failed to respond to Rydal's command when he pointed to the red trail that ran out under the stars.

At Fort Confidence, one hundred and fifty miles to the south, there was day—day that was like cold, gray dawn, the day one finds just beyond the edge of the Arctic night, in which the sun hangs like a pale lantern over the far southern horizon. In a log-built room that faced this bit of glorious red glow lay Peter, bolstered up in his bed so that he could see it until it faded from the sky. There was a new light in his face, and there was something of the old Peter back in his eyes. Watching the final glow with him was Dolores. It was their second day.

Into this world, in the twilight that was falling swiftly as they watched the setting of the sun, came Wapi, the Walrus. Blinded in the eye, gaunt with hunger and exhaustion, covered with wounds, and with his great heart almost ready to die, he came at last to the river across which lay the barracks. His vision was nearly gone, but under his nose he could still smell faintly the trail he was following until the last. It led him across the river. And in darkness it brought him to a door.

After a little the door opened, and with its opening came at last the fulfilment of the promise of his dreams—hope, happiness, things to live for in a new, a white-man's world. For Wapi, the Walrus, forty years removed from Tao of Vancouver, had at last come home.

COMMAND *AND* BIG HUNT
BY JAMES WARNER BELLAH
(She Wore a Yellow Ribbon)

James Warner Bellah (1899–1976) specialized in military fiction of all types and all time periods, from the Revolutionary War to the Korean Conflict. But his best work of this type are the stories which deal with soldiers on the Western frontier; no writer has done better cavalry tales or infused them with more historical accuracy. Testimony to his expertise is the fact that John Ford based all three films in his famous "cavalry trilogy" on Bellah short stories— Fort Apache *(1948) on "Massacre" (see* The Reel West*),* She Wore a Yellow Ribbon *(1949) on the two stories which follow, and* Rio Grande *(1950) on "Mission with No Record." Yet another Bellah story, the* Saturday Evening Post *serial* Sergeant Rutledge, *was filmed under Ford's direction in 1960.*

COMMAND

Sergeant Utterback stiffened in his saddle, staring through the yellow sundown haze at a ragged buzzard that circled low in the darkening air ahead of the little column. The only live thing in that prairie wasteland except the three dozen saddle-weary troopers and the two officers who hated each other.

A lone buffalo off there, dead after many migratory years. Dead in some stupid way of his own devising. The thought was John Utterback's. He shifted his weary loins in the saddle and spat into the dust in boredom and apathy. At the head of the halted column, Captain Brittles uncased his glasses and raised them to his eyes in both grimy hands, his gauntlets tucked under his left arm. Mr. Cohill, riding back with the point, was about four hundred yards ahead of the captain, coming back toward him. Four lean troopers and the lieutenant outlined against the crimson backwash where the sun had died in agony twenty minutes before. The heads and arched necks of their mounts cut easily upward and easily downward across the sky as they came toward the column outlined sharply in a yellow band of light that touched them like St. Elmo's fire.

"Here's your best body of grass, sir. This slope, with a small run below for water. This slope is your bivouac."

You could smell the column as it stood there, still mounted, waiting. The warm flesh and leather and nitrogen of the horses. The heavy human rancidity of the men, unbathed for nine days. Utterback's mind fingered the roll from force of habit: Atkissons, Blunt, Cartter, Dannecker, Dortmunder, Eskuries, Ershick, Hertwole—and you could smell the green horror above them, thickening as the wind shifted.

"Mr. Cohill"—the captain lowered his glasses and looked intently at his second in command—"do you see the rise there to the left behind you across the valley? What are those lumped shapes on the forward slope?"

Nathan Brittles was a gray man that no sun could redden for long. His eyes were agate-gray and his hair was dust-gray, and there was a grayness within him that was his own manner of living, which he discussed with no man and no man questioned. Narrow-hipped and straight-backed. Hard and slender in the leg. Taut, so that when he moved, it was almost as if he would twang. And he did—when he spoke. Not unpleasantly, with a whine, but sharply, like the breech spang of a Spencer.

Flintridge Cohill half circled his horse on the forehand and turned his head, "We started back when we saw them, sir. Sleeping buffalo. A small herd."

"Now that the wind has shifted, take a deep breath, Mr. Cohill. Those aren't buffalo, Mr. Cohill!" Brittles closed his glasses, cased them and swung the case behind his left hip. He was furious. The red flush of his anger throbbed in his neck muscles. "Take another deep breath, Mr. Cohill! Get it in your nostrils and then tell me what's on that other slope!"

And then everyone in the column knew what was on that slope. That they weren't buffalo—either dead or sleeping. They were Mr. Gresham and the nine men of the 2nd that they'd come out to find—stripped naked and pincushioned to the ground with arrows, their feet and their right hands hacked off, their bodies purpling and sweet rotten.

Futile anger crawled within Cohill—anger at himself for his inaccuracy; anger at Nathan Brittles for catching it ruthlessly and ripping it wide open—as he always did.

"This is not a schoolroom out here, Mr. Cohill, in which you can fail and try again. I call it to your attention, Mr. Cohill, that accuracy in observation is a military virtue. Cultivate it. . . . Sergeant Utterback, dismount and unsaddle. This is the bivouac. Graze below the actual crest of the slope, off the skyline. Night grazing area between the military crest and the creek bottom. Use the picket rope, not individual pins, after darkness. Lay it on the ground."

The captain turned slowly and looked back the long way they had come across the flat depression of Paradise Valley; looked back toward the Mesa Roja.

The amber haze of the plains, shot now with the lavender of evening, lay across the distances. Flint Cohill, watching Brittles, felt dread loneliness for a second—the emptiness of a thousand frontier miles converging on him in a vast and whirling radius. Galloping toward him on thundering hoofs, lashed by the riata of oncoming night. And he was a boy again. Back again those few brief years that would put him into the irresponsibility of boyhood once more. A boy, masquerading as a man among grown men, steel-legged in fine boots and antelope-faced trousers. Silken kerchief at his neck, gauntleted and gunned and hatted for the part he would play if they'd let him. But alone now on the empty stage, with no applause. Nothing but his aloneness and the long vista of the years ahead of him, and the echoing memory of his own anger at himself that still clung sullenly to his brain—to be justified, because of his youth, if he could justify it.

Why doesn't Brittles go across to the other slope now and make sure, instead of camping here? If it is Gresham and his men, and they are fresh dead, it's the Santee Sioux war party whose trace we crossed this morning that killed them. It pleased Flint Cohill to be able to think Santee Sioux instead of plain Sioux, as everybody usually did back in the States. That was Sergeant Utterback's doing—Sergeant Utterback going along that trace at noon until he found the broken rattle made of the ends of buffalo toes.

"Sioux, sir"—to Brittles—"Santee Sioux I'd say; about forty strong." There was no triumph in the way John Utterback had said it; only the patience of long service and the acceptance of a fact. Utterback had stood there on foot, looking up at the captain, the broken rattle end in his hand. A modest, thin-faced man, John Utterback. Slope-shouldered almost to deformity, but secure in the system that had made him, knowing the things that he knew, beyond all shadow of doubt and all human timidity, moving quietly within the laws of his life and fearing no man to best him or break him.

Brittles had said, "Or Cheyenne, Utterback. They make rattles much the same. Or Comanches. Or Arapaho. Mount up!"

In memory again, Cohill's silent anger lashed out at Nathan Brittles in the gathering dusk. A stickler for detail and accuracy, even probably if it sacrificed the over-all plan. That Indian trace was fifteen miles back. With the Sioux making approximately the same rate of march that they were, their wickiups would be no more than thirty miles to the northward. Less, Cohill remembered his teaching suddenly. If they were Sioux, they'd camp away from timber—with their mortal dread of ambush—and near water. They'd be along the Paradise's upper reaches—in the dead lands.

Cohill blurted it suddenly, "Two hours' rest and we can be on the upper reaches of the Paradise by dawn, sir."

"Mr. Cohill, I have no orders to be on anyone or anything by dawn or at any other time. My orders are to find Mr. Gresham's patrol"—Brittles threw a leg off his animal and dismounted—"and finding him, to go back in to Fort Starke and report it. I think I've found him. I'll know, as soon as the moon rises and I go over and look. Take evening stables. Water in a half an hour. Saddle blankets left on until after the mounts are watered. Remember always, Mr. Cohill, that because of the liability to deterioration of the horses, cavalry is a very delicate arm of the service."

There was this in Cohill—that, spurred to the bleeding quick, he still would not talk back. But his mind raced in futile anger, *He's an old woman and he can't hold his temper. Little things infuriate him, but with a big chance like this, he's going to cut and run back in. In a stiff action, I'd probably have to kill him and take over the command.*

Brittles turned again and said, "Mr. Cohill, reading minds is an uncomfortable habit." Flint stared and moved his arm imperceptibly toward his revolving pistol. "But suppose for a moment they were Cheyennes, which they well might be, instead of Santee Sioux, they wouldn't be in the dead lands, you see. They'd head for the timber along the lower Mesa Roja branch. So would Arapaho. Kiowas or Comanches would bivouac right in the open timber . . . and they all make rattles out of buffalo toes! Pass the word to Sergeant Utterback that dinner call will be at six-thirty, but the trumpeter will still not sound calls. Mr. Cohill, there is no short cut to the top of the glory heap. So we'll not run all over the West tonight looking for one."

To some of them for the rest of their lives, the full moon, rising red gold on the horizon, would bring back what they saw that night, and what they heard, for the dead can whisper restlessly when the cool evening air contracts stiffened diaphragms. By the empty cartridge cases, Gresham's men had sold out dearly—sold out until the panther rush flattened and shredded them across the forward slope of the rise in a ferocious effort to rip their white dignity from them by savage mutilation.

"Whoever did it never wants to meet Mr. Gresham's patrol again," Sergeant Utterback growled; "that's why they lopped off their hands and feet to handicap them in case they meet in the Hereafter. They respected them as fighting men—every mother's son is left bald-headed, so he can cross the Shadow Waters without trouble."

The burial shovels were chattering in the hillside shale. Captain Brittles said, "Utterback, do you still think Santee Sioux?"

Sergeant Utterback stood quietly looking off toward the southwest. The moonlight was a limitless white wash across the sea of mist.

"No, sir. Not now, sir."

"Why not?" Brittles snapped. "Speak up!"

Flint Cohill turned toward them, listening intently.

"I made the march from Bent's Fort to Santa Fe with Steve Kearny, and I know an Apache arrow when I see one, sir, even a thousand miles from where they're made."

"Your Sioux of this noon could have brushed with an Apache war party"—Brittles nodded toward the southwest—"and come by Apache arrows that way."

"No." Utterback shook his head. "This job is two days old. It wasn't this morning's Sioux. It's an Apache job."

"How do you reason that?"

"Mostly"—Utterback smiled faintly—"because the captain knows it's Apache work, too, not Sioux work."

Brittles looked at his first sergeant, studying his eyes carefully. "I shall want to move the command out by ten tonight. We go back in to Fort Starke with this word as fast as we can get in."

"Yes, sir."

"When the graves are cairned, Sergeant Utterback, fall the burial party in for services."

". . . for Thine is the kingdom and the power and the glory forever and ever, amen."

The moon was high and small and frozen crystal above the column as it moved out for Fort Starke. Thirty miles already that day, with no knowing how many night miles Brittles would pile up on top of them. Plenty. The order was to halt fifteen minutes in the hour, dismount and unbit for grazing. The order was to trot five minutes after every half hour of walking, to avoid animal fatigue from bad carriage in the saddle, and the liability to sore backs. The order was to dismount and lead, ten minutes in every hour. Walk, trot, lead, halt and graze—and at two in the morning Brittles halted on the Paradise for twenty-five full minutes for watering call.

Flintridge Cohill trudged along, leading, alkali white to mid-thigh. His spurs, dust muffled, sounded like silver dollars clinked deep in the pocket of a greatcoat. He could feel the resentment in the men—resentment at the night march. It was a hard and a sullen thing; and it was there in an occasional angry sneeze, in the dust coughing that became general after a while in spite of long intervals, in a deep and throaty curse rolled into the night on dry saliva.

Cohill could feel the swing and thrust of Sergeant Utterback's legs beside him; he could smell Utterback's rank gaminess above his own, cut by the sweet brownness of the sergeant's eating tobacco, all of it washed hot and cleanly sulphurous by a horse ahead. All of it rushing back again, to be breathed again against the cooling curtain of the dying night.

"Pass the word to mount." It came down the column like cards falling from a table edge, and Utterback, swinging up, stood high for a second in his stirrups. "He's heading up north."

"How's that, sergeant?"

"North," Utterback said.

Cohill pulled his hat brim down under the dying moon and looked high to the horizon, toward Mesa Roja. "You're right." He meant to put a question into it, but if he put one in, Utterback ignored it.

Cohill sat with it for a moment, settling himself to the cold saddle, turning, looking back at the dust-white masks of the faces in the moonlight. The lean-jawed faces and the hard faces. The brutal faces and the weak. The hopeful faces and the finished faces—Jordin, Knight, Lusk, Mallory, Mittendorffer, Norton and Opdyke—and as far as he could see the faces back of him, he knew that they knew that the Old Man was heading up north, and that they questioned it. The flat top of Mesa Roja was dead ahead on the line of march. And it didn't make sense. If they were going back in, fast, to Fort Starke to report an Apache war party—going back in a straight line across their own nine-day circle by a forced night march—Mesa Roja should bear on their left shoulders, not between their mounts' ears.

And then Cohill knew, and his mind was cold and taut with the knowledge, and he was ashamed suddenly for the traditions that had made him, but that could so fail other men.

Brittles had an Apache war party up from the southwest and Gresham's death at their hands to report. So he was forcing the march in to Starke, but in the midst of forcing it, he was taking good care that he gave this morning's Santee Sioux a wide berth. He wouldn't fight if it was handed to him! He was afraid to fight—afraid of himself probably. Knew himself for what Cohill was finding him out to be—superannuated, petty, nerve-racked and afraid.

What we all come to understand sooner or later, Mr. Cohill, is that we're not out here to fight Indians. We're out here to watch them and report on them for the Indian Bureau. We fight only if they attack us. I refer you to departmental standing orders, which are most explicit.

Gresham fought, damn you. He had no choice but to fight.

Mr. Gresham was young. Probably he was extremely rash.

And you are old, and not fit for this job any longer. If they are really Apaches, it's your duty to cut straight in to Starke and report it. But if they turned out to be those same Santee Sioux—as they well might, for all you really know to the contrary—you could force their attack on a technicality and wipe them out in punishment on the way in. This stupid way—we march all day and march all night, and we're still miles from home, with worn and sullen men and tired animals, and nothing to show for it but a sop to your old man's caution. Cavalry is a delicate arm.

Cohill was conscious that his lips were moving contemptuously with his silent monologue. He covered them with his hand as Utterback turned and looked at him.

"Sergeant, how did you know the captain thought they were Apaches that killed Mr. Gresham's detail?"

"I've been his first sergeant for a long time. You get to know."

"I see. Do I get to know?"

"Mr. Cohill, the captain's been out here a good many years."

"You're not answering me, is that it? If it's all the same to me, you fell up a tree?"

"No use talking. It ain't learned ever. It's lived. It's a feeling, after all's said and done, sir."

"And you're sure yourself it's an Apache party?"

"Reasonably, only I wouldn't hold to it alone. But I'm dead sure when I know Captain Brittles is sure too. He earns the difference in our pay, sir."

Cohill threw up his head in annoyance. Five hours on the way now. A shade less than three left to dawn. They'd make the foot of the mesa and bivouac there probably, hitting the trail again in the afternoon. What a fool procedure, when the whole command could have been freshened by a night's sleep and grazing after the burial detail.

The moon grew colder and slid down the sky behind them. Knees were thick now and sanded with fatigue, and there was the clamminess of dank sweat in their shirts that their bodies no longer warmed. Mist tatters wove above the prairie, girth high, and in the hollows chilled them with the hand of death. Flintridge heard his name passed softly down the column, "Mr. Cohill," and he kneed out to the right and cantered forward.

Brittles sat straight in his saddle, cut there like stone, outlined against the night sky, nose and chin and shoulder—an aging man, riding out his destiny. "Mr. Cohill, this is officer's call. Listen carefully. I have Sergeant Sutro ahead of me with the point. You will relieve him with eight men, and push forward fast. Do you recall the ford on the Mesa Roja branch?"

"I do, sir."

"There is a knoll on the mesa side—a knoll that the trail crosses from the mesa top."

"I remember."

"Be there prior to dawn. Build a bivouac fire on your arrival."

"Do what, sir?"

"I want to know it, when you get there. And I want everyone else for miles around to know it, too. Build a bivouac fire. A squad fire. No larger."

"But I can send a file back to tell you when I arrive."

"Disabuse yourself of the idea that this is a debating society, Mr. Cohill. In the event of an attack on your position, you will hold the knoll top, fighting on foot. Always hold your fire at dawn to the last possible moment. Remember, the dawn light works for you, but it can fool you in the first half hour in this country. Move out, Mr. Cohill. You're the bait on my hook. Wriggle . . . and keep alive!"

High overhead under the rim of Mesa Roja there was an eagle scream in the chilled darkness. The whipsaw blade of it grated down Flint Cohill's damp spine. His lips were drawn thin across his dry teeth. "Don't stand still, Skinnor. Move a little all the time. Move always. Slap the mounts. Keep moving them too." Soft. Words lashed whisper-high across the knoll—whisper-high and rowel-sharp.

The little squad fire burned brightly, and the tired animals held the echo of its gold in the moist jewels of their eyes. Skinnor and Blankenship were with the horses, moving them, keeping them circling their picket pins, ready to cut them free and stampede them. Corporal McKenzie and his five men lay just beyond the wash of light, fanned out behind their flung saddles, waiting and watching and listening and breathing softly. Mr. Cohill was wriggling beautifully on the hook.

A great feathery exultation pressed its soft hands upward under his lower ribs, catching his breath every time he drew it. Here, then, is the justification —the final heritage of soldiering—to stand steady, ready to deliver, to bleed and to draw blood. Everything else is the parade ground. And he was afraid for his first shots in anger. His fear was livid and gasping behind the drawn curtain at the back of his mind. To fire and to draw fire. To kill and to be killed. And he could hear the panic whimper of his fear behind its curtain. "Mr. Cohill, this is not a schoolroom out here."

Some weed, some bitter prairie flower freshening on the dawn winds, feathered his nostrils, and, with association, brought back the green horror in the moonlight that they had put decently below the ground thirty miles back across the plains.

The play went on. The trap was good. Carefully acted. Cohill crossed into the firelight, and out of it again. Always moving. The natural movement of a small bivouac. Carneal put the spider on, crisping and richening the clean air with the smell of frying bacon.

Neither Sioux nor Apache nor any Plains Indian will fight willingly at night, for a warrior killed in darkness wanders up and down the outer world forever, eternally blind in darkness. But in a little while the dawn would creep across from the eastward, and there on the knoll was a small white-soldier war party like two-yesterdays' party that lay bloating where they had overwhelmed it thirty miles down Paradise Valley. Fire alight and bacon cooking. Mounts unsaddled and warriors sleeping from a long night march to bring back the death news of the other party. Soft for the killing.

Down, then, from the mesa rim silently. Down in the last black darkness on shadow feet. With the ponies led carefully, so that not a stone could chip and skip and arch on ahead in chattering cascade to herald the approach. Not a twig must snap.

Suddenly Flint Cohill could see the pewter trace of the Mesa Roja branch below him. He could see tree boles and the shiny black dampness of a stomped hoof in dew-drenched grass and the grime on the back of his own hand. And it was the dawn opening slowly, like the reflexive lid of a dead eyeball. Then a horse screamed in bowel-torn agony, and three animals were down, thrashing. Skinnor crawled out, dragging a splintered shin bone, cursing in high falsetto. And the air was alive with whiplashing, but no lash cracks. Just the intake gasp, unfinished, threatening. Cruel and thin as the bite of a bone saw.

"Hold your fire, Corporal McKenzie!" Cohill was belly-down in the soaking grass. Five of his horses were running free, fear driven and panic blind. Then the air ripped alive with the war shriek and the gray dawn was throbbing with a thundering rush. So close that it was on them. So close that it was over them. So close that Cohill screamed the order to fire, and they fired, and the wave broke like a brown sea wave on an emerald beach, crested before them on the slope of the knoll, curled mightily upward and crashed over and toward them with the weight of its own speed. Rolling in a spume of thrashing pony hoofs and of torn and howling throats and an agony of shattered bone.

"They are Apaches!"

Those behind broke away and to the left, and passed below the knoll, circling to re-form and roar up again toward the knoll top. Brown oiled bodies hard down on the off-side of ponies, galloping into the teeth of the dawn wind. And the men on the knoll saw them now for the Gresham massacre party, for there were yellow stripes on the legs of some, with the seat and the front cut from the trousers; and there were sabers and yellow silken neckerchiefs and the brass buckles of belts and of bandoleers.

Round again and up again frantically into the flaming scythe of Cohill's fire. And again, as they took it, breaking and circling, but this time raggedly bunched, with free ponies racing among them. Cut down to half their number. Torn and bleeding, whirling across the whitening dawn. Battered in their strength, broken and hacked into. Shrieking now in anger and the primitive hurt of animals—frustrated tigers of the Plains.

The raucous brass file of the trumpet scratched across the gunmetal of the new day, and Nathan Brittles' main body came up out of the bottoms of the Mesa Roja branch, splashed hoof-deep across the lower ford and charging as foragers, struck them on their shattered flank, parched sabers drawn and drinking. There was a long and racing moment down the bottoms, horse to horse and man to man, below Cohill's knoll. A red moment of fury. Steel and flesh and livid madness with the black lash of the devil in it to whip it to frenzied crescendo.

Cohill stood above, his shirt black with sweat, watching the bitter finish, the last flaming action and the last free pony pistoled off its flashing hoofs. Below him on the knoll there was a writhing Apache hurling himself up off his dead hips and legs, thrashing his upper body in madness to free himself from the icy shackles of his broken spine. Noiselessly thrashing, like a snake dismembered. And to the left, there was Corporal McKenzie, lying blue-faced and quiet, his hands close to the feathered shaft that was sunk deep in his right side below the ribs—hands rising and falling with the last of his breathing. And Skinnor, with the twisted bloat of his leg stretched out naked before him, smoking evenly on his black-stubbed pipe watching the sun wash that reddened the horizon.

"Mr. Cohill, you did that well." Nathan Brittles swung down and plunged his face and hands in the wet grass to clean them and freshen himself. He opened his matted shirt to the waist and tugged it over his head. "You may do. In time."

"You knew they were Apaches yesterday at sundown . . . and you knew they were camped on the mesa top, sir?"

"Mr. Cohill,"—Brittles swabbed his bare chest with his shirttail—"Apaches fear only man. They camp as high as they can get, no matter how far it is from water. Had you pushed forward to Mr. Gresham's slope, you would have found Mr. Gresham, not sleeping buffalo. Had your eyes been sharp, you would have seen this between the slope and last evening's bivouac." Brittles dug a hand deep into his pocket and tugged out a blood-hardened shred of Apache headband of red flannel and handed it over. "Commit it to your diary and your brain." Brittles pulled on his shirt again, "And had you been a plainsman and suspected the Apache, you would have looked at once for smoke at sundown on the highest ground—Mesa Roja."

Cohill's quick admiration was in his eyes, in his blurted words, "You came straight here, sir, to hole them out and pay them off for Gresham. You had no intention of anything else, from the start, but to force the fight." He grinned. "You even had Utterback fooled, until you turned north."

The captain stood quite still for a moment, looking Flint Cohill over very carefully, as if he had never seen him before. "The essence of command is timing, Mr. Cohill. A successful commander keeps his own counsel until the right moment. At that time he tells his subordinates everything they should know to do their part of the work properly. Nothing more. My intention was to fool no one. Sergeant Utterback is a soldier. He keeps his mouth shut. The facts are these: My point, temporarily bivouacked at dawn today, came under sudden enemy attack. Fortunately, it was able to hold until I arrived with the main body."

Cohill drew himself up and bowed slightly. "I understand that, sir, perfectly. I am familiar with departmental standing orders which allow defensive actions only, and expressly forbid the attack."

"And yet"—Captain Brittles' eyes never wavered from Cohill's—"they are in direct violation of cavalry tactics, for cavalry is very weak on the defensive. It can defend itself well only by attacking. Most young lieutenants will agree with that, whether or not they examine the reasons."

"I am desperately sorry, sir."

"Mr. Cohill, never apologize. It's a mark of weakness. There is a captain out here who tried it once to escape a Benzine Board. He escaped it, but he's been ashamed a little bit ever since. He will die a captain, in spite of his apology. The man who did for him could have worked with him and made him a soldier, if his humanity had been large enough. Mr. Cohill, I'm going to make a soldier out of you, if you don't break. You may present my respects to General Cohill when next you write your father. Mr. Cohill, take morning stables."

BIG HUNT

A brisk knuckle tattoo rattled the frame of the commanding officer's door. At the word, it opened to Lieutenant Pennell's hand. "Mr. Rynders is here to see you, sir."

MacLerndon Allshard was still so murderously angry that there was no feeling in his finger tips. He looked at his adjutant. "Is the surgeon set up and ready for us, Mr. Pennell?"

"Yes, sir."

Major Allshard drew his long legs from under the desk, stood up and reached for his hat.

"There is another telegram in from department, Pennell. They have changed plans again on Senator Chadbourne and his party. They come in on today's stage from Elkhorn with the mail escort."

"But they still want to shoot buffalo?"

"They still do," Allshard nodded, "so hold Oldroyd here at the post for a guide and alert a hunting-party escort for the senator."

Ross Pennell opened the door to the outer office, letting the commanding officer pass him. Then he followed on, skirting to his left to open the door to the veranda.

Toucey Rynders, the Comanche agent, was leaning against the railing. He was a tall man with very tiny hands. Ben Oldroyd, the railroad's contract hunter, sat on the steps below him, hunched over his long-stemmed pipe, staring off toward the horizon dust smudges to the south and to the east.

"Good morning, major," the agent bowed.

"Good morning, Mr. Rynders."

"I was just leaving the South Branch store to go up to the agency, when your message reached me. How can I serve you, sir?" Toucey Rynders' hands scrabbled around the broad brim of his hat like little damp animals.

Fury still swirled crimson in the major's blood, but twenty-two years of discipline held it close. He said, "You are probably aware, Mr. Rynders, that the garrison here at Fort Starke hasn't been paid for over two months?"

Rynders' eyebrows went up slightly. "My books at the store are eloquent testimony to the fact, major. Is that what you wished to discuss with me."

"No." Allshard shook his head. "I wanted to discuss the paymaster with you. He arrived early this morning. Dead . . . and without his money. Ben

Oldroyd here brought him in, in a poncho." The major's voice was soft. "And I wanted to discuss the matter of where your Comanches are getting Henry repeating rifles from, Mr. Rynders."

Oldroyd on the steps below spat out into the roadway dust, and the sound of it was like the sound of dropped playing cards, for his jaws were lined with snuff and there was a twist the size of a duck's egg in his cheek—against the full blast of his pipe.

Rynders put his hat back on his head. He put it on carefully with both small hands, raking the brim across his right ear, flaring it over his left, thrusting his hands out of sight again, deep in his trousers pockets.

"Am I to understand," he said, "that there is some connection in your mind, major, between the death of the paymaster and the question about the Henry rifles?"

The contract hunter took the long-stemmed pipe from his mouth and swept a smudge of tobacco ash from his hickory pants. "Sure'n hell there's some connection"—Ben's voice was a startling cackle, like a rasp drawn across a cold horseshoe—"because Comanches done in Major Devine, plain's the seat in your pants!"

Rynders swung around toward Oldroyd, furious at the interruption, but Ben didn't look up. He still sat there, his back to them, squinting off to the south and east. And having shattered Rynders' dignity into quick anger, he put his pipestem back into his mouth again and drew in a long and slow pull of hot smoke.

"My guess is," Allshard said, "that the rifles are coming up from the south in case lots, as they did three years ago, when the smugglers were operating at Yapparika." He went down the veranda steps, his booted legs lacing shadows in the sunlight. Rynders hesitated briefly, looking down at Allshard, at Ben Oldroyd's hunched shoulders. Then, with Pennell behind him, he followed the major, who was still talking. "As they did when Caddo George Washington was gun-running to hostiles with one hand, while he held ours with the other in a travesty of friendship. And my guess also is that the rifles are being cached at a central distributing point, and sold as the tribes migrate."

Allshard was saying all of it slowly, throwing it out to Rynders for what his own considered thinking was worth to the other man. Rynders walked beside him, listening, looking at him now and then as he spoke, letting his own thinking trail evenly along with the major's.

"And that distributing point," Allshard said, "is the weak link. As the rifles spread through the bands, every Comanche brave will come to know where he can get one when he has the price. A tribe war or the prospect of a big buffalo hunt will send them all scurrying to that point, pawning and mortgaging everything they own for a Henry repeater. That's when I hope to catch the smuggler—by catching the Comanches when they make contact, by watching them with my patrols until they do."

Lieutenant Pennell cut off the roadway and went on ahead of Rynders and the C.O., up the path to the post hospital. He opened the door to the back room and stood aside, holding it. That was the room with the black oilcloth tacked from the sills halfway up the window frames.

Arthur Jopp, still in his rubber apron, but with his bare arms and hands newly scrubbed at the pump, stood in a blue cloud of pipe smoke just inside the door.

"This is Doctor Jopp," Major Allshard said. "My surgeon, Mr. Rynders."

Jopp nodded, and he stepped across to the table and flicked a poncho back from what had, several days before, been Major Robert Gansell Devine, Pay Department.

Jopp reached for his Blasius pincers and pointed with them. "The ball entered just to the right of the inferior angle of the right scapula, penetrated the thoracic cavity and lodged." Jopp twisted the forward thumbscrew of the *Darmschere*, picking up the bullet. "Conoidal. Slightly contused from bone impact. Forty-four caliber. But neither the shot nor the scalping killed him, for there is soot in the lungs. He was still breathing when they built the fire on him."

"Never mind the fire, doctor," Allshard lashed his hat at the flies. "Get on with the bullet."

"Forty-four caliber," Jopp said, "and because it lodged, instead of penetrating through and through, I'd swear forty-four, forty, two hundred in any court. A Henry rifle, sir."

The sound of Rynders' flat cough was the sound of two pine shingles struck together. He pressed his handkerchief to his mouth and nose.

"They tell me"—Pennell looked up curiously at Arthur Jopp—"that an expert never peels or tears a scalp. He cuts a quick circle to the bone and tugs straight up at the hair"—thumb in mouth, the lieutenant popped his cheek with the sound of a drawn cork—"and pops the scalp free, which makes much face in making coup."

They stepped out and stood for a moment in the sunlight, filling their lungs with clean air and spitting the brassy saliva that trickled down inside their cheeks.

Allshard said, "So, you see, Mr. Rynders, it looks very much as if the men here at Fort Starke wouldn't be paid for another month or so. And thirteen dollars a month isn't too much, even when you get it, for the privilege of being sniped at by Henrys; the volume of fire of which can damned soon make up for poor individual marksmanship."

Rynders said, "But this is evidence of only one rifle, major . . . if your surgeon is right about it and the paymaster was shot with a Henry."

Allshard shook his head. "Ben Oldroyd found the paymaster seventeen miles south of Jarrod's. It's two-hundred-odd miles from Jarrod's to Coleman's. In my office I have a rusted-out Henry rifle that my patrol officer found on a dead Comanche near Coleman's on the twenty-second of last month. The Comanche had crawled off into the rocks to die of his wounds. He had a towheaded scalp on him with braided pigtails and a pink hair ribbon. They scalped Coleman's entire family. It's a hundred and seventy miles north and east from Coleman's to Tallow Creek. Sergeant Tyree's detail shot a Comanche named Red Horse on the Tallow Creek raid and brought him in. There were twelve rounds of ammunition in his tobacco pouch—forty-four, forty, two hundred—the Henry charge and caliber. It's ninety miles north and west from Tallow Creek to Four Graves on the Elkhorn mail run. We have the splintered Henry-rifle stock that broke the skull of the mail driver the first of the month, and my patrol officer buried two Comanches at the scene, dead of the fight. And finally, from damn near two hundred and eighty miles due west, I have three empty brasses, the slugs from which were sniped at my Paradise River survey detail eleven days ago, and the brasses are Henry rifle brasses." They were walking slowly back toward headquarters. "And if you will spot those points on the map, Mr. Rynders, you will find that a line that joins them will encircle the whole of outdoors your Comanches have been playing in since they broke their treaty in March. For each trace of a Henry we have found, I'll lay you that there are fifty rifles loose in the tribes."

Rynders folded his kerchief carefully and put it in the pocket in the tail of his coat. "You have an imposing array of evidence, major. I sincerely trust that you are not accusing me of inefficiency and carelessness in the administration of my agency?"

"On the contrary, I am putting the situation to you man to man, for your help, sir, in running the gun smuggler to earth. And again I am pointing out the weak points—the gopher holes that can throw our man. First, he has created a monopoly. Henry-rifle buyers will have to come back to him for forty-four caliber ammunition, because buffalo hunters use the forty-five, ninety, five hundred fifty generally, and the Ward-Butrons, the Remingtons and the Sharps that the Ordnance Board has us experimenting with here, are all fifty-caliber pieces. Our old Springfields are forty-fives again. So the Comanche has small chance of picking up contraband ammunition. And, secondly, when the Comanches come back for ammunition or come for new rifles, under the necessity of a big hunt or of a war—they'll throw caution to the winds; they'll come in quantity to the contact point, and that fact will give our gun runner away cold."

Rynders smiled. "There isn't much that you have left out of your thinking, sir. If you can't break a horse, force him and run him until he kills himself." The agent held out his hand. "Thank you, major. It'll be a pleasure to work with you."

And as he said it, Ben Oldroyd on the headquarters steps stood up suddenly, swept off his battered hat and scaled it into the dust of the roadway.

"Donk me, Allshard, effen it didn't work!" and he pointed across the parade ground to the southeast. "There ain't enough salt west of K.C. to corn this mess!"

A long veil of saffron prairie dust hung above the flatlands all the way up from south to almost due east, trailing low like dust over a mounted column at the walk. And there was thin high dust in a quick whiplash on the Sudro road, and that was the Elkhorn stagecoach, with Dandy Balderston standing in the boot for a galloping finish at the Fort Starke Station, flaying his red-mouthed mules and cursing them on ahead of the slow-moving buffalo herds that closed in relentlessly after the coach passed.

Ben Oldroyd was dancing on his hat. "It's that laudanum-eatin' Sioux medicine chief at Twin Rocks, sure as you're born, Allshard! Old Powder Face. Saw him two days before I found the paymaster; gave him a bottle of belly rot and he made big medicine, and he swore the buffalo would hear it through the ground all the way down in their underground caves in the Llano Estacado; that they'd come north again on their old trails when they did."

That was the last time the buffalo came near Fort Starke on the trails they had always used before the railroads cut across them, before the Eastern factories found out that their thick hides made cheap and durable belting for the new machinery of commerce, before the hides began to sell for three dollars apiece railside, and the skeletons for a dollar, for bone-dust fertilizer, so that every tenderfoot who could borrow a gun made a stake in no time.

They were coming north in hundreds of small herds, moving in many parallel columns, with their flankers interlocking them, until the great mass of it looked like one great column. Where the lands were flat and the blue-stem thick, the herds wandered off to right and to left, widening the line of march to fifty miles and more in width.

You couldn't see that at Starke, but you could measure it afterward. If your own way lay across the way the buffalo had come, you could see how many miles wide their passage was. At Starke, when they passed, you couldn't see much at all, for the slow wind brought the yellow dust down on the post and turned the sun into a great silver pan. It powdered the backs of hands until the hair on them looked like tiny tufts of crab grass in beach sand. It dried up eye rims until they gummed together, and it cracked lips into blood smudges. Before the post laundresses could get the wash in off the lines in Sudsville, everything was tinted red ocher.

When Major Allshard doubled down to the coach station to meet the senator's party, Brome Chadbourne roared out at him, "What are you trying to do to me, major—make me believe this?"

And Allshard laughed. "Department wired me to place all facilities at your disposal for a buffalo hunt, senator, this is the best I could do."

But when Sergeant Tyree and his weary, red-eyed detail rode in at five o'clock that afternoon—rode in lean and worn and scorched black from a self-made hell of sleepless days and nights, and of prairie-fire smoke and of hard riding, Major Allshard said, "Mr. Pennell, witchcraft is a poor substitute for reconnaissance, and luck never relieves command of responsibility. Tyree has done the impossible, even though it took him two weeks to do it. He has been under my orders to halloo and smoke and stampede all the buffalo he could find eastward into Comanche country, and the centaurs must have ridden with him, for he seems to have done it, in spite of the fact that the buffalo haven't wanted to come this far east in their migration for over two years. So, have Tyree made a first sergeant, because he's made it possible for me to get that big hunt I've wanted. And every Comanche west of the Paradise will want a Henry rifle by sundown, or I'm a recruit!"

He stood up to his wall map. "Cohill and his patrol are up here in the Estrellas. The rifle cache could be in there somewhere. Mr. Topliff is in the flatlands east of the Comanche agency. I believe he's chasing wild geese, because the country is too open for hiding much in there. Captain Flecknoe may draw the winning card along the upper reaches of the Paradise River, because you can hide a regiment in there without even trying to. Or you and I and the senator may draw it ourselves, mister." . . .

Brome Chadbourne was a little man with honesty and a simple dignity that needed neither whisky nor bombast to make him six feet tall. "Hell, major, pop used to send us five shavers to school on one horse. If you fell off, you walked. Give me anything to ride and I'll stick on it, short legs or not!"

The hunting party and the escort wound on up north of Fort Starke, keeping well to the west of the miles of slow-moving buffalo.

"It's the ones out ahead of the herds we want for the senator," Oldroyd cackled; "the ones ahead get the most grass and fatten up quickest. Their hides make the best robes. . . . Dumbest animals in the world, senator. Wouldn't have no truck with 'm effen I wasn't under contract with the railroad to provide meat. Buffalo are so stupid they're plumb dangerous. Effen they can't smell you or see you, a herd'll stand still and let you shoot ev'y last one of 'em down. Then again, for no cause you can spot, a herd'll stampede in wild panic and go rocketing across the prairie for miles, trampling the calves and the slowpokes in blind, unreasoning fear. But the damnedest thing they do—the most stupid—is to be timid about going north. All the time, the front ones seem to watch the rear ones, and if there is any disturbance back there, the front ones turn and stampede back south through the herd, toward the rear, turning the whole kit and kaboodle back on itself, causing the damnedest, most unbelievable mix-up you ever saw in your born days!"

The senator said, "Major Allshard, I'm well-aware of the fact that Army officers don't babble about their work. But I'm not out here to hunt buffalo. I'm on the commission . . . and I know damned well what a hell of a mess Washington has made of this Indian problem. How can I help you?"

"That's a difficult question to answer, offhand, sir."

Brome Chadbourne said, "I wish Rynders had stayed long enough at Fort Starke the day I arrived so I could have met him and had a talk with him."

"He runs two stores as well as the agency," Allshard said. "He's a busy man."

The senator said, "When President Grant turned the Indian administration over to the Quakers, he did it because he honestly believed they'd convert them to Quakers, which would take the fight completely out of them."

"Rynders is not a Quaker, senator," Allshard said.

"That's why I want to meet him and talk to him. I know now that Grant's theory is nonsense. So I want to see how the straight political appointee works . . . without religion."

Allshard rode on for a little while in silence. Then he smiled. "Senator, is the Sumner Bill going to be passed? Are we going to have to take the names of all Union victories off regimental colors, and eliminate mention of them from the Army Register?"

And just as he said it, Ben Oldroyd, ahead in the trail, threw off and bent close to the ground. "Third time, Allshard. Third time since breakfast, and all three trails have been Comanche trails!"

Senator Chadbourne looked quickly at the major, and saw his eyes and Lieutenant Pennell's eyes know something between them at last, and know it together and light up quickly with their mutual knowledge. It couldn't have been plainer had they both shouted.

The afternoon sun was still high above them, but the dust of the great moving herds caused a pale-yellow refraction of light which was like the light before a desert thunderstorm. The dust trailed high to their right—to the east, that is—paralleling the endless line of march of the herd's, which the hunting detail's own march also paralleled. But up ahead the dust clouds lay hooked above the ground like a vast question mark, where the animals moved slowly out of line to the right, skirting the eastern end of Jackknife Canyon, and circled back again to the left on the northern rim of the canyon. A great scythe of dust hanging over the animals like a Damoclean blade.

"Mr. Pennell," Allshard said, "I make it about three miles from where we are to the southern rim of Jackknife Canyon. Take four men and push out ahead of Corporal Jodlebauer's point. Make a reconnaissance along the entire southern rim. Rejoin me where my present line of march reaches the canyon."

"What is it, major?" Chadbourne asked sharply. "What's wrong with Rynders? Is there Comanche trouble?"

"Is there?" Oldroyd cackled. "There sure'n hell is. The Comanches are crawling with Henry repeating rifles from the Querhada to the Paradise River, and they aren't making 'em out of beaver tails, senator!"

"Where are they getting them from?"

MacLerndon Allshard looked at Brome Chadbourne as Pennell moved out with his reconnaissance detail. "It does little good to accuse a man of anything serious out here, unless you're in a position to kill him right afterwards, before he can kill you. And it does less good, as a policeman—which is the position I find myself in—to have proof of your accusation—because the court that will try your prisoner is a thousand miles away from the scene and the facts and the consciousness of the results of the crime."

"What is it you expect to find in Jackknife Canyon, major?" Chadbourne's voice was even.

"If I am lucky, sir, I expect to find a cache of Henry rifles, and if I'm better than lucky, I expect to find the smugglers getting rid of those rifles to Comanches who want to shoot buffalo—getting rid of those rifles fast, for any price that is offered, before they are caught with the evidence on them!"

Aeons ago an upthrust of traprock, buckling in frantic agony from a deep volcanic fireburst, carried with it a layer of sandstone, upending it until its grain pointed to the skies when both formations burst through the topsoil and lay across the face of the prairie, a steaming cicatrice. The rains and the surface springs that feed South Branch ate out the sandstone and left a deep and narrow indentation where it had been—an indentation that was like a beckoning finger, crooked at the second joint, or like a jackknife, if you will, with one blade half-open.

The hunting party rode on up toward the canyon rim. There were a few buffalo that had turned west from the great migration and slipped in south of the canyon, but the dust of the vast herds hung to the northward on the opposite side to Allshard's approach, and under the dust you could see the close-packed, weaving mass of animals that had skirted the eastern end of Jackknife and turned west again, paralleling the north rim.

Chadbourne rode in close to Allshard. "Rynders?"

Again Allshard looked at him. There was nothing in the senator from his gone years that his eyes were trying to lie out of. And there is that in most men, to deny confidence.

"Senator," Allshard said, "Jackknife Canyon lies on the route from Fort Starke to the Comanche agency. Rynders left Starke for the agency directly after I put it to him that we had evidence of a wide distribution of Henry rifles. Directly after I put it to him that tribe war or the prospect of a big hunt would send Comanches to the distributing point in hordes, and give it away to my watching patrols. He didn't even wait to meet you, not when we saw the herds coming north."

"In other words, if Rynders is the guilty man, you used every ounce of persuasion at your command to pack him off posthaste to get rid of the evidence of his guilt, hoping that one of your patrols would catch him in the act. But it is still a long guess, still circumstantial."

"It is circumstantial as far as Rynders is concerned, except for one additional fact, senator. The enlisted men at Fort Starke haven't been paid for two months, so the officers have syndicated them for tobacco, beer and small slops at the post exchange and Rynders' South Branch store, and the junior officers have rotated the duty of keeping a jaundiced eye casually on the jawbone score Rynders has totted against the garrison. A week ago, my adjutant, Mr. Pennell, bought a packet of tobacco at Rynders' store. When he opened it, he found that one of Rynders' clerks had made a mistake. There was no tobacco in the packet. Instead, there was straw packing around six rounds of forty-four, forty, two hundred ammunition."

Pennell and his four men were riding in through the yellow dust, bunched at the gallop. The major heeled into his mount and bolted toward them with the senator at his knee. Pennell drew in and threw up his hand to halt his detail.

"What have you got, mister?"

"Rynders is in the canyon himself, with Three-Fingered Dekker, who clerks his South Branch store, and the two drivers that came in Thursday from Santa Fe; they're passing out Henrys from Rynders' own freight wagons, sir."

Allshard kneed around Pennell. "Send your men back to the main body," he called, "and show me!"

Dismounted and flat on their faces at the canyon rim, Allshard passed his glasses to Senator Chadbourne. Ross Pennell cased his own glasses and crawled back from the rim to stand up.

There was the towheaded scalp with the braided pigtails and the pink hair ribbon, crawling with noisome flies. And there was the Rafferty girl at Tallow Creek that Red Horse had dragged off and cut and left to bleed to death. There was the Elkhorn mail driver, one side of his skull soft as a smashed egg, thrashing in reflex in the dust of the road, throwing himself a good two feet in the air at each frenzied spasm, and dying that way. And there was the paymaster pegged down and burned in half and still alive to know his agony.

All of that Brome Chadbourne saw in Allshard's face as they crawled back and stood up. And he saw dead cavalrymen, bloated black and bursting their faded shirts, from the Querhada to the Paradise River, and deep in Allshard's eyes he saw Allshard's soul. The major stood looking across the narrow canyon toward the slow-moving herds on the opposite side. *The court that will try your prisoner is a thousand miles away from the scene and the facts and the consciousness of the results of the crime.*

Then it was as if the senator had questioned him—had reached out and asked for his decision in advance—for Allshard turned and said, "Exactly what I planned to do! Arrest Toucey Rynders and send him East for trial!"

He cupped his grimy hands and hallooed down into the narrow canyon. "Rynders!" he shouted. And he drew his hand gun and emptied it into the canyon's hollow echo. And he took off his broad-brimmed hat and waved it back and forth over his head, so Rynders could see him.

On the other side of the erosion, the buffalo, weaving across the flatlands, were a huge and dusty blanket that rippled with movement as far as you could see into the yellow dust. Then at the far edge of it there was a sudden and fearful hesitation, a vast animal fright that you could almost smell, as you can, at times, smell the fear in men. Fright at the unknown, taking place behind them.

The far ripple became suddenly a broad surge, washing back upon itself—a raging surf in another breath. The thundering herds began to double back upon themselves toward the hollow, torn reverberation of the shots, toward the waving of Allshard's hat; trampling themselves in the fury of panic, coming back the slow way they had come, at full frantic gallop now, stampeding themselves to the death.

Close in, across the canyon, Brome Chadbourne could still see clear avenues of green grass, with the yellow dust streaks staining them like drift lines at high water. But as he watched, the herds compressed mightily under the pressure against their flanks and overflowed into those avenues, filling them with the flood of their resurgent tide.

For a torn second one herd was lashing frantically head on to another. Both circled and melted into each other in a tangled rip that bubbled up upon itself like gray mud in a great sink hole.

On to the canyon rim in a rending avalanche, churning the prairie to the grass roots, leaving the roots burned out in the scalloped dust. Then there was no rim, nothing but a huge moving roller pouring heavily over the hidden earth and down into Jackknife like the shoulder of a vast waterfall moving up to its drop, going over endlessly. No one spoke; no one could speak. They stood there watching the awful destruction, the gray surge to the brink and the fall that went on endlessly in dust clouds that rose up chokingly from the canyon floor, into the smell of hot blood that steamed up presently with the dust—beast blood and the blood of renegade men, pooled in crushed oblivion.

Then, as suddenly as it had begun, it ceased. The herds turned at the brink, trotted off right and left for a few yards and stood still again in the abysmal stupidity that would kill off seventy-five million of them in a handful of brief years.

"Mr. Pennell"—Allshard put on his hat and holstered his gun—"get on back to Fort Starke at once and order out two companies with every skinning knife on the post. If I can get four thousand of these hides into South Branch store before Rynders' heirs and assigns arrive to close his books, I can balance the garrison's account and give them a little credit ahead until the next paymaster arrives. . . . A pity, senator, that this had to happen. We had Rynders cold!"

Brome Chadbourne wiped his steaming forehead with his great handkerchief. "If there is ever another war, major, save a place for me, sir . . . with you!"

YANKEE GOLD
BY JOHN M. CUNNINGHAM
(The Stranger Wore a Gun)

John M. Cunningham's 1947 Collier's *short story "The Tin Star" (see* The Reel West) *was the basis for what many aficionados consider the finest Western film ever made: Carl Foreman's* High Noon *(1951), which of course starred Gary Cooper in what may be the finest performance ever given in a Western film. Cunningham has written a number of other top-notch stories, among them "Yankee Gold" (which was also first published in 1947, in the long-defunct slick magazine* Pic). *He also has two unusual Western novels to his credit,* Warhorse *(1956) and* Starfall *(1960).*

Hull leaned against the bar waiting for Mourret and looked with faint disgust at his drink. He was sick of shots and bottles; he'd tried to fix up a mint julep and there it stood, tall, pale and stinking, no ice, no mint, no nothing. You might as well drink champagne out of a kerosene can as try to make a julep in a Montana gold-boom town.

He began remembering New Orleans, the smooth mahogany bars, the silver, the river, and somebody said beside him, "Mourret's back. I just saw him go in the hotel. We'd better go up and get things settled for tonight."

Hull looked at Wootten's cold, meek face. "Tonight?" Wootten nodded, his lips compressed. He had a way of looking down, of holding his face and eyes controlled, as though half-blind, or with a kind of secretive mock-modesty which concealed his secret thoughts. Wootten's face always looked as though the coroner had just taken the ice off it. In spite of his downcast eyes he saw everything and when he looked up suddenly you saw not timidity, but pure danger.

"The Negro took Bonnetty's running horse down to be shod. Has to be ready by six tonight. And Rogers heard the black boy and Bonnetty talking out at the barn. It's tonight for sure."

"You didn't find out which way he's going to take it?"

Wootten shook his head and bit the corner of his lower lip. "Not yet. We will. I'm going on over. Don't follow me too closely." He turned and left, head down, walking neatly, modestly, feet straight, close together, everything as proper and controlled as a hangman's thoughts.

Hull looked after him, a helpless sneer faint on his face, a sneer that protected him from his own fear. Wootten was too good for him. Everything about him was efficient—his two clean, modest guns boasted no show. They were a workman's tools. Hull thought of how sometimes a man and wife got to look like each other. A man couldn't kill as many men as Wootten had and not be partly dead himself.

"Now what do you call that there thing you fixed up?" the barkeep said, looking with a yellow eye at the julep.

Hull looked at it and swallowed. "That there thing is known as Dr. Emilius Quack's Jiffy-fix. You feed it to them as they die and save the embalming cost. When are you going to get some really good kerosene in this territory?"

The barkeep's eye turned evil and he slunk down the bar like a fox in a cage. Hull looked after him. He was like the whole damned territory—dry as death, yellow and hungry as a dog—for gold.

Outside he could hear the rattle of wagons, the shout of drivers and crack of whips—bootheels tap-tapping up and down the boardwalks—hammers pounding up the flimsy shanties they had to call palaces or golden globes— nothing as natural as the wide, peaceful saloons in New Orleans, like Garigou's.

In two weeks he'd be there with twenty thousand dollars to set him up again. He smiled to himself. Twenty thousand in Yankee gold.

He walked out into the blazing sunshine and stood blinking at a girl. She was standing still in the middle of the walk. A small package lay at the edge of the walk beside her and her foot, invisible beneath her long skirt, seemed to be trying to kick something. Her face was flushed with embarrassment, yet she did not move.

He frowned with perplexity. She wasn't the kind to make a joke of herself. She was no palace girl, not with that delicacy of face. She was completely out of place here among the saloons, being stared at by every lout that knew how to lean against a porch-pole.

"Excuse me, ma'am," he said, taking off his hat and picking up the package. "This is yours, isn't it?"

"Please hold it," she said, her voice very small. He held the package, and became infected with her own embarrassment.

"What is the matter, ma'am?" She was still doing something with her foot. Somebody sniggered. Her eyelids lowered and she looked down. He looked around. They had a gallery of four or five men, all grinning.

"Who laughed?" he said.

The grins dropped. One of them took an easy step away from the saloon-front, his thumbs hooked in his gun-belt. "I did. What of it, mister?" His hands dropped from his belt.

"Don't you know it's not polite to laugh at young ladies?"
"What lady?"

Hull got him before he could move. He slammed back against the wall, slid down and sat holding his face, blood running down his forearms and chin. Hull stepped to him and gave him a stiff boot in the thigh. "Move out fast."

The other got up, took his hands down and made a pass at his gun. He went back to the wall and Hull took the gun and slung it out into the street.

He turned back to the girl, giving the others a look. They drifted away slowly, with a look on their faces as though they had forgotten to put on their pants that morning and were pretending nobody could see them.

"I'm sorry for that," he said to the girl. She ignored him painfully.

"Please, it's my shoe. Would you be kind enough to give me your arm—just for a moment?" She laid her hand on his forearm and wiggled her foot again. He looked down at her hand, middle-sized and smooth, very white, and a surprising warm pleasure made him smile.

"Please don't laugh," she said. "My father told me not to come down here. I shouldn't have. I was curious. But please don't laugh at me."

"I wasn't laughing at you, ma'am. I'm glad to be of service."

She gave a little hop to one side and stood balancing herself on one foot.

"There," she said. "You see? Would you please get it for me?"

He looked down. Her shoe, a small slipper, sat on the walk, its heel jammed into a knot-hole. He knelt and worked it loose, stood up and offered it to her.

She laughed at him. "I don't want to carry it home, thank you," she said. He put it down again and she wiggled her foot into it, stamped lightly and smiled. Her face was pale again, and her eyes, no longer clouded by embarrassment, looked up at him clear and laughing.

"Thank you so much," she said. All at once the warm pleasure in him deepened and he was looking not at her eyes, but into them. He looked away quickly.

"You're very welcome, ma'am," he said. "Let me walk with you up the street a way. The—the walks are full of holes."

She hesitated and then suddenly seemed to collect herself, frowning very faintly. She gave him a quick, shielded, almost suspicious glance, then down again. "Please, my package?" she said remotely.

"Oh," he said and held it out. She took it and looked up at him again. The shield was still there, but she was peeking over it.

Her head gave a little bow. "Thank you," she said, and went past him. He turned and watched her moving, head down, up the walk, her long, grey dress swinging. Her hair went bright and dark as she passed under the porches from sun into shadow. Then she turned a corner out of sight.

He stood with her scent still in his nostrils—suddenly astonished that she was not there.

Finally he turned and saw Wootten standing in the street, looking at him with a wooden smile, eyes slyly amused. The pleasure in Hull iced and died.

"What do you want?"

Wootten's little smile faded into his customary prim meekness. "Mourret says to hurry up. He's got a job for you right away." Four men were coming up the walk. Wootten pulled a watch from his vest and looked at it. "Ten o'clock, stranger," he said loudly, and then, after they had passed: "We've got six hours left." He turned and walked off, neatly and collectedly, through the passing wagons.

Hull looked down at the knothole in the walk. A moment before she had been there beside him; now her scent, the pressure of her hand on his arm, had gone and there was nothing left but the memory of her face.

He looked around the street, and it had a new aspect. After all, it wasn't so bad—just new and brawly. The sky had a clean, open look, a quality of bigness he had never noticed before. He thought again of her face. He didn't even know her name—but there were ways of meeting people. New Orleans could wait a while—at least until he had seen her again. And with fifteen or twenty thousand, whatever his cut might be tonight, there was no telling what he might do here—maybe better than in New Orleans.

He untied his horse, rode a few bucks out of it and managed it up the street to the hotel.

Rogers stopped pacing up and down and looked at him as he closed the door behind him, then started pacing again. Wootten sat on the bed, quietly cleaning his guns.

"I tell you, Mourret," Rogers said, "if you play this too cagey we're likely to lose the whole thing. I say just follow him out of town tonight and hold him up in the mountains, wherever he goes. To hell with all this plotting."

Mourret sat by the front window, looking down over the porch roof at the other side of the street. A quart of brandy stood on a small table beside him and he was quietly enjoying one of his good cigars. He glanced at Hull.

"Fine looking man, isn't he?" he said, nodding across the street. Hull looked out. Bonnetty stood in front of his bank talking to three or four other men. His short, spare figure was straight as a string, and as he moved about slightly, he reminded Hull of an Arab horse—the same smallness, fineness, the same air of quiet dignity. His hair was black and grey, and as he talked he smiled with amusement and content. "A fine looking man," Mourret answered himself. "Pity if we have to kill him." He delicately broke the ash from his cigar into a saucer. "Now there's a man who has sense enough to get gold without a pickaxe. They rush in every afternoon, he buys their dust and they all love him for it. He runs it to Helena and comes back for more, and all it costs him is brains, energy and horseflesh. The only trouble is, he's foxy. He never goes to the same town two times running. Sometimes Helena, sometimes Butte, sometimes Boulder. We've got to get him on the trail, but we can't do that unless we find out where he's going."

"Didn't you hear what I said?" Rogers cried out behind them. "I tell you, to hell with finding out where he's going; follow him out of town and get him anyway."

Mourret sighed. "Have a drink and calm down, Rogers."

"I think he's right, Mourret," Wootten said. "The place is full of dust. Why waste so much time?"

Mourret sighed again. "Now, boys. Now, boys. If it's full this week, it'll be full again next week. And that reminds me, Wootten, no shooting tonight if we can possibly help it. I like the old man. And anyway, we don't kill the golden goose, do we?" Wootten said nothing. "We've got to play it right. If we follow him, we'll have to track him around all day so as not to lose him. We'll have to watch his house, watch wherever he goes, and if he doesn't catch on, somebody else will notice us and pin it on us afterward. We can't have suspicions. I've got a good plan for Hull. We'll get at the Negro, Catlin, or whatever his name is. We'll just wait until he comes for Bonnetty in the buggy at noon."

Rogers sat on the bed beside Wootten, jaw clamped. "I don't give a damn for this waiting. I say let's hit him once and clear out. He's on to me. I've seen old Catlin looking at me down his nose. Every time he's around the barn out there I think he's going to knife me. He comes around like the devil's shadow. He knows I'm up to something and all he has to do is say a word to Bonnetty and I'm through. It's all right for you, Mourret, to sit around drinking in a hotel—I got to sweat in his lousy barn and work. I'm sick of it." He stopped and waited, looking at Mourret. Mourret drew on his cigar calmly, and Hull saw the lids of his eyes come down. It was a beautiful face, creamy white under pure black hair, as clear in feature and fine in modelling as the best New Orleans blood could make it.

Hull saw Rogers make a mistake as Mourret held his peace. Rogers sat up straighter and his face relaxed in boldness. "So I say," he said loudly, "let's just follow him out. The hell with all this pussy-footing around." He sat staring at Mourret.

Mourret carefully laid his cigar on the saucer, his long fingers balancing it gently. He walked over to Rogers with a slow, easy grace and stood smiling down at him.

"Now, Rogers, you're upset, and so naturally you're upsetting things. You've been very good, very helpful with your spying and your information. But don't try to take on too much. Don't try to tell me what to do." He swung. The blow cracked like a shot and left the red print of his open hand on Rogers' face. "Do you understand what I say?"

Rogers sprang up at him. Mourret caught his wrist and twisted him back down on the bed, kept on twisting and crushing. Rogers let out a cry of pain and lay whimpering.

"Do you understand?" Mourret asked again, still grinding Rogers' wristbones in his one hand. There was no tension, no anger, not even much sign of exertion, and the crushing and twisting went on. Rogers lay squealing. Mourret let go and stepped back.

"Don't tamper with me, Rogers. If I wanted to, I could tear the muscles out of your neck with one hand. You're in this, and you do what I say. Understand?"

Rogers nodded dumbly. "All right," he said. "You're the boss."

"Go back out to Bonnetty's house and hang around the barn. The Negro may let something slip."

Rogers pulled himself off the bed and went out, face sullen and remote.

Mourret glanced at Wootten. He was still cleaning his guns, carefully picking oily dust out of a crack. He did not look up. For all he showed of interest in the affair, he might have been in Texas.

Mourret came back to his chair, gave a wink and a private smile to Hull and sat down again. He picked up his cigar and drew on it till an even red circle appeared under the ash.

"Sit down, Hull, and listen to my plans. I think you're the clever one to pull the trick." He turned in his chair, crossing his legs, and gave Hull a smile that lightened his whole face. He regarded Hull for a moment. "I'll never forget your coming into Beauregarde's tent that night and reporting on your reconnaissance. So modest, so humble, and what an exploit! Do you remember that? The beginning of our acquaintance." The smile faded. "Poor Beauregarde. It broke his heart, Appomattox. That swine, Grant—that brutal, plugging, brainless swine."

Hull looked away through the window. He could not look at Mourret honestly. He had forgotten the meaning of defeat, and Mourret never would. He remembered Beauregarde well enough, the meeting in the tattered tent, even the decoration he had received of that stillborn confederation. But, now, it was all in shadow, an old photograph of people he had hardly known. The war was over, the war was dead, and he realized that the things that had held him to Mourret were dying, one by one.

"There are three things we can do," Mourret said. "None very good, but all possible. First, you take some dust in to Bonnetty and sell it, and while you are there, try to see something that will tell you where he is going. Maybe the bags are labelled. He has to write a deposit slip or a receipt or something, and the name of the bank and the town'll be on that. Try and see."

He uncrossed his legs and leaned forward. "If that doesn't work, go at it a different way. Ask him for a job. Get him talking. Talk about the danger of robbery. You've still got your old mail-guard ticket, haven't you?"

Hull nodded. "He may have heard about me."

Mourret stuck out his lips and slowly shook his head. "I don't think so. What was it, after all? A mail-guard in Louisiana is accused of conniving with robbers. It isn't as if you had been convicted. What is it? Case thrown out of court. It's a long way from here to Baton Rouge, and who cares to spread such little news? Ask him to hire you on as a rider, a guard, anything. You have an honest face, a good way with you."

Hull looked out of the window silently, thinking again of her face, remembering her eyes, clear and sparkling as stars. So he had a good way with him, did he? A way to her? He'd like to try it. Why? The question hung there without reasonable answer. He had seen her once, and he wanted to see her again. As simple as that.

And suddenly he did see her again, across the street, in a buggy, pulling up at the dry goods store two doors up from Bonnetty's bank. He watched her face as she tied the horse. Serious, a little pensive, but she did it practically, with sure movements. He caught a smile on his own face and suppressed it. She picked up her skirt, with a little bowing movement and disappeared into the shadow of the porch. He began imagining plans. Loose the team and catch them; loose a tug and fix it for her; take a package out of the buggy, follow her home and give it to her, pretending she had dropped it.

"What's the matter with you?" Mourret's low, hissing voice cut through the smile in his mind and he looked at him hurriedly. Black eyes were fixed on him intensely, at once imperious and suspicious.

"Why aren't you listening? What's the meaning of this day-dreaming? Don't you want to go through with this thing? Or are you crazy?"

Hull's mind turned cold. "Take it easy, Mourret. I'm not Rogers."

"Then listen to me as though you weren't."

Hull looked at Mourret's eyes and a strange perception dawned on him. The look in them was new to him, he felt that he was looking at a stranger, a part of Mourret that had been hidden, or had lately grown—not the casual, graceful, charming Mourret, but a dark, imperious and impersonal one. Hull suddenly felt very awkward and self-conscious, and at the same time Mourret's fixed and accusing stare broke down and some of the old amusement filtered back.

"Sorry," Hull said. "I was thinking about something. You said I was to ask for a job. What's the third plan?"

Mourret shook his head ruefully. "You're changing, Hull, my friend. Day-dreaming. Are you in love? Stick to plans and you can have any woman in New Orleans. I was saying, when Catlin, or whatever his name, comes to take Bonnetty home for lunch, I'm going to start a fight with him, order him around. You take a stand against me, be a friend to the Negro, protect him, do a little mild fighting with me. I'll retire beaten. You buy Catlin a few drinks to cheer him up. And in one of them, you put something I'll give you. It's a drug they use in Haiti. I used it in the Army on prisoners to make them answer questions. It'll work, it'll give us what we want to know. Butte, Helena or Boulder. All right?"

Hull pulled out his old mail-guard certificate and looked at it, thinking. "I'm not much of a liar, Mourret. I don't know how well I can put anything over on Bonnetty."

"You were good enough to be a spy under Beauregarde," Mourret said sharply.

"That was war, Mourret. There was a reason."

"It's still war as far as I'm concerned, Hull. Why do you think I came up to this country instead of staying in the south?"

"The gold, I supposed."

"Yankee gold. Do you think I'm a natural thief, Hull? Do you think I'd rob my friends?" He paused and slowly ground out the light of his cigar on the saucer. "Maybe Lee quit, but I never will. As far as I'm concerned, there's no such thing as robbing a Yankee. They have no rights. They gutted the South and they're robbing it blind right now. What about you? Weren't you framed out of that job so that damned Yankee could get it for his nephew? What about you?"

Hull thought a moment. Then he stood up and began wandering around the room. "I don't care, Mourret. I don't care any more."

Mourret was sitting up straight, looking at him sharply. "You don't care that you were beaten?"

Hull looked full at him. "We were beaten. We took on the North in a fight and we were beaten flat. What more is necessary to make an end of it?"

Mourret stood up. "You just quit and run? You get framed out of a job and just take it?"

Hull's voice came heavy and clear. "The Yankees won. The South is shot. They've got the power. What good does it do to fight a machine you can't lick? Let them have the job. And in any case," he added more softly, "it's better to take your licking and get out than nurse a grudge and stab them in the back."

Mourret's eyelids lowered. "You've got a fine lot of talk there. You know what you are? You're a lick-spittle coward."

Hull took three steps, his hands open and then stopped. They looked at each other steadily for a moment. Then Mourret drew the back of his hand slowly across his mouth, bent his head slightly and said to the floor, "I'm sorry."

Hull looked at him distantly and said to him as though he were on the other side of the Grand Canyon, "That's all right. Maybe I am a coward. It remains to be seen."

Mourret looked up. "Would you mind telling me why you came up here with me?"

"You asked me to. You were pretty good to me—the hospital, the lawyer, all that."

"It didn't have anything to do with money?"

"Yes, it did. I was sore. I figured if they believed I was a thief I might as well make the most of it. I'll tell you one thing, Mourret. I'm not going back to New Orleans with you."

Mourret smiled twistedly. "That's all right. We won't miss you."

"You've sure got a sidling tongue. Some day it's going to get mixed up in your teeth."

"Any day. Any day you pick, after we get through tonight." Mourret turned his back, reached for the brandy bottle and stopped. "My God, Catlin's there. Get going." He ran to the bureau. Hull looked out of the window. The girl's buggy was gone and in its place stood another with a big Negro waiting patiently in the seat.

Mourret tossed him a small sack. "Sell that." He pulled out his wallet, picked a small envelope out of it and handed it over. "Just a pinch will do. Too much will knock him out. Even if you think you found out from Bonnetty, we'll check with Catlin."

Mourret smiled in his old way and Hull felt a faint repulsion that he could have said the things he had said and still expect to go back to their old friendship. "I'll tell you what, Mourret," he said, taking the packet. "I owe you a lot. We've been through a lot together. We'll finish this job, but after that I don't know."

"Pure gratitude. A noble motive. Of course the money means nothing to you."

Blood surged to Hull's head. "As long as you put it that way, Mourret, I'll make it definite. After this, we're through. The more I see of this outfit, the less I like it. Wootten—nothing but a common murderer. Rogers—a bribed fool. And you. What's come over you since the war?"

Mourret ignored him. "You're going to finish this job all right, whether you like it or not. I'll see you and Catlin later."

Hull went down the hall burning with anger. The more he thought of it, the less he liked the job. The whole thing was dirty; a filthy mess he'd tied himself to in a period of bitterness. He'd cut clear of Mourret, the South and the past, and try his luck in new country. Up here nothing mattered—the place was full of men who had new names, changed them every month, and nobody cared. It was a new land, undiscovered, untouched. Wyoming was filling up with cattle, here the mines were opening like flowers and the earth was full of wealth. He remembered New Orleans with sudden disgust. Defeated, bitter, poor, gaudy, holding itself together with a specious pride—like the white marble tombs that had to depend on their rotting stilts to keep them out of the rotten Mississippi mud. A dead city.

He heard the racket of voices coming up the stair-well. Up here it was raw, but it was new and the dirt was on the hide, not in the bone.

And as he started to go down the steps the thing that had been in the back of his mind, urging all these thoughts, came forward: the girl. His anger eased and he smiled slightly. That was the real reason he wanted to be free of Mourret. Because she and Mourret didn't mix. He suddenly hauled up his mind and looked at himself coldly. Here he was, thinking like this, basing his actions on the look of the eyes of a girl he'd seen for five minutes that morning, whose name he didn't even know. And yet a certain shrewd instinct reassured him—he knew her, knew enough of her to be warranted in acting surely.

He went on down the stairs and out of the lobby to his horse. He'd get the information for Mourret and be quit of him for good.

He mounted his half-broken horse and worked it across the street, dodging teams and wagons. As he pushed it toward the hitch-rail beside the buggy, the girl came out of the store and got in beside Catlin. Catlin took up the whip and brought it back—the lash hit Hull's horse in the face and the horse exploded, bucking and kicking. There was a crash. He fought it down and tied it trembling.

"I'm sorry, suh," Catlin said.

"Oh, I'm so sorry," the girl said. "I know he didn't mean it."

He looked from one to the other, then at Bonnetty's sign over the bank door, then back.

"You're not going to be angry with me after I apologized, are you?" she asked.

"Are you by any chance Miss Bonnetty?"

"Why, yes. Is that any reason for looking so upset?"

He glanced up at Mourret's window and back to her. "No, ma'am." He got hold of himself and took off his hat. "In fact I'm glad the horse was hit—although maybe it's odd to be introduced by a horse. My name is Hull, ma'am. John Hull. And you owed me no apology, Miss Bonnetty, seeing as my horse kicked two spokes out of your wheel." He looked at her and put a question in his eyes. "With your permission, I'll drive your buggy to the wheelwright's tomorrow and have it fixed."

"Catlin can do it, thank you, Mr. Hull."

"I'm sure he can. But why deprive me of that pleasure. I have so few, you know."

She looked up and laughed. "I see," she said. "Very well, you may find the buggy out at my father's ranch. Rogers will have to give it to you, since father and I live in town." She looked at him with not too secret amusement, and as his face fell, she smiled. "And please return it to my house, if you will. I'll be there to inspect it. Catlin, do you want to take me home? You can come back for father." Catlin gathered up the lines. "Goodbye, Mr. Hull," she said.

He watched them disappear in the traffic.

"Your horse is a little rough yet," somebody said behind him. He turned and saw Bonnetty. "Thanks for offering to fix my buggy, Mr. Hull. Catlin should have looked behind him."

"You know me?"

Bonnetty smiled. "I was eavesdropping in the door. And I know of no reason why you cannot come to the house without having to kick a spoke out of my buggy for an excuse. As a matter of fact, I've known you for some time."

"I don't understand. How do you know me?"

"Come inside and be at ease. In fact, come into the back office. I want to talk to you."

Bonnetty led him along the counter, past the scales, into the shadows of the rear office. A back window let in a dim light. In one corner stood a large safe. Saddle bags lay on the floor, two rifles stood in one corner, and a heap of empty gold-pokes lay in a large roasting pan. A roll-top desk stood open, littered with papers.

Somebody banged a bell out front.

"Sit down, Hull," Bonnetty said. "Early customer." He went out, shutting the door behind him.

Hull got up and walked nervously to the window, loosened his gun, turned and sat down again. Bonnetty, Bonnetty, he thought. His daughter. And what did he know about him? If she was his daughter, he'd have to get out of the robbery some way—play along with Mourret until the chance came. He had three hours to do it.

He looked at the papers on the desk. There were too many to go through, and then he realized that if he was to edge out on Mourret, he'd better know nothing. He couldn't give him the information now.

He got up and went to the window again. The poke of gold sagged in his pocket. Better return it to Mourret. And how would Mourret like it when he told him? It would mean a fight of some kind, argument, fists, guns. He thought of Wootten.

Then he realized that merely backing out of the robbery solved nothing. Even if he got out of it with his skin, they'd go ahead. If they couldn't find out which town Bonnetty was going to, Mourret would give up his plan, make a good haul and take to the hills. The robbery would come off whether he were in it or not. He'd have to tell Bonnetty—and Bonnetty would know of his part in the plan to rob him, and she would find out, and when she knew, what chance had this little beginning to grow under the doubt and suspicion that would be in her mind?

He turned about restively. Was she worth it, anyway? Was any woman worth it? He recalled her face, remembered her laugh. An amused laugh. Suppose he protected Bonnetty, took the awful chances of bucking Mourret and Wootten, and found out that he was nothing but an amusement to her? And then he remembered what was behind the laugh. Amusement, yes, naturally, but behind it, interest, a shy friendliness, and sincerity. He'd have it out with Bonnetty and take his chances.

The door opened and he turned. Bonnetty came in smiling, sat down at the desk and swivelled around. "Sit down, Hull, sit down. You make me nervous as you are." He began rolling himself a cigarette, shot Hull a side glance and said, frowning as he spilled tobacco, "In fact, you look like a man about to make a confession. Let me save you the trouble." He licked the paper and twisted the end.

"You were hired to guard federal mails between Baton Rouge and New Orleans. You were held up, shot in the battle, killed the driver. You were accused of conniving with the bandits. You pleaded not guilty—said the driver was the conniver, not you, that he got the drop on you when the stage was stopped. You fought him anyway, killed him and were shot by one of the gang. You were acquitted on lack of real evidence, in spite of a general prejudice against you, and you left Baton Rouge two months ago."

Hull looked at him quietly. "That's all very true. What about it?"

Bonnetty winked at him and lighted his cigarette. "The rest of the story is that one of the nephews of the military governor of Baton Rouge got your job immediately. If you had had a state job, they would simply have fired you. Since it was a federal job, they had to frame you. Well, Hull, you worked as guard for six years and during that time defeated nine attempts at robbery. A very good record. In case you want to know how I know all this, the banks all have reports on things pertaining to mail conditions, and I read them carefully. I have to keep an eye open for odd characters around town, in my business."

Hull stood up. "That's fine. I'll be around."

"Sit down. It's a sin to be so touchy. Did I say you were an odd character? Did I? Actually?"

Hull grinned and sat down again.

"It's a fact I need a guard. Somebody to ride gold from here to the banks in Helena and Butte, sometimes Boulder, a few times to Ft. Missoula. Somebody I can trust. Up to now I've ridden it myself—I don't believe in asking any man to risk his life riding my gold for the little I'd pay him. But it's too damned hard on me, 50, 60 miles a night. I've got to get a good man."

His cigarette fell apart in his fingers. "Blast these things. I won't smoke the cigars they sell out here. Well, Hull, you're such a man. A fine record and one bad break."

Hull drew a deep breath, stretched his legs out and laughed. "You mean you're offering me a job?"

"Yes. Not much pay to start. I want to tempt you, and tempt you good."

"You're putting a lot of faith in me, Mr. Bonnetty. Lack of evidence doesn't exactly prove innocence, either."

"You came up here without changing your name. Catlin tells me you've been hanging around in the saloons drinking a good deal in a gloomy manner. Not changing your name shows me you feel innocent. And if you were a real thief, you wouldn't be drinking in bitterness, but out thieving and having a good time. My daughter Maura told me how you helped her this morning and beat up some oaf that laughed at her—drat her, she's just out from Philadelphia and doesn't realize anything—and I, myself, saw your courtesy just now. That might be merely her attractiveness, but I'll wager not, since courtesy's a habit you don't get overnight. Anyway, it's an offer. I take chances all the time and you're a pretty good one."

"When would I start?"

"Tonight. No point in waiting."

Hull looked at the rifles in the corner and thought of Mourret. If there were only some way of getting free of Mourret, cutting loose from him and Wootten. Maura, he had said. Maura was her name. What was the matter with him? he suddenly thought. He'd get rid of Mourret some way.

"I'll take it," he said. Bonnetty shook his hand. "And glad to have it."

"That's fine." Bonnetty's face was quiet and shrewd. "I don't mind telling you there's room in this town for a real banking business. This is no boom. The mines are big. When the gold's gone there's copper. Nobody wants that now, but they will later."

"I had a little mathematics in school."

"I can always get somebody that can add. I want somebody with some guts, brains and go. We'll see what you can do, Hull. Come out to my house at two o'clock and I'll go over a map with you."

Hull stood up. He wasn't going to tell Bonnetty anything. This was too good to spoil. He'd settle Mourret privately.

"You want to sell that?" Bonnetty asked, pointing to his pocket.

Hull put his hand over the bulge. Mourret's damned gold.

"Come on out and we'll weigh it up."

He followed Bonnetty out and surrendered the bag. Refusing without a good reason would only look suspicious. He looked through the open door and saw Catlin again waiting in the buggy. He glanced past him and saw Mourret waiting on the hotel porch, slapping a quirt lightly against one leg.

Bonnetty took the bag to the scales, began to untie the knot, stopped and looked quizzically at Hull. "Do you work with old Burrel?"

"What? No, why?" Hull asked in surprise.

"This knot—he always ties his pokes this way." He poured the dust into the pan and began weighing it. "It's funny you and he should use a lover's knot. Most of them just use grannies. What's the idea? You saving up to get married?"

Hull forced a laugh. "I ought to meet him some day—seeing we've got something in common." Mourret was coming down the steps to his horse.

"He's up on Salt Creek, sober old man with a big bushy beard, religious as he can be, in his way. Doesn't smoke, drink, swear or gamble. Just greedy. Once in a while he'll come down to sell a poke for food—most of it he's got stacked up in his cabin." Bonnetty began counting out bills, and lifted his head at a sharp command from outside.

"Get out of my way!"

Mourret was sitting his horse beside the buggy. Catlin was looking up at him with an expression of deep reserve and dignity. Bonnetty stood stiffly watching, the bills unnoticed in his hands. Hull began to move slowly toward the door, feeling anger rise. The act was out.

"Suh, I'm sorry. This is Mr. Bonnetty's hitching place, suh. There's room over there."

Hull reached the door, a dull fog of apprehension in his mind. Mourret was half-drunk, his pale, cool face now flushed, his usually firm mouth loose and smiling.

"Don't speak to me, you black b------ —move!"

"I regret, suh, this is Mr. Bonnetty's—"

The quirt slashed out, cutting across Catlin's face. Hull stood shocked. This was no act. Mourret's face flamed with rage. Bonnetty was running around the counter. Hull jumped through the door as Mourret's quirt whistled again.

"Cut it out!" he shouted as the lash cracked viciously. Catlin huddled stubbornly in the buggy seat, defending his head with his arms.

"You ape, when I say move, you—"

Hull reached up and grabbed Mourret's arm.

"Cut it out, you fool!" he shouted. Mourret slashed at him with the quirt, he took it on the neck and with sudden fury dragged him out of the saddle. The horse danced away as Mourret fell in the dust and he hauled him to his feet.

"You're going too far," he breathed heavily in Mourret's face. "This was supposed to be an act."

"Let go of me, you trash. No negro's going to sass me to my face."

Hull stood back and forgot in his anger that there had ever been a plan.

"And no cheap New Orleans bum is going to beat a black in front of me and get away with it. You understand that? You're drunk. Clear out."

Mourret's teeth bared and he slashed at him. Hull ducked it, lunging in, and drove Mourret's head back with a snap. Mourret fell to his knees and sat back in the dust. He shook his head and got up clumsily. He suddenly feinted at Hull, Hull parried it with his left arm and Mourret, seizing his wrist, twisted him to his knees. He wrenched against Mourret's grip and coming up threw him off. Mourret staggered back and again stood still, panting, his eyes bloodshot.

"You're right," he gasped. "I'm drunk. It's the only reason I didn't kill you. The next time this happens, I'll be sober."

He turned and walked unsteadily back to the hotel.

"That's twice today you've defended my people," Bonnetty said behind him. "I'm grateful." Hull turned, wiping sweat from his face. Bonnetty's face was calm, but his eyes followed Mourret with a cold, flickering anger. "You all right, Catlin?"

"Yessuh," Catlin said, holding his face and trying to make a smile. "Thanks to Mr. Hull, thank you, suh."

"You'd better come out to dinner now, Hull. I want you to help me repack the gold, anyway. Catlin and I'll wait for you if you want to clean up in the hotel."

Hull stared at Mourret's window. Now was the time to settle with Mourret. He nodded. "I'll be right with you."

He stopped outside Mourret's door and loosened his gun in the holster. He'd break with them now, take empty saddle bags tonight, let Mourret and the others follow him, and fight it out. He could backtrack and waylay them, as they had planned waylaying Bonnetty, and reduce the odds considerably.

He knocked and said his name in a low voice. The key rattled. Wootten opened the door and smiled at him blankly. Mourret was drying his face with a towel.

"I couldn't get Catlin away."

"I saw that from the window."

"I couldn't find out anything. What's more, I didn't try. I'm through."

"Is that all?"

"That's all."

Mourret looked at Wootten and smiled. He shrugged, slung the towel into a corner and strolled to the bed, casually picked up a gun and pointed it at Hull's stomach. Hull's arms made an instinctive jerk for his own guns, then slowly rose. Mourret's casualness had caught him completely off guard.

"It's not quite all, Hull. I had an idea when you left you were sore enough to cross me. Why didn't you tell me Bonnetty hired you to ride the gold tonight? That you're going out to his house to go over the map? I sent

Wootten over. He went in when you and Bonnetty went in the back office. He heard every word." He raised the gun-muzzle an inch and his eyes froze. "You're not through, Hull. You're going out and find out where you're taking it, you're going to ride out with it and we're going to meet you. And you're going to hand it over."

Hull looked at the gun muzzle. "And suppose I don't. Suppose I round up the local law and drive you out of town?"

Mourret smiled. "You can't. You've got no evidence. You're forgetting they can't do anything until something's happened. Don't try to cross me any more. If you do, I'll kill you. But you won't cross me, you're going to do exactly what I say. Because if you don't, we're going to get Bonnetty's daughter. You see now?"

Hull looked at him with widening eyes.

Mourret laughed. "You think I don't know what's got into you? Wootten told me about this morning. I saw you and her out there, myself. Doves. Charming. And I see it in your face right now. If you want her alive, you'll do exactly what I say. Get out now, Romeo, and do as I tell you—quickly, obediently, like a lamb. Open the door for him, Wootten."

Hull backed out of the door, still dumb, and stood staring at it as it slammed in his face. He had a raging impulse to kick down the door and have it out now; but he realized he could prove nothing—it would be only murder, even if he succeeded. The only thing to do was to tell Bonnetty.

He turned and made his way slowly down the hall.

Catlin took the last of the dishes off the table and Bonnetty rose. He had been grave all through the meal, speaking very little. Maura had watched his face worriedly. Hull had sat in silence, occasionally forcing himself to speak. Twice he had caught Catlin looking at him with a peculiar expression—one of reserved judgment and perplexity. There was none of that morning's friendliness.

"I'll get a few things ready, Hull, and then call you." Bonnetty went out.

Maura looked at Hull. "What's the matter?" she asked. "He isn't at all like himself."

Hull shook his head.

She regarded him a moment and smiled. "You too. What's got into you?"

He pulled himself out of his depression and anxiety and tried to smile. They rose. The only thing to do was to hope for the best and, at least in front of her, pretend that nothing was wrong. They stood at a window, looking down the street.

"Your father's given me a job," he said. "Riding gold. He seemed to suggest there might be a kind of future in it."

She smiled. "That's fine. He likes you. That means you'll be around for some time, doesn't it?"

He nodded and then looked at her suddenly and fully. "I hope so. There's nothing I'd like more."

She looked away. "I know about your trouble in Louisiana. It doesn't make any difference to me."

"Did your father tell you?"

"I asked him. I asked him why a man like you would be staying in saloons in the mornings—so he told me. Not that I object to a man's drinking," she added hurriedly. "Indeed, in school in Philadelphia, once in a while we used to steal a bottle of sherry out of the pantry and drink it up in our room—so you see I am not as innocent as you might think."

He turned her gently toward him and smiled down at her. She looked up at him quite seriously a moment, examining his face and eyes, and then smiled back.

"Hull!" Bonnetty called. He jumped and immediately a wave of fear swept through his stomach as the whole situation came back to him.

"Coming," he answered, and turned back to her. "Listen," he said. "Do you feel this is a kind of beginning?"

She looked up. "I do feel that way. I don't know of any reason why I shouldn't, so I do."

"Hull!"

He gave her a sudden light kiss and left her, feeling as he went the sudden tightening of her fingers on his arm.

He stopped at the door of Bonnetty's library and drew a deep breath. Just how he could tell him about Mourret and his danger, and yet keep his faith, he could not see—but he had to tell him.

On the floor beside Bonnetty's desk rested the black satchel which Catlin and he had dragged in from the buggy. On the desk stood several large full buckskin sacks. On the floor lay two empty saddlebags. Bonnetty was writing on a pad of forms.

"Help me tie them up, will you, Hull?" Bonnetty said without looking up.

Hull glanced over the paper. Helena, First National. He pulled up a chair and picked up a cord, wound it twice around the sack neck and tied it firmly. He went on to the next.

He was suddenly aware of Catlin behind him and looked up into Bonnetty's eyes. They were grave, sad and remote.

"What's the matter?" Hull asked, dropping his string.

"Catlin has a gun on you, Hull. Don't try to get your own. That's all right, Catlin, leave them where they are. I don't think Mr. Hull's likely to use them."

Hull sat up straight. "What's all this, Mr. Bonnetty?"

Bonnetty pointed to the sacks. "The sack you brought in this morning had a lover's knot—Burrel's knot. I assumed you tied it. I asked you to tie these sacks in order to check that. I find you tie a square knot. That means your sack was tied up by Burrel, not you. Yet you said you did not know Burrel. Then how, I wonder, did you come by Burrel's sack?"

"What's all this about? It's quite true I don't know Burrel—also, I lied about tying that knot. But I came by the sack honestly."

"I don't see how. Burrel was robbed and killed in his cabin last night. Catlin heard it this morning."

Bonnetty's face was heavy and old. "I'm sorry. Looking at you now, I can't believe it. I liked you immediately, Hull, liked your record, your actions. I am sorry also to find my judgment of men so defective. It's rarely been so wrong. I can only conclude, comparing this evidence with the honesty of your face, that you are the damnedest, smoothest, cleverest liar I have ever met."

He shoved his chair back a foot. "If you have no interpretation of this evidence other than what I have given, I am forced to take you down and place you under arrest for murder and robbery. Catlin, take his guns."

Hull looked at Bonnetty helplessly. "I'll tell you the whole truth. I was going to anyway, before you sprung this on me."

Bonnetty listened carefully and thought it over for a long time when Hull had finished.

"Assuming your story is true, Hull, which I'd like to believe, can you make Mourret confess that he gave you the sack? Or even admit that he knows you? He would laugh off the accusation of planning to rob me. You haven't got a case, Hull—all you have is a story."

Bonnetty sat back. "All I can reasonably do is take you down and have you arrested. I don't want to, I prefer to believe you, but I can't do otherwise." He rose. "Catlin, hold him till I get my coat. I hate to do this, Hull. But I can't let you go in the face of evidence. My conscience won't let me."

Hull stood up. "There's something you're forgetting, Mr. Bonnetty. Mourret and Wootten are still on the loose. I told you what they threatened to do. They'll do it."

"I'll have to take my chances," Bonnetty said, and went out, shutting the door.

Hull looked at Catlin, sizing him up. He was big, hard, and had a gun. If he could kick the gun out of his hand, he might have a chance of taking a dive through the window.

Catlin smiled. "That's all right, Mr. Hull, suh. You don't have to look at me that way. It's few times I've had a white gentleman stand up for me against another white man, and take a beating for my sake. You go now, suh, and I'll fire a couple of shots after you. Mr. Bonnetty's conscience won't hurt him none if he thinks I tried—and knows I missed. Here's your guns." He grinned and opened the window. "I reckon you'd better get out of town, suh. He'll think he'll have to report you to the sheriff, suh."

"Don't worry, Catlin. I've got a plan I want to try out." He grabbed his guns and the two saddlebags and scrambled out of the window. As he ran for the barn two shots crashed behind him and dirt spouted far to one side. Catlin began shouting. He ducked into the barn and ran for his horse.

Inside the house, Bonnetty calmly went into his library again. "You can shut up the shouting, Catlin. I heard you." He sat down at his desk and sighed. "I hope he does what he said he'd do." He looked up at Catlin. "You can take the afternoon off. And you can take my shotgun if you think it will do any good. You'd better load it with buck."

Hull slung the saddlebags into a corner and poured himself a shot of Mourret's brandy. Mourret and Wootten watched him suspiciously.

"Better have one, Mourret," Hull said, grinning at him. "It's all set. It's perfect. I'm to take the bags out to Bonnetty's tonight, load up and hit for Helena by the Judge Fork pass. You three can meet me along the road and we'll split and take off. Sorry I was sore at you, Mourret. Let's forget it."

Mourret's face relaxed and he stood up with a smile. "I thought you were going crazy this morning, Hull, old boy. I never saw such a fast change in a man. Wootten, drink up!" He began pacing up and down, rubbing his hands excitedly. Hull watched him as though he were a stranger. "It's four now," Mourret said. "We'll leave at six and meet you about 10 miles out."

Wootten hadn't moved from the bed, but sat stiffly on the edge, his knees close together, his round, alert eyes watching Hull's face. "It sounds too good, Mourret. Too easy."

Somebody knocked at the door.

"Who is it?" Mourret said.

"Me. Rogers. Open up." He burst in, his eyes wide and face excited. "Something's happened," he chattered at Mourret, not bothering to look around. "Hull was out there. Something went wrong. He busted out of the house and Catlin took two shots at him. I saw him from the stables. Bonnetty must have found out some—"

He saw Hull and his mouth opened. Mourret's eyes darted to Hull. Hull saw the sudden flash in them, dropped his glass and grabbed for his gun. Before he had it halfway out, Wootten had leaped from the bed and was crouched in the middle of the room, covering him.

"Drop it," Wootten said, his eyes glaring like a cat's. "Drop it."

Blood pounded in Hull's head, half fear and half anger. He let go of the gun and raised his hands. Mourret stepped behind him, snatched his gun out and skidded it under the bed.

"Talk," Mourret said in a hard, stiff voice, pinching the word off with tight lips. "What's the deal. What's the meaning of this line about you riding the gold—and getting chased off the place."

"He's crossed us," Wootten said. "What's behind all this? He's lying to us for some reason."

"Let him have it," Rogers said. "Get rid of him. We can get the dust out at the house. I saw them lug it in."

"Shut up," Mourret snapped. "We'll get it all right, but no shooting here. How much does Bonnetty know? You'd better tell it straight, or I'll take that dame out and—"

Hull whipped around, slamming his fist down at Mourret, and missed. Wootten's knees hit him in the kidneys and he crashed down across Mourret's chair, knocking over the table and the bottle. He heaved up, trying to throw Wootten off and somebody jumped on the back of his knees. He saw Mourret's hand and arm, grabbing up the bottle, made a final struggle to throw off Wootten, and then as the bottle smashed down, his brain exploded with a thousand lights and he lay still.

He woke slowly and lay in dusk, trying to blink the haze out of his aching brain. He heard low voices, and then realized that the sun had gone. He was tied hand and foot and lay on the floor arched backward, facing the open windows, his wrists lashed to his ankles.

He became aware of the extent of his sickness and weakness and lay in an immense weariness, remembering what had happened and hardly caring. The voices behind him went on, low, sharp and urgent.

"In the back?"

"Yeah, there's a window."

"All right. I'll go in by the front and cover Catlin. Wootten, you go in and cover Bonnetty and the girl. If it isn't in the house we'll damned soon find out where. The old man won't let thirty thousand dollars worry him when we start on his only daughter."

Hull stiffened all over, his head clearing with rage and the pain shrinking to a small, burning point at the top of his skull.

"Rogers, you stay here and keep a guard on that double crossing------. When we come back we'll decide what's the best way to get rid of him."

"How do I know you're coming back?" Rogers whined.

"Don't be a fool. Do you think we'd ride out on you with him still alive as a witness? Wootten, you all set? It's about time. Let's go and have a couple of drinks downstairs before we start."

The door slammed. Rogers came over to Hull and sat down beside him, gun in hand. "One peep out of you and I'll crack your head open, Hull."

"Listen, Rogers, you know what this'll mean, don't you? You'll be on the run for the rest of your life. Think it over. Be smart. Cut me loose—we'll go down and get the sheriff and stop this thing."

"Shut up!" Rogers said, raising the gun. "This is my chance to get out of this lousy life. Shovelling manure forever. This is my big chance. Shut up."

Hull lay quiet, listening to the usual evening uproar in the street below, the jangle of pianos, hoarse singing from a dozen saloons, an occasional shot as some lush miner celebrated his luck. Another shout wouldn't mean a thing to anybody down there.

Outside the windows a shadow rose in the dark, faintly outlined by the reflection from the lighted street below. The long black barrel of a shot gun snaked into the room.

"Lay down that gun, suh," Catlin said in a low rumble. "Else I shoot off your leg."

Rogers jerked upright in his chair, his face working.

"Don't want to shoot you, Mr. Rogers, but I reckon—"

Rogers threw himself onto the floor, whipping around and firing at the window. The shot gun spurted orange fire and as Hull's hearing slowly came back he heard Rogers groaning on the floor. Catlin came in through the window like a big black bear, moving slowly and lightly, and began cutting Hull free.

"I sneaked up like a porter, suh. I been lying out there two hours waiting for the odds to come down. I reckoned you might need a little help. You want we should go out and wait for those gunmen to come at Mr. Bonnetty?"

Hull stood flexing his wrists and fingers to get the cramp out of them.

"Wait, hell. We don't dare let them get near that house. You ride out and bring Bonnetty and the sheriff to the bar downstairs. I think I know a way to hold them that long."

He crawled under the bed, gritting his teeth against the blinding pain that flooded his head, and retrieved his gun. As he walked down the hall, he had to steady himself with one hand against the wall. He stood at the top of the stairs, listening to the roar of voices and tinkle of glasses downstairs.

He went on down and edged inconspicuously into the crowded bar. Mourret and Wootten stood together half way down. He beckoned the bartender.

"Two whiskies, quick," he said. He fumbled in his pocket and took out the little envelope Mourret had given him. The barkeep set the glasses down and as he turned away, Hull slid the powder into them.

"My compliments to those two gentlemen down there. Just say they're on the house."

He drew away from the bar and mingled with the crowd. He watched Mourret and Wootten accept the drinks with surprise and toss them off, and then moved up directly behind them.

"Don't move, Mourret," he said in a low voice, looking between their heads at their faces in the backbar mirror. "Don't move at all."

Mourret's eyes glittered back at him from the mirror, and then he smiled. "You can't stop us, Hull. If you start anything we'll just kill you in self-defense."

"No. If what you said about that drug is true, Mourret, you won't be able to lie for a while. Because you and Wootten just drank it. So we're just going to stand here like this till the sheriff gets here, and then you're going to answer questions."

Wootten's face lost its neat look and slowly went blank. "What's the idea? What drug?" Mourret stared at his glass, his face pale.

"We've got to get out of here, Wootten. It makes you talk. You double-crossing rat, Hull—I'll kill you for this. Get out."

"It makes you talk," Wootten repeated in a low voice. He gave a short laugh. "What kind of nonsense is this? I've kept my mouth shut for 15 years and no damned drug is going to make me into a fool. Hell, they had me in Natchez for a week after the Connelly murder, and you think I cracked? They never found out it was me, and if they couldn't, do you think some punk constable—"

"Shut up! You're talking now, you fool."

"Talking? What did I say?"

"Hull, I'm coming at you in just ten seconds. Get away while you can. Wootten, you just confessed a murder. Let's get out of here fast."

"I what?" Wootten said, gaping. "What?" His mouth opened with amazement. His hand went for his gun. Before he could draw, Hull stepped in and landed a smashing left to the jaw. Then everything happened at once. Wootten came up shooting as Hull dodged, pulling his gun. Maura appeared in the doorway. Dead silence fell on the crowd. A man writhed on the floor, holding his stomach. Mourret had both guns out. The crowd shrank away and lined up against the wall.

"Don't anybody move," Mourret said. "Hull, I said I'd get you."

"Drop it!" a deep voice said in the door. Wootten fired at the star on the man's chest and he fell. Mourret's gun blasted at Hull as Hull pulled his trigger and he and Mourret went down at the same time. Mourret staggered up. Hull lay still, his right chest flaming with pain. He had dropped his gun.

"Come on," Mourret yelled at Wootten. They moved off toward the rear door, covering the crowd. Hull got to his knees and dived for his gun. Mourret's gun crashed as he grabbed it and the bullet seared his thigh. Wootten whirled as he fired, and he fired again into the blast of his gun. Wootten staggered back and fell, the back of his head blown out.

Mourret sagged against the bar, trying to hold himself up. He turned his head and looked heavily at Hull; his head fell, his hands let go of the bar and he slumped to the floor.

The crowd began to move out of its paralysis, some breaking and running for the doors, the rest mulling around Hull and Mourret's body.

Bonnetty pushed through and knelt beside Hull. "I take it back, Hull, whatever I said. I'm damned glad to know I was wrong about you. They killed Burrel and the sheriff'll be mighty grateful to you for getting them."

Catlin came up with a doctor and Hull sat quiet while he went to work.

"Does Maura know about my being mixed up with Mourret?"

"Yes, yes," Bonnetty sighed. "She made me tell her."

Hull's heart sank. "What did she say?"

"I don't know what's the matter with her, son. She's lost all her morals. She says she doesn't care. She's out in the buggy. Made me let her come. When the doctor's fixed you up, do you think you can walk out?"

"Listen," Hull said, grinning, "when the doctor lets me up, I'm making it on the run."

A MAN CALLED HORSE
BY DOROTHY M. JOHNSON
(A Man Called Horse)

One of the foremost writers of contemporary Western fiction, Dorothy M. Johnson (1905–1984) created novels and short stories of high literary merit that show her understanding of the forces that shaped the American West. She was the recipient of numerous awards from such organizations as the Western Writers of America and the Western Heritage Foundation and was revered by the native Americans who populate her home state of Montana. A Man Called Horse *is one of three films made from her short fiction. The other two are the surprisingly good* The Hanging Tree *(1959), with Gary Cooper, Maria Schell, and George C. Scott, based on the novella of the same title, and* The Man Who Shot Liberty Valance *(1962), featuring John Wayne, James Stewart, and Lee Marvin, from the short story of the same title (included in* The Reel West*).*

He was a young man of good family, as the phrase went in the New England of a hundred-odd years ago, and the reasons for his bitter discontent were unclear, even to himself. He grew up in the gracious old Boston home under his grandmother's care, for his mother had died in giving him birth; and all his life he had known every comfort and privilege his father's wealth could provide.

But still there was the discontent, which puzzled him because he could not even define it. He wanted to live among his equals—people who were no better than he and no worse either. That was as close as he could come to describing the source of his unhappiness in Boston and his restless desire to go somewhere else.

In the year 1845, he left home and went out West, far beyond the country's creeping frontier, where he hoped to find his equals. He had the idea that in Indian country, where there was danger, all white men were kings, and he wanted to be one of them. But he found, in the West as in Boston, that the men he respected were still his superiors, even if they could not read, and those he did not respect weren't worth talking to.

He did have money, however, and he could hire the men he respected. He hired four of them, to cook and hunt and guide and be his companions, but he found them not friendly.

They were apart from him and he was still alone. He still brooded about his status in the world, longing for his equals.

On a day in June, he learned what it was to have no status at all. He became a captive of a small raiding party of Crow Indians.

He heard gunfire and the brief shouts of his companions around the bend of the creek just before they died, but he never saw their bodies. He had no chance to fight, because he was naked and unarmed, bathing in the creek, when a Crow warrior seized and held him.

His captor let him go at last, let him run. Then the lot of them rode him down for sport, striking him with their coup sticks. They carried the dripping scalps of his companions, and one had skinned off Baptiste's black beard as well, for a trophy.

They took him along in a matter-of-fact way, as they took the captured horses. He was unshod and naked as the horses were, and like them he had a rawhide thong around his neck. So long as he didn't fall down, the Crows ignored him.

On the second day they gave him his breeches. His feet were too swollen for his boots, but one of the Indians threw him a pair of moccasins that had belonged to the halfbreed, Henri, who was dead back at the creek. The captive wore the moccasins gratefully. The third day they let him ride one of the spare horses so the party could move faster, and on that day they came in sight of their camp.

He thought of trying to escape, hoping he might be killed in flight rather than by slow torture in the camp, but he never had a chance to try. They were more familiar with escape than he was and, knowing what to expect, they forestalled it. The only other time he had tried to escape from anyone, he had succeeded. When he had left his home in Boston, his father had raged and his grandmother had cried, but they could not talk him out of his intention.

The men of the Crow raiding party didn't bother with talk.

Before riding into camp they stopped and dressed in their regalia, and in parts of their victims' clothing; they painted their faces black. Then, leading the white man by the rawhide around his neck as though he were a horse, they rode down toward the tepee circle, shouting and singing, brandishing their weapons. He was unconscious when they got there; he fell and was dragged.

He lay dazed and battered near a tepee while the noisy, busy life of the camp swarmed around him and Indians came to stare. Thirst consumed him, and when it rained he lapped rain water from the ground like a dog. A scrawny, shrieking, eternally busy old woman with ragged graying hair threw a chunk of meat on the grass, and he fought the dogs for it.

When his head cleared, he was angry, although anger was an emotion he knew he could not afford.

It was better when I was a horse, he thought—when they led me by the rawhide around my neck. I won't be a dog, no matter what!

The hag gave him stinking, rancid grease and let him figure out what it was for. He applied it gingerly to his bruised and sun-seared body.

Now, he thought, I smell like the rest of them.

While he was healing, he considered coldly the advantages of being a horse. A man would be humiliated, and sooner or later he would strike back and that would be the end of him. But a horse had only to be docile. Very well, he would learn to do without pride.

He understood that he was the property of the screaming old woman, a fine gift from her son, one that she liked to show off. She did more yelling at him than at anyone else, probably to impress the neighbors so they would not forget what a great and generous man her son was. She was bossy and proud, a dreadful sag of skin and bones, and she was a devilish hard worker.

The white man, who now thought of himself as a horse, forgot sometimes to worry about his danger. He kept making mental notes of things to tell his own people in Boston about this hideous adventure. He would go back a hero, and he would say, "Grandmother, let me fetch your shawl. I've been accustomed to doing little errands for another lady about your age."

Two girls lived in the tepee with the old hag and her warrior son. One of them, the white man concluded, was his captor's wife and the other was his little sister. The daughter-in-law was smug and spoiled. Being beloved, she did not have to be useful. The younger girl had bright, wandering eyes. Often enough they wandered to the white man who was pretending to be a horse.

The two girls worked when the old woman put them at it, but they were always running off to do something they enjoyed more. There were games and noisy contests, and there was much laughter. But not for the white man. He was finding out what loneliness could be.

That was a rich summer on the plains, with plenty of buffalo for meat and clothing and the making of tepees. The Crows were wealthy in horses, prosperous and contented. If their men had not been so avid for glory, the white man thought, there would have been a lot more of them. But they went out of their way to court death, and when one of them met it, the whole camp mourned extravagantly and cried to their God for vengeance.

The captive was a horse all summer, a docile bearer of burdens, careful and patient. He kept reminding himself that he had to be better-natured than other horses, because he could not lash out with hoofs or teeth. Helping the old woman load up the horses for travel, he yanked at a pack and said, "Whoa, brother. It goes easier when you don't fight."

The horse gave him a big-eyed stare as if it understood his language—a comforting thought, because nobody else did. But even among the horses he felt unequal. They were able to look out for themselves if they escaped. He would simply starve. He was envious still, even among the horses.

Humbly he fetched and carried. Sometimes he even offered to help, but he had not the skill for the endless work of the women, and he was not trusted to hunt with the men, the providers.

When the camp moved, he carried a pack trudging with the women. Even the dogs worked then, pulling small burdens on travois of sticks.

The Indian who had captured him lived like a lord, as he had a right to do. He hunted with his peers, attended long ceremonial meetings with much chanting and dancing, and lounged in the shade with his smug bride. He had only two responsibilities: to kill buffalo and to gain glory. The white man was so far beneath him in status that the Indian did not even think of envy.

One day several things happened that made the captive think he might sometime become a man again. That was the day when he began to understand their language. For four months he had heard it, day and night, the joy and the mourning, the ritual chanting and sung prayers, the squabbles and the deliberations. None of it meant anything to him at all.

But on that important day in early fall the two young women set out for the river, and one of them called over her shoulder to the old woman. The white man was startled. She had said she was going to bathe. His understanding was so sudden that he felt as if his ears had come unstopped. Listening to the racket of the camp, he heard fragments of meaning instead of gabble.

On that same important day the old woman brought a pair of new moccasins out of the tepee and tossed them on the ground before him. He could not believe she would do anything for him because of kindness, but giving him moccasins was one way of looking after her property.

In thanking her, he dared greatly. He picked a little handful of fading fall flowers and took them to her as she squatted in front of her tepee, scraping a buffalo hide with a tool made from a piece of iron tied to a bone. Her hands were hideous—most of the fingers had the first joint missing. He bowed solemnly and offered the flowers.

She glared at him from beneath the short, ragged tangle of her hair. She stared at the flowers, knocked them out of his hand and went running to the next tepee, squalling the story. He heard her and the other women screaming with laughter.

The white man squared his shoulders and walked boldly over to watch three small boys shooting arrows at a target. He said in English, "Show me how to do that, will you?"

They frowned, but he held out his hand as if there could be no doubt. One of them gave him a bow and one arrow, and they snickered when he missed.

The people were easily amused, except when they were angry. They were amused, at him, playing with the little boys. A few days later he asked the hag, with gestures, for a bow that her son had just discarded, a man-size bow of horn. He scavenged for old arrows. The old woman cackled at his marksmanship and called her neighbors to enjoy the fun.

When he could understand words, he could identify his people by their names. The old woman was Greasy Hand, and her daughter was Pretty Calf. The other young woman's name was not clear to him, for the words were not in his vocabulary. The man who had captured him was Yellow Robe.

Once he could understand, he could begin to talk a little, and then he was less lonely. Nobody had been able to see any reason for talking to him, since he would not understand anyway. He asked the old woman, "What is my name?" Until he knew it, he was incomplete. She shrugged to let him know he had none.

He told her in the Crow language, "My name is Horse." He repeated it, and she nodded. After that they called him Horse when they called him anything. Nobody cared except the white man himself.

They trusted him enough to let him stray out of camp, so that he might have got away and, by unimaginable good luck, might have reached a trading post or a fort, but winter was too close. He did not dare leave without a horse; he needed clothing and a better hunting weapon than he had, and more certain skill in using it. He did not dare steal, for then they would surely have pursued him, and just as certainly they would have caught him. Remembering the warmth of the home that was waiting in Boston, he settled down for the winter.

On a cold night he crept into the tepee after the others had gone to bed. Even a horse might try to find shelter from the wind. The old woman grumbled, but without conviction. She did not put him out.

They tolerated him, back in the shadows, so long as he did not get in the way.

He began to understand how the family that owned him differed from the others. Fate had been cruel to them. In a short, sharp argument among the old women, one of them derided Greasy Hand by sneering, "You have no relatives!" and Greasy Hand raved for minutes of the deeds of her father and uncles and brothers. And she had had four sons, she reminded her detractor —who answered with scorn, "Where are they?"

Later the white man found her moaning and whimpering to herself, rocking back and forth on her haunches, staring at her mutilated hands. By that time he understood. A mourner often chopped off a finger joint. Old Greasy Hand had mourned often. For the first time he felt a twinge of pity, but he put it aside as another emotion, like anger, that he could not afford. He thought: What tales I will tell when I get home!

He wrinkled his nose in disdain. The camp stank of animals and meat and rancid grease. He looked down at his naked, shivering legs and was startled, remembering that he was still only a horse.

He could not trust the old woman. She fed him only because a starved slave would die and not be worth boasting about. Just how fitful her temper was he saw on the day when she got tired of stumbling over one of the hundred dogs that infested the camp. This was one of her own dogs, a large, strong one that pulled a baggage travois when the tribe moved camp.

Countless times he had seen her kick at the beast as it lay sleeping in front of the tepee, in her way. The dog always moved, with a yelp, but it always got in the way again. One day she gave the dog its usual kick and then stood scolding at it while the animal rolled its eyes sleepily. The old woman suddenly picked up her axe and cut the dog's head off with one blow. Looking well satisfied with herself, she beckoned her slave to remove the body.

It could have been me, he thought, if I were a dog. But I'm a horse.

His hope of life lay with the girl, Pretty Calf. He set about courting her, realizing how desperately poor he was both in property and honor. He owned no horse, no weapon but the old bow and the battered arrows. He had nothing to give away, and he needed gifts, because he did not dare seduce the girl.

One of the customs of courtship involved sending a gift of horses to a girl's older brother and bestowing much buffalo meat upon her mother. The white man could not wait for some far-off time when he might have either horses or meat to give away. And his courtship had to be secret. It was not for him to stroll past the groups of watchful girls, blowing a flute made of an eagle's wing bone, as the flirtatious young bucks did.

He could not ride past Pretty Calf's tepee, painted and bedizened; he had no horse, no finery.

Back home, he remembered, I could marry just about any girl I'd want to. But he wasted little time thinking about that. A future was something to be earned.

The most he dared do was wink at Pretty Calf now and then, or state his admiration while she giggled and hid her face. The least he dared do to win his bride was to elope with her, but he had to give her a horse to put the seal of tribal approval on that. And he had no horse until he killed a man to get one. . . .

His opportunity came in early spring. He was casually accepted by that time. He did not belong, but he was amusing to the Crows, like a strange pet, or they would not have fed him through the winter.

His chance came when he was hunting small game with three young boys who were his guards as well as his scornful companions. Rabbits and birds were of no account in a camp well fed on buffalo meat, but they made good targets.

His party walked far that day. All of them at once saw the two horses in a sheltered coulee. The boys and the man crawled forward on their bellies, and then they saw an Indian who lay on the ground, moaning, a lone traveler. From the way the boys inched eagerly forward, Horse knew the man was fair prey—a member of some enemy tribe.

This is the way the captive white man acquired wealth and honor to win a bride and save his life: He shot an arrow into the sick man, a split second ahead of one of his small companions, and dashed forward to strike the still-groaning man with his bow, to count first coup. Then he seized the hobbled horses.

By the time he had the horses secure, and with them his hope for freedom, the boys had followed, counting coup with gestures and shrieks they had practiced since boyhood, and one of them had the scalp. The white man was grimly amused to see the boy double up with sudden nausea when he had the thing in his hand. . . .

There was a hubbub in the camp when they rode in that evening, two of them on each horse. The captive was noticed. Indians who had ignored him as a slave stared at the brave man who had struck first coup and had stolen horses.

The hubbub lasted all night, as fathers boasted loudly of their young sons' exploits. The white man was called upon to settle an argument between two fierce boys as to which of them had struck second coup and which must be satisfied with third. After much talk that went over his head, he solemnly pointed at the nearest boy. He didn't know which boy it was and didn't care, but the boy did.

The white man had watched warriors in their triumph. He knew what to do. Modesty about achievements had no place among the Crow people. When a man did something big, he told about it.

The white man smeared his face with grease and charcoal. He walked inside the tepee circle, chanting and singing. He used his own language.

"You heathens, you savages," he shouted. "I'm going to get out of here someday! I am going to get away!" The Crow people listened respectfully. In the Crow tongue he shouted, "Horse! I am Horse!" and they nodded.

He had a right to boast, and he had two horses. Before dawn, the white man and his bride were sheltered beyond a far hill, and he was telling her, "I love you, little lady. I love you."

She looked at him with her great dark eyes, and he thought she understood his English words—or as much as she needed to understand.

"You are my treasure," he said, "more precious than jewels, better than fine gold. I am going to call you Freedom."

When they returned to camp two days later, he was bold but worried. His ace, he suspected, might not be high enough in the game he was playing without being sure of the rules. But it served.

Old Greasy Hand raged—but not at him. She complained loudly that her daughter had let herself go too cheap. But the marriage was as good as any Crow marriage. He had paid a horse.

He learned the language faster after that, from Pretty Calf, whom he sometimes called Freedom. He learned that his attentive, adoring bride was fourteen years old.

One thing he had not guessed was the difference that being Pretty Calf's husband would make in his relationship to her mother and brother. He had hoped only to make his position a little safer, but he had not expected to be treated with dignity. Greasy Hand no longer spoke to him at all. When the white man spoke to her, his bride murmured in dismay, explaining at great length that he must never do that. There could be no conversation between a man and his mother-in-law. He could not even mention a word that was part of her name.

Having improved his status so magnificently, he felt no need for hurry in getting away. Now that he had a woman, he had as good a chance to be rich as any man. Pretty Calf waited on him; she seldom ran off to play games with other young girls, but took pride in learning from her mother the many women's skills of tanning hides and making clothing and preparing food.

He was no more a horse but a kind of man, a half-Indian, still poor and unskilled but laden with honors, clinging to the buckskin fringes of Crow society.

Escape could wait until he could manage it in comfort, with fit clothing and a good horse, with hunting weapons. Escape could wait until the camp moved near some trading post. He did not plan how he would get home. He dreamed of being there all at once, and of telling stories nobody would believe. There was no hurry.

Pretty Calf delighted in educating him. He began to understand tribal arrangements, customs and why things were as they were. They were that way because they had always been so. His young wife giggled when she told him, in his ignorance, things she had always known. But she did not laugh when her brother's wife was taken by another warrior. She explained that solemnly with words and signs.

Yellow Robe belonged to a society called the Big Dogs. The wife stealer, Cut Neck, belonged to the Foxes. They were fellow tribesmen; they hunted together and fought side by side, but men of one society could take away wives from the other society if they wished, subject to certain limitations.

When Cut Neck rode up to the tepee, laughing and singing, and called to Yellow Robe's wife, "Come out! Come out!" she did as ordered, looking smug as usual, meek and entirely willing. Thereafter she rode beside him in ceremonial processions and carried his coup stick, while his other wife pretended not to care.

"But why?" the white man demanded of his wife, his Freedom. "Why did our brother let his woman go? He sits and smokes and does not speak."

Pretty Calf was shocked at the suggestion. Her brother could not possibly reclaim his woman, she explained. He could not even let her come back if she wanted to—and she probably would want to when Cut Neck tired of her. Yellow Robe could not even admit that his heart was sick. That was the way things were. Deviation meant dishonor.

The woman could have hidden from Cut Neck, she said. She could even have refused to go with him if she had been *ba-wurokee*—a really virtuous woman. But she had been his woman before, for a little while on a berrying expedition, and he had a right to claim her.

There was no sense in it, the white man insisted. He glared at his young wife. "If you go, I will bring you back!" he promised.

She laughed and buried her head against his shoulder. "I will not have to go," she said. "Horse is my first man. There is no hole in my moccasin."

He stroked her hair and said, *"Ba-wurokee."*

With great daring, she murmured, *"Hayha,"* and when he did not answer, because he did not know what she meant, she drew away, hurt.

"A woman calls her man that if she thinks he will not leave her. Am I wrong?"

The white man held her closer and lied. "Pretty Calf is not wrong. Horse will not leave her. Horse will not take another woman, either." No, he certainly would not. Parting from this one was going to be harder than getting her had been. *"Hayha,"* he murmured. "Freedom."

His conscience irked him, but not very much. Pretty Calf could get another man easily enough when he was gone, and a better provider. His hunting skill was improving, but he was still awkward.

There was no hurry about leaving. He was used to most of the Crow ways and could stand the rest. He was becoming prosperous. He owned five horses. His place in the life of the tribe was secure, such as it was. Three or four young women, including the one who had belonged to Yellow Robe, made advances to him. Pretty Calf took pride in the fact that her man was so attractive.

By the time he had what he needed for a secret journey, the grass grew yellow on the plains and the long cold was close. He was enslaved by the girl he called Freedom and, before the winter ended, by the knowledge that she was carrying his child. . . .

The Big Dog society held a long ceremony in the spring. The white man strolled with his woman along the creek bank, thinking: When I get home I will tell them about the chants and the drumming. Sometime. Sometime.

Pretty Calf would not go to bed when they went back to the tepee.

"Wait and find out about my brother," she urged. "Something may happen."

So far as Horse could figure out, the Big Dogs were having some kind of election. He pampered his wife by staying up with her by the fire. Even the old woman, who was a great one for getting sleep when she was not working, prowled around restlessly.

The white man was yawning by the time the noise of the ceremony died down. When Yellow Robe strode in, garish and heathen in his paint and feathers and furs, the women cried out. There was conversation, too fast for Horse to follow, and the old woman wailed once, but her son silenced her with a gruff command.

When the white man went to sleep, he thought his wife was weeping beside him.

The next morning she explained.

"He wears the bearskin belt. Now he can never retreat in battle. He will always be in danger. He will die."

Maybe he wouldn't, the white man tried to convince her. Pretty Calf recalled that some few men had been honored by the bearskin belt, vowed to the highest daring, and had not died. If they lived through the summer, then they were free of it.

"My brother wants to die," she mourned. "His heart is bitter."

Yellow Robe lived through half a dozen clashes with small parties of raiders from hostile tribes. His honors were many. He captured horses in an enemy camp, led two successful raids, counted first coup and snatched a gun from the hand of an enemy tribesman. He wore wolf tails on his moccasins and ermine skins on his shirt, and he fringed his leggings with scalps in token of his glory.

When his mother ventured to suggest, as she did many times, "My son should take a new wife, I need another woman to help me," he ignored her. He spent much time in prayer, alone in the hills or in conference with a medicine man. He fasted and made vows and kept them. And before he could be free of the heavy honor of the bearskin belt, he went on his last raid.

The warriors were returning from the north just as the white man and two other hunters approached from the south, with buffalo and elk meat dripping from the bloody hides tied on their restive ponies. One of the hunters grunted, and they stopped to watch a rider on the hill north of the tepee circle.

The rider dismounted, held up a blanket and dropped it. He repeated the gesture.

The hunters murmured dismay. "Two! Two men dead!" They rode fast into the camp, where there was already wailing.

A messenger came down from the war party on the hill. The rest of the party delayed to paint their faces for mourning and for victory. One of the two dead men was Yellow Robe. They had put his body in a cave and walled it in with rocks. The other man died later, and his body was in a tree.

There was blood on the ground before the tepee to which Yellow Robe would return no more. His mother, with her hair chopped short, sat in the doorway, rocking back and forth on her haunches, wailing her heartbreak. She cradled one mutilated hand in the other. She had cut off another finger joint.

Pretty Calf had cut off chunks of her long hair and was crying as she gashed her arms with a knife. The white man tried to take the knife away, but she protested so piteously that he let her do as she wished. He was sickened with the lot of them.

Savages! he thought. Now I will go back! I'll go hunting alone, and I'll keep on going.

But he did not go just yet, because he was the only hunter in the lodge of the two grieving women, one of them old and the other pregnant with his child.

In their mourning, they made him a pauper again. Everything that meant comfort, wealth and safety they sacrificed to the spirits because of the death of Yellow Robe. The tepee, made of seventeen fine buffalo hides, the furs that should have kept them warm, the white deerskin dress, trimmed with elk teeth, that Pretty Calf loved so well, even their tools and Yellow Robe's weapons—everything but his sacred medicine objects—they left there on the prairie, and the whole camp moved away. Two of his best horses were killed as a sacrifice, and the women gave away the rest.

They had no shelter. They would have no tepee of their own for two months at least of mourning, and then the women would have to tan hides to make it. Meanwhile they could live in temporary huts made of willows, covered with skins given them in pity by their friends. They could have lived with relatives, but Yellow Robe's women had no relatives.

The white man had not realized until then how terrible a thing it was for a Crow to have no kinfolk. No wonder old Greasy Hand had only stumps for fingers. She had mourned, from one year to the next, for everyone she had ever loved. She had no one left but her daughter, Pretty Calf.

Horse was furious at their foolishness. It had been bad enough for him, a captive, to be naked as a horse and poor as a slave, but that was because his captors had stripped him. These women had voluntarily given up everything they needed.

He was too angry at them to sleep in the willow hut. He lay under a sheltering tree. And on the third night of the mourning he made his plans. He had a knife and a bow. He would go after meat, taking two horses. And he would not come back. There were, he realized, many things he was not going to tell when he got back home.

In the willow hut, Pretty Calf cried out. He heard rustling there, and the old woman's querulous voice.

Some twenty hours later his son was born, two months early, in the tepee of a skilled medicine woman. The child was born without breath, and the mother died before the sun went down.

The white man was too shocked to think whether he should mourn, or how he should mourn. The old woman screamed until she was voiceless. Piteously she approached him, bent and trembling, blind with grief. She held out her knife and he took it.

She spread out her hands and shook her head. If she cut off any more finger joints, she could do no more work. She could not afford any more lasting signs of grief.

The white man said, "All right! All right!" between his teeth. He hacked his arms with the knife and stood watching the blood run down. It was little enough to do for Pretty Calf, for little Freedom.

Now there is nothing to keep me, he realized. When I get home, I must not let them see the scars.

He looked at Greasy Hand, hideous in her grief-burdened age, and thought: I really am free now! When a wife dies, her husband has no more duty toward her family. Pretty Calf had told him so, long ago, when he wondered why a certain man moved out of one tepee and into another.

The old woman, of course, would be a scavenger. There was one other with the tribe, an ancient crone who had no relatives, toward whom no one felt any responsibility. She lived on food thrown away by the more fortunate. She slept in shelters that she built with her own knotted hands. She plodded wearily at the end of the procession when the camp moved. When she stumbled, nobody cared. When she died, nobody would miss her.

Tomorrow morning, the white man decided, I will go.

His mother-in-law's sunken mouth quivered. She said one word, questioningly. She said, *"Eero-oshay?"* She said, "Son?"

Blinking, he remembered. When a wife died, her husband was free. But her mother, who had ignored him with dignity, might if she wished ask him to stay. She invited him by calling him Son, and he accepted by answering Mother.

Greasy Hand stood before him, bowed with years, withered with unceasing labor, loveless and childless, scarred with grief. But with all her burdens, she still loved life enough to beg it from him, the only person she had any right to ask. She was stripping herself of all she had left, her pride.

He looked eastward across the prairie. Two thousand miles away was home. The old woman would not live forever. He could afford to wait, for he was young. He could afford to be magnanimous, for he knew he was a man. He gave her the answer. *"Eegya,"* he said. "Mother."

He went home three years later. He explained no more than to say, "I lived with Crows for a while. It was some time before I could leave. They called me Horse."

He did not find it necessary either to apologize or to boast, because he was the equal of any man on earth.

THE SINGING SANDS
BY STEVE FRAZEE
(Gold of the Seven Saints)

"The Singing Sands" is a first-rate tale of man's lust for gold, a popular theme in Western fiction (and in Western film). Steve Frazee's evocative, cinematic prose style has led Hollywood to transfer a number of his novels and short stories to the silver screen, in some cases not very well. The best of the films based on his fiction are probably Many Rivers to Cross *(1955) from the novel of the same title, which starred Robert Taylor, Eleanor Parker, and James Arness, and* Running Target *(1956), a very good low-budget "B" adapted from the novelized version of Frazee's prize-winning novelette "My Brother Down There" (included in* The Reel West). *Less successful adaptations are* Wild Heritage *(1958), taken from the novel* Smoke in the Valley, *and* High Hell, *produced that same year—an updated, soap-opera version of the novel* High Cage.

There were three passes ahead and their names were like the rhythm of a chant, Mosca, Medano and Music. The alliteration kept running in Johnny Anderson's mind as his tired pony chopped through the rabbitbrush, across alkali flats where the dust rose thin and bitter in the windless air. Like magic words that would kill the trouble behind, the names chased each other; but every few moments Anderson looked across his shoulder at the long backtrail.

Jasper Lamb was doing the same thing, twisting wearily in the saddle, squinting his bloodshot eyes at the gray distance. He was a middle-aged man, slouching, leanly built. For a year Anderson had prowled the mountains with him. They had never faced any severe test until now; and now Anderson was wondering if he had picked the right partner. Lamb was not showing the proper concern about things.

Anderson worked his lips and ran his tongue around his mouth to clear dust and the cottony feeling that had been in his mouth ever since he knew there were men on their trail. "Which pass, Lamb?"

"Medano, I know it best." Lamb glanced at the heavily loaded mule he was towing. The mule was the strongest of the three animals, but it would not be hurried.

Each mile seemed to bring them no closer to the mountains with their golden streaks of frost-touched aspens. Looking backward at the space they had crossed, Anderson was uneasy because of the very emptiness. He said hopefully, "Maybe we threw them off when we made that fake toward Poncha Pass early this morning."

"I figured on wind," Lamb said. "There ain't been any. We've left a trail like a single furrow ploughed across a field. The wind blows like old Scratch here sometimes, but today it didn't." He had come out during the Pike's Peak bust, cutting his teeth on the mountains and losing his illusions at the same time, so now he did not rail against luck or the weather. "They'll be along."

Johnny Anderson was young. He had passed his twenty-second birthday the week before when they were making their final cleanup on their placer claim in the San Juan. He wasted energy cursing the vagaries of the weather; but half his anger was fear as he saw how Lamb's buckskin was limping. The horse had thrown a shoe in the rocky foothills just north of the Rio Grande the night before. Anderson tried to weigh the limp against the distance yet to go; and then he turned to look behind.

There was no dust far back. Mosca, Medano and Music. . . . He studied immense buff foothills ahead. He had never seen their like before but he was not greatly interested.

He asked, "Who are they, do you suppose?"

Lamb did not waste motion in shrugging or any other gesture. "You saw some of the toughs there in Baker's Park when we stopped overnight. Pick any bunch of them."

"We made a mistake!" Anderson said. "We shouldn't have stopped there, and then we guarded the panniers on the mule too close. We should have dumped them on the ground like they didn't amount to nothing. We made another mistake when we slipped out of there by night. We—"

"Sure, we made mistakes." Lamb leaned ahead to feel the shoulder of his horse. "We come out of the San Juan with a loaded mule at the end of summer. Nobody had to be smart to know what we're carrying." He kept watching the buckskin's shoulder. "We made our pile in a hurry, boy. I mistrust too much good luck."

Anderson let the thought grind away for a while. "Is your horse going to make it?"

"I doubt it, not without he rests and I try to do something for that tender foot." Lamb looked at the unshod Indian pony under Anderson. It cut no figure at all beside the buckskin. It rode hard and its gait was uneven but the mustang mark was there and there were guts in the pony for many miles yet.

Lamb watched it for a moment with no expression on his bearded, dusty features.

Slowly the great pale brown hills came closer. No trees, no rocks broke the rounding contours. The ridges were sharp on the spines, delicately molded. The shadings of the coloration flowed so subtly into each other that Anderson could not tell whether the hills were a quarter of a mile away or two miles. The whole mass of them seemed to pulse in the still heat. Anderson's sudden loss of distance judgment gave him a queer feeling.

When he looked behind once more and saw only lonely vastness, the claws of fear began to loosen and the hills began to capture his attention. A gentle incline led the two men among the pinon trees. The pitchy scent of them was warmly strong. Lamb swung his sorefooted horse into a broad gulch and soon they were riding on a brown carpet that flowed out from the skirts of the hills. Pure sand.

The pack mule balked the moment its hooves touched the silky softness. It sniffed and held back on the tow rope, but at last Lamb urged it on ahead. Riding in an eerie silence broken only by the gentle plopping of hooves, the two men struck a course to turn the shoulder of the dunes where they ended against the mountains.

"That's the biggest pile of sand I ever saw!" Anderson said.

In the strike of the afternoon sun the sweeping curves of the hills blended into a oneness that robbed Anderson of depth perception. There were moments when the dunes had only height and length. He estimated the highest ridge at seven hundred feet, but it seemed so far away he guessed that a man could not reach it in a day.

Staring at the dunes, he forgot for a time the threat behind him—until Lamb stopped the buckskin suddenly. The dust was out there now, standing like thin smoke above the rabbitbrush on the way that they had come. As they watched, the first wind of the day came out of the southwest. The claws hooked in again and the tightness returned to Anderson's stomach.

He rode to the rear of the pack mule, thinking to urge it into greater speed when they started. Lamb's calmness stopped him. With one eye almost closed so that the side of his mouth was raised in the semblance of a smile, Lamb was slouching in the saddle and studying the dust as if not sure of the cause of it. He scrubbed the scum from his teeth with his tongue.

"There were five of them before," he said. "Guess there's still that many. You know something, Andy? They swung away this morning to get fresh horses at Pascual's ranch." Lamb eyed Anderson's wiry scrub. He glanced to the right, past cotton woods and pinon trees, up to where Mosca Pass trail came down in a V of the mountains. "Medano is still best for us. Once we hit the Huerfano, I've got more friends among the Mexicans than a cur has fleas."

"Let's go!"

Lamb swung down. "My horse won't last two miles."

"He's got to! We'll get to the rocks and stand 'em off."

"We might do that with Indians, yes." Lamb lifted the buckskin's left forefoot and looked at the hoof. "These are white men, Andy." He let the hoof drop. "They know what we got." He walked to a cottonwood at the edge of the gulch.

"White men or not, by God—"

"I ain't aiming to die over no gold," Lamb said. "I've got along too many years without it. I ain't figuring to let them have it either." He grinned and his toughness was never more apparent. "Just wait a spell. The wind is coming."

"Out in the valley it would have helped, but here, when we hit the trees—"

"Wait," Lamb said.

The wind reached them after a while. Strong and warm it came out of the southwest. There was an odd rustling sound and the sand lay out in streamers from the ridges of the dunes. It was difficult to tell about the dust cloud, but Anderson knew it must be closer.

All at once Anderson realized that the tracks he and Lamb had made in the broad gulch were gone. Unbroken sand that lay in gentle waves like frozen brown water covered every mark they had made since entering the gulch.

Lamb led his buckskin and the mule toward the dunes. The idea ran then in Anderson's mind that they would lose their pursuers by circling through the hollows of the hills; but when the animals struck the first ridge and began to labor in the shifting, slippery sand, he knew his thought was wrong.

They ploughed over the ridge and dropped into a small basin where the ground was bare. All around the edges of the hollow the sand was skirling, running in tiny riffles, and up on the great hills above them it was whipping from the spines in two different directions.

Lamb took the mule close to the side of the bowl where the sand came down steeply. He began to take the gold from the panniers. It was in wheels, circular pieces of buckskin gathered from the outside edge and tied with thongs. When the first few sacks dropped at the edge of the sand Anderson cried a protest.

"I'd rather fight for it!"

"I'd rather live," Lamb said. "We're not going to get clear unless I ride the mule. We'll get a little fighting even then. Give me a hand."

Each sack that thudded down was a wrench at Anderson's heart. He could not remember how easily the gold had come to them from a rich pocket in the San Juan; he could only estimate the weight of each sack as it fell at the edge of the fine silt.

"Not all of it, for God's sake!" he cried.

Lamb kept dropping the buckskin sacks. "Take what you want but remember you're riding a tired horse. Even Indian nags play out, Andy." A few moments later when Lamb saw his partner stuffing sacks under his shirt, he said, "It'll be here when we come back, son."

It was not the words, but sudden wild music, that brought Anderson's head up with a jerk. It was a weird and whining sound, the bow of the wind playing across the sand strings of the ridges high above. Anderson listened only long enough to recognize what the sound was. It was mocking, discordant. He stuffed more gold inside his shirt.

When the panniers that had held almost two hundred pounds of weight were flapping loosely against the mule, Lamb's voice snapped across the wind with the crack of urgency, "Rake the sand down on top of the stuff while I shift my saddle to the mule."

Soft and warm, the sand slid easily under Anderson's raking hands. When he had covered part of the long row of sacks the wind had already concealed the marks where he had clawed. They climbed from the hollow, pausing on the ridge to peer through a brown haze at the dust still coming toward them. Anderson turned then to look into the little basin. All marks were gone, but he did not trust the smooth quickness of the sand.

"Maybe we could stand them off here," he said.

"Maybe we could die of thirst here, too." Lamb pointed across the shallow sand to the edge of the gulch. "It was six hundred and ten long steps, Andy, from that cottonwood with the busted top. Sight above the tree to that patch of gray rocks on the mountains. You got it?"

Anderson tried to burn the marks into his mind. He stared until he found a third point of sighting, the smoke-gray deadness of a spruce tree between the cottonwood and the patch of rocks. Six hundred and ten paces from the cottonwood. He could never forget this place.

Out in the rabbitbrush the riders had dropped into a swale. Only the dust they had raised behind them was visible. Lamb swung up on the mule and the mule tried to pitch him off. "I hope we never have to eat this devil," he said, "as tough as he is." He rode down the slope and into the broad expanse of shallow sand, towing his limping buckskin.

Anderson had difficulty in mounting. His shirt bulged with weight and his boots were full of sand. The hills were singing their high, queer song. He rode away, twisted in the saddle to watch his tracks; and he saw them drifting into smoothness almost as quickly as he made them. The treasure was safe enough but he worried because there seemed to be a gloating tone in the singing sands.

Now the dust was much closer and the fear of men was greater than all other worries.

Beside the eastern shoulder of the hills they crossed ground where water had carried brown earth from the mountains. The earth was cracked and curled upward in little chips. They let the animals drink when they hit the first seep of Medano Creek.

"Now we got our work cut out," Lamb said.

Medano Pass was rocky. The wind was funneling through it cold and sharp. Now the pursuers gained in earnest, for Anderson's pony began to lag and the hobbling buckskin began to lay back stubbornly on the lead rope.

From a high switchback Anderson saw the riders for the first time. Five of them, the same as before. "Let's get rid of the damned buckskin, Lamb!"

"About another mile and then we will."

When they came to a place where the trail was very narrow above a booming creek, Lamb said, "Drop a sack of gold here, Andy. The lead man will have to get down to get it. Every minute will help."

"Drop one of your own."

"I got only one," Lamb said patiently.

The gold was a terrible weight around Anderson's middle but he would not drop a sack. Nor would he part with it when he had to dismount to lead his pony up steep pitches. The sides of the horses were pounding. They stopped to rest at the top of a brutal hill. They could hear the sounds of the men behind them. Anderson tried to pull off his boots but the sand had worked so tightly around his feet and ankles that he could not get the boots off, and he was afraid to spend too much time in trying.

On a ledge above a canyon Lamb stopped again. He took the panniers from the buckskin, dropped a heavy rock into each of them, and hurled them away. He stripped the packsaddle and threw it by the cinch strap. Anderson heard it crash somewhere in the rocks out of sight. In the next stand of aspens Lamb took the buckskin out of sight and turned it loose.

He seemed to be gone a long time. Anderson stood beside his trembling pony with his rifle ready, watching the trail. Lamb returned. His face was grim with the first anger he had shown since the pursuit began. He took his rifle and walked down the trail. "Go on," he ordered. "I'll be along directly."

Anderson went ahead on foot. There were seven shots, flat reports that sent echoes through the rocks. Anderson stopped, waiting, afraid. Presently Lamb came trotting up the trail. Blood was dripping from his left hand and his shirt was ripped above the elbow. He whipped the blood off his hand and said, "Get on, don't wait for nothing. Not far ahead they got a chance to flank around us if we stop to pick flowers."

On the next steep, narrow pitch Anderson dropped a sack of gold. It was a place where horses would have to hold in a straining position against the grade while the lead man got down. It was not much, but maybe it would help. Four more times he picked his spots and dropped more sacks.

Twice more Lamb went back on foot with his rifle. There were fewer shots each time.

Sunset dripped its colors on the mountains and they flamed with the hue that gave them their name, *Sangre de Cristo,* Blood of Christ. The colors died and the cold dusk came. Again Lamb went back on the trail and his rifle made crimson flashes. They passed the place where a Spanish governor had camped an avenging army two centuries before. They went over the top and the necks of the animals slanted downward.

It was dark then. A wind that came from vastness was running up the mountain. To Anderson, the pass had been the obstacle, and now they were across it. He breathed relief. The magic words, Mosca, Medano and Music came again; but moments later he forgot that it was his life he had worried about, and he thought of the gold they had left in the sand, and of the sacks of gold they had dropped on the trail. At least he had not thrown away everything; there were two sacks yet inside his shirt.

A pale moon rose, throwing ghostly light on the rocks. Far below the timber was a black sea. It was still a long way to the Huerfano, and there were things like weariness and hunger.

Lamb said, "Hold up a second."

In the dead stillness they heard the sound of hoofs sliding on stones on the trail behind them. The men were still coming. Not knowing who they were made it worse for Anderson. Their persistence chilled him. Lamb was a dark form near the head of the mule. "One of those three knows this trail," he muttered.

There had been five men. Anderson did not comment on the difference.

Lamb listened a moment longer. "They're on a shortcut that I didn't care to try." For the first time he sounded worried. He mounted and sent the mule down the trail on the trot.

The clatter of stones came loudly on the higher benches of the mountain.

Lamb set a dangerous pace, cutting across the sharp angles of the switchbacks, sending rocks in wild flight down the slopes. They made a long turn to the left and entered timber on the edge of a canyon where a waterfall was splashing in the moonlight. At the head of the canyon the trail swung back to the right. They were then in dense timber where the needle mat took sharpness from the hoofbeats of the horses.

"Hold it," Lamb called back softly, and then he stopped.

Above the canyon they had skirted, where the trail lay in Z patterns against the mountain, Anderson heard the riders. Suddenly there was an eerie quietness

Lamb said, "Just ahead of us the trail is open to the next point. They can reach us good from where they are." He led the mule aside. "Put your horse across first but don't follow him too close."

Anderson pulled his rifle free. From the edge of the timber the trail ahead lay against cliffs of white quartz. It seemed starkly exposed and lighted. He peered up the mountain. The shadows were tricky among the huge rocks and he could make out nothing. But then he heard a tired horse blow from somewhere up there in the rocks.

He prodded his pony into the open. It went a few slow paces and stopped. With savage force he bounced a rock off its rump. The animal jumped and started on at a half trot.

Anderson ran. He heard the crashing of the rifles and from the corner of his eye he saw their flame. They seemed to be a long way off but yet he heard the smack of lead against the cliffs beside him. The pony was almost to the point when its hind legs went down. It screamed in agony and pawed its way along the ledge. It reared halfway up, twisting. Anderson saw the glint of moonlight on steel where the leather was worn off the horn, and that was when the pony was going into the canyon.

A man on the mountainside yelled triumphantly, "We got the mule!"

Then Anderson was across. He fell behind the rocky point and shot toward the sound of the voice. The horses were moving up there in the rocks now and someone was cursing. Anderson rammed in another cartridge and fired.

The mule came with a rush, nearly trampling him before he could roll aside and leap up. He caught the bridle with a desperate lunge when the animal would have jogged on down the trail. Soon afterward Lamb skidded around the point. He knelt and fired. "No good," he muttered. "Two of them got into the timber on foot." He reloaded and stood up. "Now let *them* try that trail."

If there had been a taunt or a challenge from the black trees, Anderson would have been sure he was fighting men instead of some determined deadliness that would follow him forever. But the trees were silent.

"Take the mule," Lamb said. "He'll stay with the trail. By daylight you'll be seeing sheep. Ask the first herder you come to how to get to Luis Mendoza's place. Wait for me there."

"We'll both—"

"I was ramming around these mountains when you was still wearing didies," Lamb said. "Listen to what I say, boy. Get to hell out of here with that mule. That's what they're after. They think the gold is still on it. We *want* 'em to think so because one of these days we've got to go back after it. Go on now."

Anderson gave the mule its head and let it pick its way down the trail. He was a half hour away from the point when he heard the first shots rolling sullenly high above him. In the bleak, cold hours just before sunup, he heard more shooting. And then the mountain was silent.

The two sheepherders sitting on a rock beside their flock in a high meadow eyed the mule keenly. "Luis Mendoza?" They looked at each other. One of them pointed toward the valley. It went like that all morning, whenever Anderson stopped at adobes on the Huerfano. The liquid eyes sized up the mule and him, and weighed a consideration; but when he asked the way to Luis Mendoza's place, there was another careful weighing and he was pointed on.

The hot sun pressed him lower in the saddle. Sweat streaked down through the dust on his face, burning his eyes. At noon on this bright late-fall day he came into the yard of an adobe somewhat larger than the others he had passed. Hens were taking dust baths in the shade. There was a green field near the river, and goats upon a hill.

From the gloom of the house a deep voice asked, "Who comes?"

In Spanish Anderson said, "I am the friend of Jasper Lamb."

A little man walked from the house. His hair and mustache were white. His legs were short and bowed. From a nest of wrinkles around his eyes his gaze was like sharp, black points. He said, "You are followed?"

"We *were* followed."

"And Lamb?"

"He is in the mountains yet. He will come." Anderson wondered if he ever would.

The little man said sharply, "I am Luis Mendoza. Lamb is like my son. Do not doubt that he will be here. And now, you are welcome."

Thereupon a half dozen Mexican men of various ages appeared. One of them said, "Yes, it is the mule of Jasper Lamb."

"I have eyes." Mendoza's Spanish flowed rapidly then as he gave orders. Four men rode away, going slowly, chattering, obliterating the marks of Anderson's coming. He knew that if any of the three pursuers got past Jasper Lamb and reached the Huerfano, there would be only shrugs and muteness, or lies, to answer their questions.

"Go back for Lamb," Anderson said.

"He will be well, that one," Mendoza answered.

"He's wounded."

"That has happened before, also. Now we will take off your boots."

One of the pursuers did come in late afternoon. Lying on a pile of blankets on a cool dirt floor, Anderson heard the man ride up. "I look for a stolen mule, Mendoza."

Anderson tried to judge the enemy by the voice. A young man, he thought; and he knew already that he was a dangerous, determined man.

"Of that I know nothing."

Anderson clutched his rifle and started to get up. A broad Mexican sitting across the room from him shook his head and made cautioning gestures with his hands, and all the time he was grinning. After a moment Anderson recognized the wisdom of silence. For one thing, his feet were so scraped and sore and swollen from the sand that had been in his boots that he doubted if he could get across the room.

The man outside said, "The mule came this way. It had a heavy load. The man was young, with sandy hair."

"A *gringo* perhaps," Mendoza said lazily. "They do not stop for long on the Huerfano. The climate sometimes makes them ill," his voice slurred on gently. "Very ill."

"He could be in your house."

"I do not think so. My sons do not think so. My nephews do not think so."

There was a long silence.

"This stealer of mules is gone toward the Arkansas long ago, I think, although I did not see him," Mendoza said. "It is a long ride, my friend, and you are late now."

"Many things are possible," the pursuer answered, fully as easily as Mendoza had spoken. There was no defeat in his tone, but a cold patience that made Anderson wish he could get him in the sights of a rifle for an instant. "It could be that he is gone toward the Arkansas, and it could be that he is in your house, in spite of what all your sons and nephews think. Since the vote is in your favor, Mendoza, I will go toward the Arkansas myself."

"May God go with you," Mendoza said politely.

The man rode away. After a time Anderson dozed and then he woke, clutching where the weight should have been inside his shirt.

"At the head of your bed, *señor*," the man across the room murmured.

Anderson found the sacks and dragged them against him, and then he slept until sometime in the dead of night when he heard a terrible shout, soon followed by laughter.

Lamb had arrived. He was shouting for wine.

Anderson and Lamb stayed three weeks on the Huerfano. Lamb had married Mendoza's oldest daughter ten years before. She had died in childbirth a year later. These were facts Anderson had never known before.

It was a simple, easy life here in the hills. There were sheep in the upland country, with old men and young boys to watch them. Maize and squash grew in the fields. Anderson did not know where the wine came from but it was here, and every night there was dancing at Mendoza's place.

Quite easily Lamb fell into the routineless drift of the life. He slept when it was hot. He hunted when he was in the mood, ate when he was hungry, and during the long, cool evenings he danced with the best of them on the packed ground in front of Mendoza's house. He was no longer the cool, efficient man who had directed the running fight across Medano. He acted as if he had forgotten the gold lying at the foot of the great dunes.

"We can get it any time," he told Anderson. "What's the rush?" It seemed to Anderson that he was casting around for an excuse. "It's best not to go back there anyway until that last fellow gives up. Only a week ago one of Luis' cousins saw him heading back over the pass."

"Why didn't Luis' cousin shoot him?"

"Why should he? Why should anyone on the Huerfano ask for unnecessary trouble? They can scrape up family battles enough to keep 'em busy all their lives, if they want to." Lamb went away to take a nap.

The change in him puzzled Anderson. Or was it a change? Lamb would have a man believe that he didn't care about that gold. Suspicion narrowed Anderson's mind. He fretted over the delay. He brooded about Lamb's motives; and he worried about the cold-voiced man who had followed the mule even after his companions were dead.

One day he could bear impatience no longer. He told Lamb he was going alone to the dunes.

"Hold your horses. The big *baile* comes off day after tomorrow. We'll leave then." Lamb sighed.

They gave two sacks of gold to Luis Mendoza. It was too much, Anderson thought, but when Lamb parted with his sack carelessly, Anderson felt that he must match it. They rode away on good horses, towing the mule as before. Anderson was in his own saddle, brought down from the mountain by one of Mendoza's sons two days after the Indian pony had gone over the cliff. There were new elk hide panniers on the mule, and they surely must be advertising the purpose of the trip to every Mexican on the Huerfano, so Anderson thought.

"We'll go up the Arkansas and over Hayden Pass and then swing down to the sand hills," Lamb said. "It's possible that fellow caught on to the fact the mule was traveling light. He may have somebody waiting on Medano."

Anderson said, "I don't favor this running in circles."

"I don't favor trouble, particularly not over a bunch of damned metal that grows wild in the mountains."

"That's what brought you out here in the first place."

"Yeah. Well, it was different then," Lamb said. He was unusually silent, almost surly, during the first two days on the trail.

They watered the animals on San Luis Creek when they came down to the floor of the inland plateau. Thirty miles away the dunes were a pale brown mass. Once again they seemed to be no closer after hours of dusty traveling. As if in a stupor, Lamb stared at the sunset on the *Sangre de Cristo*.

Anderson wanted to travel as far into the night as it took to reach the dunes but Lamb overrode him. They camped. Anderson did not sleep well. He kept his rifle close and was sensitive to all of Lamb's small movements and sounds. During the night Lamb rose to go out to the animals when the mule fouled up his picket rope. He came back to the camp slowly, a lean, tall figure slouching through the night.

Anderson held back the trigger of his rifle and cocked the piece silently. Afterward, when Lamb walked past and settled into his blankets with a grunt, Anderson let the hammer down again, and lay with the tightness ebbing slowly out of him.

It seemed to Anderson that they lagged when they started down the valley the next day. At last he cried, "You're in no hurry, damn it!"

"I ain't for a fact." Lamb gave him an oblique glance. "There's kinds of grief that I don't care to hurry into."

"That last man, don't worry about him."

"I ain't," Lamb said. "I'm worrying some about the other four."

They approached the northern end of the dunes. After they encountered the first shallow drifting of sand out from the skirts, they rode for almost ten miles beside the hills before they reached the broad gulch at the mouth of Medano Creek.

Anderson felt a constriction of breath. He wanted to gallop ahead. Nothing was changed. He saw the narrow-leaf cottonwood with the broken top and from a wide angle the gray rocks on the mountain. Mosca, Medano and Music. . . . He wanted to shout.

They left the horses at the cottonwood. Lamb was silent, almost sullen, as if there were no pleasure in this. He stayed at the cottonwood while Anderson led the mule out to the ridge and then part way up the side. When Anderson stopped to look back, he was pleased to see that his trail lay straight behind him and that he was almost in direct line with the sighting marks. He had to shift only a few feet until he had them lined up, the snag-topped cottonwood, the dead spruce and the gray rocks.

He called then to Lamb to start his pacing. Anderson counted the steps as his partner came toward him. Three hundred and fifty across the shallow sand, another hundred to where Anderson waited. The two men went together up the ridge. It seemed higher than before. The total was six hundred steps when Anderson whirled around to take another sighting. They were dead in line

"Six hundred and ten?" he asked, and his voice cracked on the edge of panic.

"That's right," Lamb answered, and a man could read anything into his tone.

Anderson kept plunging on, but he knew already, and it made him savage. There was no ridge. He was climbing a slope that led on and on toward the deceptive hollows and troughs of the soft, pale sand. The basin was gone. He was a hundred feet above the gold on sand that ran like water.

He sighted again and then he turned and ran up the dune until his lungs ached and his leg muscles became knots of fire. He fell, staring along the surface of the wind-etched slope. Far off to his left there was a hollow, swooping all the way down to natural ground, but the basin with the gold was deeply covered. There was trickery in this; he had known it when the hills sang their song to him.

Anderson got up and staggered back to where Lamb was standing by the mule. "It wasn't six hundred and ten steps, was it?"

Lamb shifted his rifle. "Just what I said, Andy."

"Tell me the truth!" Anderson cocked his rifle and swung the piece on Lamb.

"Our gold is covered up," Lamb said. His squint was at once understanding and dangerous. "We're standing smack on top of it. Lower that barrel. It's full of sand."

Anderson let the barrel of his rifle tip down. Sand poured out in a silent stream. He let the tension off the hammer. "You knew the wind would cover it up, Lamb!"

"No, I didn't. I never realized how much this sand moves."

"We'll dig it out!" Anderson cried. "I don't care how deep it is!"

Lamb sat down. "We'll play hell trying to dig it out." He scooped his hand into the dune. Not far under the surface the sand was dark from dampness. He watched the fine dry grains from the top slide back into the hole. "It took a million years for the wind to make these hills. I guess the wind has got a right to do with them as it pleases. We'll never be able to dig ten feet down."

"Oh yes we will! Underneath it's damp. It'll hold. We'll start at the toe of the hill and tunnel. We'll line the tunnel with boards. We'll—"

Lamb shook his head. "Let me show you something." He dug with his hands, gouging long furrows downslope. The dark sand under the surface was damp for a short time only before the air dried it, and then it sloughed away. "Your boards wouldn't help much, if we knew where to get them. They'd dry out brittle. They'd crack and the sand would pour through the cracks and knotholes. If we were lucky enough to make twenty feet, one day the whole works would cave in on us."

"You act like you don't want to get the gold," Anderson accused.

Lamb looked out on the valley, toward the blue mountains on the edge of the San Juan. He was silent for a long time, a dusty, stringy man with a sort of puzzlement in his eyes. He said, "This gold is sort of used now. It ain't like brand new stuff, somehow. Even so I guess I'd stay and try to get it back, if I thought there was any chance."

"What do you mean, it's used?"

"I killed four men because of it. I lost a good buckskin horse."

"It was our neck or theirs!" Anderson said.

"Sure. I know that." Lamb frowned. "I ain't saying gold is bad, you understand, but it can cause you a pile of grief. I take it as an omen that the wind covered this mess of it up." Lamb rose. He smoothed with his feet the furrows he had made. "Let's move on."

"And leave a fortune just a hundred feet away from us?"

"It's the longest hundred feet God ever created, Andy."

"You don't want the gold?" Anderson asked.

"Not that, exactly. If we could get it, I'd take my share of it, but I'm kind of relieved that we can't get it."

Anderson licked his lips. "Suppose I get it out by myself?"

"I give my share to you right this minute. Now, let's go. We'll have to hump to get a tight camp set up in the San Juan before winter." He started down the dune.

"Then it's mine!"

"Sure, it's yours forever, Andy. Come on."

"You won't come around claiming half of it after I get it out?"

Lamb stopped and swung around. "You don't mean you're going to try?"

"I'm not going to run away from a fortune."

"We'll find another one," Lamb said.

"No! I know where this one is."

An hour later Anderson was in the same place, sitting with his rifle across his knees. He allowed that an obstacle stood between him and the treasure but the proximity of the gold outweighed all other considerations. He watched the dust where Lamb was riding away. Lamb might be trying to trick him. Lamb could have lied about the number of steps from the cottonwood.

Darkness came down on the great valley that had been a lake in ancient times. Purple shades ran in the hollows of the dunes, and the crests of the ridges looked like the black manes of horses struggling toward the sky. A mighty silence lay on the piles of sand that had been gathering here for eons.

Anderson was still sitting on the sand above the treasure. He rose at last, sticking his rifle barrel down into the dune. When he went across the shallow sand to where his horse was tied in the cottonwoods, the animal stamped and whinnied. It could wait. Anderson found a dead limb. He used it to replace his rifle as a marker. He counted his steps back to the cottonwood. They were a few less than Lamb had said.

That night he camped on Medano Creek, waking a dozen times to listen to small noises. The dunes were huge, taking pale light from the ice points of the stars. At dawn he was riding through the pinons, searching for a less exposed campsite. He found it near a spring in a narrow gulch that looked out on the dunes. From here he could see part of the mouth of Medano Gulch, and he could see the marker he had left on the dune. He built a bough hut near the spring, fretting because it seemed to be taking time from more important work.

That afternoon he killed a deer, standing for several moments after the shot, wondering how far the sound of his rifle had carried; and then he was in a fever to get back to where he could watch the dunes.

There had been wind that morning. The marker was standing above the sand by eighteen inches or more. Anderson experienced a quick leap of hope;

the wind had built the dunes, the wind had hidden the gold, and the wind could also uncover it again. It was a great thought.

Before evening the marker was almost covered. At dawn it was gone.

Without eating breakfast Anderson hurried from the trees and paced across the sand, taking sightings. Scrabbling on his hands and knees, he found the limb a few inches below the surface of the dune. He knew that he could always locate the spot but the limb was a tangible mark that gave him more of a link with the treasure than anything he carried in his mind. He set another marker at the base of the dune, a huge rock, three hundred and fifty steps from the cottonwood.

Sitting in his camp that afternoon, he worried about the loss of landmarks. The gray rocks on the mountain might change or slide away, the cottonwood and the dead spruce might blow over. He returned quickly to the broad gulch and set a row of rocks fifty paces apart, burying them on solid ground below the sand, in a line which pointed toward the treasure.

Now he felt better. Rocks were solid and heavy; they would not blow away. Going back to his camp in the evening, a brand new doubt struck him: suppose the wind uncovered his line of rocks. Anyone riding past would wonder why they had been placed so. The extensions of the thought worried Anderson until late in the night. He rose and went down the hill to have a look.

He put his face close to the sand, sighting. The surface was gently rippled. He could not see any stones, not even the large one he had left exposed purposely. He felt that his presence protected the gold; he was loath to leave. For a long time he stood shivering in the night. When he finally started back to his camp, a light wind swept down through the pinons. It was a dawn wind, natural; it came every morning and had nothing to do with the great winds that had built the dunes. But Anderson felt that it was a deliberate betrayal, and so he went back to the edge of the sand and stayed there until the wind died away.

During the days and weeks that passed he grew hollow-eyed and gaunt. He begrudged the time it required to get meat when he was out of food. His rest was never unbroken, disturbed by dreams of a powerful wind that swept the sand away to the rocks, leaving his sacks of gold lying in a long row where anyone could see them. That happened over and over, and then he dreamed of running down the hill to find himself entrapped in waist-deep sand among the trees. He struggled there, while out on the flat men were riding without haste to pick up the sacks. And then he would waken, trembling and almost ill from frustration.

Light snows dusted the valley. Whiteness lay in the grim wrinkles of the *Sangre de Cristo* and the dunes sparkled in the frosty air of early morning; but the snow never lasted long upon the sand. A season of winds followed. They gathered out of the southwest, twisting into crazy patterns when they struck the dunes. Sometimes Anderson saw sand streaming in four directions on ridges that lay close to each other.

When the wind was at its strongest he never heard the singing. The sounds came only with diminishing winds or when the blow was first rising. High-pitched music skirling from the ridges, running clear and sharp, then clashing like sky demons fighting when the wind made sudden changes. Anderson heard the singing at times when he stood at the foot of the dunes in still air, sensing the powerful rush of currents far above.

Sometimes, crouched in the doorway of his hut, he watched the queer half daylight of the storms and read strange words into the music. There was something in the sounds that wailed of lostness and of madness, of the times after centuries of rain had ceased, when the earth was drying and man was unknown.

Each time the wind ceased, while his ears still held music that could never be named or written into notes, Anderson went down the hill to see what changes had been made.

The dunes were never the same and yet they were always the same, soft contours on the slopes, wind-sharpened ridges, hollows that went down to natural earth, white streaks where the heavier particles of sand gathered to themselves. A million tons of sand could shift in a few minutes but nothing was really changed.

The wind did as it pleased; it did not do Anderson's work for him. Sometimes his limb marker was buried twenty feet deep; sometimes he found it lying ten feet lower than it had been. He always put it upright.

Long snows fell upon the valley. Deer came down from the hills. On clear days Anderson saw smoke at distant farms where pioneers were toughing out the winter. He thought of Lamb, snug by now in some tight, red-rocked valley of the San Juan. Lamb probably was searching for gold again, not really caring whether he found it or not. The thought infuriated Anderson.

Anderson was on the dunes one day when a wind, running steadily along the surface of the ground, began to eat into the side of the slope that covered the sacks. Tense and choked-up, he watched it, first with suspicion, and then with hope. Faster than any tool man could ever create, the numberless hands of the wind scooped sand until a rounding cove appeared. Anderson's largest marker rock sat on bare ground now. The cove extended, an oval running deeper and deeper into the side of the dune where his gold lay.

Anderson followed the receding sand as a man would pace after a falling tide. He counted until he knew he was within fifteen steps of the gold. Whirling around the edges of the cove, digging, lifting, the wind took sand away until Anderson knew he stood no farther than ten feet from the first sack. He could not stand inactive any longer. He began to burrow like an animal, and the wind worked with him effortlessly. He shouted incoherently when his hand closed on soft buckskin. The first sack.

It became an evil moment. Somewhere on Mosca or Medano or Music, or perhaps all three, there was a sudden change. The wind now came from a different direction. Sand poured down the slope faster than Anderson could dig. It grew around his legs, covering them. Sand rippled down the surface of the dune. It fell directly from the air. Cursing, half blinded, Anderson dug furiously. He might as well have been scooping water from a lake with his hands.

He was forced back as slowly as he had come. The cove filled up again. He stood in the wide gulch at last, on shallow sand where there never seemed to be appreciable change.

Almost exhausted, he stumbled away, muttering like a man insane. The wind began to lessen and the dunes sang to him, singing him back to his miserable hut of boughs among the pinons. He threw the sack of gold inside and lay by the spring until he was trembling from cold.

That night there was no wind. He crouched over his fire, and his eyes were as red as the flames that blossomed from the pinon sticks. It was no use to wait on the wind, for the wind would only torture him. He must do everything by his own efforts.

The next day he rode to a farm in the valley. The snow lay unevenly where ground had been ploughed, a pitiful patch of accomplishment, considering the vastness, Anderson thought. There was a low log barn, unchinked. A black-bearded young man came to the doorway of a one-room cabin with a rifle in his hands.

"I'm a prospector," Anderson explained. "I'm looking for some boards to build me a place. Been living in a bough hut."

"Build a cabin." The farmer's dark eyes were watchful, but they were also lonely.

"I lost my packhorse and all my tools coming over Music."

The man shook his head. "I've got an axe and a plough—and that's about it. Come spring, my brothers will be back with some things we need—I hope." He studied the shaggy condition of Anderson's horse. "Come in and eat."

The cabin was primitive. A man must be a fool, Anderson thought, to try to make a farm in this valley. The farmer's name was George Linkman. His loneliness came out in talk and he wanted Anderson to stay the night. From him Anderson found out that there was a man about ten miles east who had hauled a load of lumber from New Mexico the fall before and hadn't got around to building with it yet.

Ten miles east. That put the place close to the dunes, somewhere against the mountains.

Anderson rode away with one suspicion cleared from his mind: Linkman was not the man who had followed him and Lamb to the Huerfano. Linkman's voice was much too deep. But who was this man against the hills close to the dunes? Anderson was uneasy when he found the place at the mouth of a small stream, and realized that it was not more than two miles from his own camp.

He was reassured somewhat by the fact that the log buildings were old. There had been more cultivation here than at Linkman's place. No one was at home. He saw the pile of lumber, already warping. He stared at it greedily.

The man came riding in from the valley side of the foothills. He was a stocky, middle-aged man, clean shaved, with gray in his hair. His faded mackinaw was ragged. He greeted Anderson heartily and asked him why he hadn't gone inside to warm up and help himself to food.

"Just got here," Anderson said. *The voice.* . . . No, it wasn't the voice of the man who had come to Mendoza's place. That man had been young.

The farmer's name was Burl Hollister. While he cooked a meal he kept bragging about the potatoes he had grown last summer. There was a little hillside cellar still half full of them to prove his boast. Nothing would do but Anderson must stay all night with him.

By candlelight Hollister talked of the new ground he would break next spring, of the settlers who would come to the valley in time. Anderson nodded, watching him narrowly. This place was too close to the dunes, but of course it had been here long before Anderson and Lamb made their terrible mistake in the hollow of the sand.

Anderson brought up the matter of lumber and tools, speaking guardedly of a streak of gold he had discovered on Mosca Pass.

"Tools I can spare," Hollister said slowly, "but that lumber—that's something else. I figured to build the old lady a lean-to kitchen with it before she comes back in the spring. I was aiming to surprise her. This place ain't much for a woman yet, but in time—"

"You could get more lumber before spring." Anderson drew a sack of gold from his shirt. There was not much in the sack, perhaps a pound and a half, for he had left most of it in the buckskin pouch he had recovered from the dunes.

After some hesitation Hollister untied the strings and dipped his fingers into the yellow grains. "Good Lord!" he breathed. "Is that all gold?"

"You could buy more lumber, Hollister."

"Tools, yes," the farmer murmured. "I can spare tools, but doggone, it's a long haul to get boards here." He kept pinching the gold between his thumb and two fingers. "Is this from your claim on Mosca?"

Anderson did not answer too hastily. "No, that came from the San Juan. I don't know yet what I have on Mosca."

"All of it for the lumber?"

Anderson nodded.

Not looking up, Hollister said, "All right."

He hauled the lumber and tools the next day to the bottom of the hill below Anderson's camp. Hollister brought also a bushel of potatoes. He spent most of the morning digging and lining a tiny cellar to keep them from freezing. When that was done he said, "I'll help you carry the boards up here."

"You've done enough," Anderson said. "I've got to level off a place here first."

"You're welcome to stay with me till spring."

"Thanks, but I'd rather be closer to my work."

Hollister nodded, staring across at the dunes. "Sort of pretty, ain't they?"

"Not to me. There's too much sand," Anderson said, and then he began to worry about the implications of his statement. He was glad when Hollister left.

Now that he had the lumber, Anderson began to doubt that it would serve his purpose. He had planned to work only at night but desperation was growing in him. In the spring riders would be coming to Medano and Mosca constantly. It was better to take a chance now on Linkman and Hollister, so far the only men who knew he was here.

But he retained caution. Until he knew how the lumber would serve, he would not try to tunnel directly toward the gold. He started a hundred yards away from his line of rocks, in a direction at a right angle to the treasure. He drove short boards into the sand, overhead and on the sides of his projected tunnel. Then he shoveled, framing more lumber to support the boards as soon as the sand fell away from them. Sand poured through the cracks and between the warped edges where the boards did not fit tightly. He nailed more lumber over the cracks. In a month of brutal labor he made ten feet. And then one day when he was shoveling back, he heard a cracking sound. He got clear just before the tunnel collapsed.

He was standing with a shovel in his hand, too spent to curse, when Linkman rode up. Anderson did not hear him until the farmer was quite close, but when he saw the long shadow of the horse upon the sand, he dropped his shovel and leaped to grab his rifle.

"Hey!" Linkman cried. "What's the matter?"

Anderson lowered his rifle, but he kept staring at the visitor, who was looking curiously at the ends of boards sticking from the sand.

"That's a funny place for a potato cellar." Linkman tried to smile but he was too uneasy to make it real. He fumbled on, "I thought your mine was up on Mosca."

Anderson did not say anything. He saw the slow breaking of something in Linkman's expression, a fear, a disturbed sensation that Linkman tried to conceal. The man could not have made himself more clear if he had put a forefinger to his temple and made a circular motion.

"I was just riding around," Linkman said vaguely. "I guess I'll be going. I was just scouting for a place to get some firewood." He rode away.

Anderson went back to his camp. When he knelt at the spring he knew why Linkman had thought him mad. His beard was matted, his eyes hollow and bloodshot, his lips tight against his teeth. He was jolted for a few moments, and then he drank and turned his mind once more to the problem of the treasure.

It struck him suddenly. He would build his tunnel in the open, where he could make the boards tight and the framing strong. He would build sections that would fit together snugly, large enough for a man to crawl through easily. The next time the wind gouged out a hole in the direction of his gold, he would have his sections ready to lay in place. Let the damned wind cover them. The tunnel would be there, even if it was under two hundred feet of sand.

There were omissions in his plan that he did not care to dwell on at the moment; overall, it was a beautiful idea and that was enough. He rose to cook a meal and was annoyed to find he had no meat.

He found the horse tracks when he was hunting deer in the pinons above his camp. He spent the whole afternoon chasing up and down the hills until he knew that someone had been watching him, not only recently but for a long time. Instead of fear, he felt an insane fury that made him grind his teeth.

That night another gale came out of the southwest, coursing toward the high passes. Restless in his cold hut, Anderson heard the howling of it; and later, the singing of the sands when the wind began to decrease.

Clean morning sunlight on the great buff hills showed Anderson that they were unchanged. The ends of the boards from his collapsed tunnel were hidden now, and for the hundredth time his limb marker above the gold was covered. For several moments he was motionless.

There were forces here that he could never conquer, a challenge that would lead him to wreckage. Lamb had known what he was doing when he wasted not a moment, but rode away. For the first time Anderson felt an urge to leave, but he knew that the wind could undo what it had done; and if he went away, he might be haunted forever by the thought that what he had waited for happened one hour, a day, or a week, after he quit.

He went down the hill and began to build the sections of his tunnel lining. He piled them on the shallow sand. He built them so that one man could drag them into place when the time came. It was not heavy work but it tired him more each day. He went at it with desperate urgency, thinking that the wind might choose a time to dig toward his treasure when he was unprepared.

Dizzy spells began to bother him during the three days it took to build the boxes. He had been eating scraps, or very little; and his mind had been burning up the resources of his body. This he realized, but time might run away from him, and so he staggered on at his work, resting only when his vision darkened.

Utterly spent, he finished the boxes one afternoon when there was no wind. He slumped down behind a pile of them, letting his hands fall limply into the fine sand.

Sleep struck him like a maul. He dreamed of the running fight across Medano, of the easy life on the Huerfano. He trembled in his sleep, a young man who was old and gaunt. A voice roused him slowly.

"Anderson! Anderson! Where are you?"

Groggily, Anderson tried to come out of his exhaustion. He thought he was back on the floor of Mendoza's house, with his feet swollen and scratched. The last pursuer had come across the pass and was inquiring about him and the mule.

"Hey, Anderson! Don't tell me you've got lost in one of those sluice boxes."

Anderson stared at his boots. There was no doubt of it: the voice was that of the man who had survived the chase, the same cool voice of a young man who would not give up. Anderson's rifle was in one of the boxes. He could not remember which one.

His muscles dragged wearily when he rose. He could not believe the man sitting there on the horse was Hollister.

"Sleeping in the middle of daylight!" Hollister grinned. His clean shaved face was bright. His gray hair showed below the frayed edges of his scotch cap. He frowned at the boxes. "You're a long ways from water with those sluices, Anderson."

Hollister was the man. Now that Anderson could separate his voice from his appearance, he was able to get rid of the inaccurate picture he had built of Hollister. Anderson moved around the boxes until he found his rifle. He remembered the flight across Medano long ago. It was Hollister's fault and his fault that the gold was here.

Hollister said, "You've worked yourself plumb string-haltered, Ander—" He stopped, staring into the muzzle of Anderson's rifle. "What's the matter?"

"You're the man that followed me and Lamb to the Huerfano! You're no farmer. You've been watching me ever since I've been here."

Hollister kept his hands on the saddle horn. He looked at Anderson gravely. "The farm belongs to a man who wanted to go back to Kansas for the winter. I'm the man, all right. Now there's just two of us. The wind got your gold, didn't it, Anderson?"

Anderson stepped away from the boxes, edging to the side so that if Hollister made his horse rear the act would not interfere with the shot. Anderson was ready to kill the man. He wanted to. All he lacked was some small puff of provocation.

Hollister gave him none. He sat quietly, moving only his head. "When I came back over the pass, I found the panniers and the packsaddle you threw away. There was only one place where you two could have covered your tracks that day—here. I knew you'd come back.

"There's two of us, Anderson. You're as well off as you were before. I'm much better off, thanks to your partner." He gave the thought time to grow. "You left the gold here. The wind covered it. Your partner should have known better, but of course we were pushing you hard and you didn't have much choice. There's ways to get at it, Anderson. How deep is it?"

Anderson did not answer. He still wanted to kill Hollister but he knew he could not do it.

"The two of us can get it out of there," Hollister said. "I know a way." He looked at the boxes. "That won't work. You figure to make a tunnel of them, don't you? The sand will blow in one end and pour into the other. I know a better way, Anderson."

He was bargaining only because the rifle was on him, Anderson thought. But no, Hollister must not be sure of where the treasure lay.

"I've got every ounce of every sack you dropped on Medano," Hollister said. "That goes in the split too. You know where the rest is. I'm not sure. You can't get it out. I know a way. I could have killed you, Anderson, months ago. If I had been sure of where the sacks were, maybe I would have." He smiled. "That's all in the past now. There's gold enough for ten men."

Anderson grounded his rifle. "You know a way to get it out?"

"Yes."

That was the bait, Anderson thought, the bait that would bring the deadfall crashing down on his neck. But belief began to grow in him. The thought that he could trust Hollister became more important than any idea the man had about recovering the treasure.

"Think about it," Hollister said. "You've no one to ask about me. I'm an odd man inside. When I give my word, Anderson, before God, it's good." He turned his horse and rode away. The faded mackinaw covering his broad back was an easy target all the way to the cottonwoods.

Anderson had believed him while he was here, but now the worms of suspicion began to twist and turn again. For a week Anderson did not go down upon the sands. He stayed in camp or hunted, and he saw no more fresh horse tracks on the hills. The winds came, piling sand in a long, curving ramp against his boxes, and the wind uncovered the boards where he had experimented with a tunnel. There was something ancient and ghostly in the look of the lumber sticking from the dune.

He knew with a dreary certainty that men could not defy the work of a million years of wind. The caprice of the gales would expose the treasure when the time came, but that might be a century from now.

There was also the thought that it could be tomorrow, and that was what held Anderson, gnawed with the fear of defeat only, no longer dreaming of what gold could buy. It struck him that if he could transfer the burden of worry, which in a way was exactly what Lamb had done, then he might be free.

He rode to see Hollister.

The man was sitting by a warm fire, smoking his pipe. "Out of potatoes, Anderson? The darned things are beginning to sprout. It must be getting near spring."

Near spring. Months of Anderson's life had flowed into the sands. He had lived like a brute.

"You look some better," Hollister said. He spoke like a neighbor being pleasant but knowing that there was bargaining to come.

"This way of yours to move the sand. . . ." Anderson let it trail off. There was no way to move the sand. His own ideas had been sure and clear about that once, but now he knew better.

"Yeah?" Hollister's eyes tightened.

"You've got the sacks I threw away on Medano?"

Hollister nodded.

"For them I'll tell you where the rest is, and you can have it all—if you can dig it out."

Hollister cocked his head. "I'd rather have you working with me—for half of everything."

"You're afraid I won't tell the truth? I thought Lamb had lied to me too, Hollister. He didn't. He paced the distance. I recovered one sack of gold, right where it was supposed to be."

Hollister rubbed his lips together slowly.

"One sack is all. The wind will break your heart, Hollister."

"I can beat it."

"Give me what I left behind on the pass. The rest is yours."

Hollister's eyes were bright. "Let's go up and take a look at the dunes."

The hooves of the horses made soft sounds in the broad gulch. The full weight of the hills bore on Anderson and he wondered how he had ever been fool enough to think he could outwit the dunes. He knew better now and he had learned before his mind broke on the problem.

"They're yours, Hollister."

The older man's satisfied expression threw a jet of worry into Anderson. Maybe he was selling out too cheaply. It was an effort to stick with his decision.

Hollister said, "Your sacks are buried just inside the door of the potato cellar."

Anderson pointed to the limb on the dune. He told Hollister about the rocks under the sand and the sighting marks and the number of steps from the tree.

"I knew most of that from watching you," Hollister said, "but I wasn't sure. Why'd you start the tunnel over there?" His gaze was sharp and hard.

"I did that after I knew you were spying."

Hollister knew the truth when he heard it. "It would have saved me gold if I had killed you, wouldn't it?" In the same conversational tone he went on, "I'm going to bring a ditch down from Medano. I'll flume it through the sand and let the water wash away what I want moved."

Water would seep into the sand. It would run out of cracks in the flume, causing the sections to buckle. The eternal wind would work easily while Hollister was floundering and cursing his broken plan. Anderson had never felt sorry for himself. Now he had sympathy for Hollister.

"Don't come back," Hollister said. "We've made our bargain. I'll kill you if you hang around or come back."

Anderson went up the hill to his camp. The first signs of spring were breaking on the edges of the valley. He hadn't noticed them before. He stared for a while at the bough hut. It was a hovel unworthy of a Digger Indian. *I stayed in that all winter.*

He took his camping gear and kicked the hut apart.

Out on the sand, Hollister was walking slowly. He had found the line of rocks. He turned and sighted, and then he looked at the boards where the wrecked tunnel had been. There would always be in his mind, Anderson knew, doubt that Anderson had told the truth. The sand would defy him, the winds would mock him, and the singing on the ridges would jeer him.

When Anderson rode away, he saw Hollister dragging the boxes with his horse, dragging them up to where he would build a flume that would break his heart. The struggle of the horse and man against the sand was a picture that Anderson would never forget.

He found the sacks in the potato cellar where Hollister had said. He opened each one and ran his hand inside and afterward looked at the grains of gold clinging to his cracked and roughened skin. The sand had done that too.

He stuffed the sacks inside his shirt. At once the weight was intolerable. Perhaps somewhere out on the floor of the valley where there was no sand to blow over it. . . . No, gold was not to be buried. He would put it inside the pack on his horse. Half of it was Lamb's.

Anderson hesitated and then he dropped one bag on the floor. He thought it was a small enough price to pay for transferring a crushing burden. He rode away, going toward the purple mountains of the San Juan Basin. For a while the tug of the treasure of the dunes was still strong, but he kept going until at last he knew beyond doubt that he had made a good decision.

At sunset he turned to look back. Against the high range the buff hills were small, pale, beautiful, changeless. Anderson raised his eyes to the crimson glory flaming on the summits of the Blood of Christ Mountains, watching quietly until the color seeped away; and then he rode on, knowing that tonight he would sleep as he had not slept for months.

The winds still sing across the dark manes of the sand dunes, wailing, if the ear can understand, of the man who lived for thirty years in a little hut among the pinons. He dressed in cast-off garments that ranchers brought him. He raised dogs that ran wild, eating them when times were lean. He was crazy as a bedbug, for he talked of gold he was going to wash from the sands. The wind alternately covered and uncovered the rotting sections of a flume he had tried to build around the shoulder of the dune.

He said that the wind knew a great secret and that four times the wind had almost showed him the secret; and then in the next breath he would curse the wind with such insane vehemence that people were glad to get away from him. There was something vicious about the old man, but there also was something pitiful and lost in the record of his life.

On a bright fall day when the aspens on Medano were golden streaks against the mountains he died on the sand with a shovel in his hands. George Linkman, a pioneer rancher, found him there with the hungry dogs whining and edging closer to him. Linkman shot the dogs. One yellow cur went howling across the sand almost to the rotting trunk of a huge, fallen cottonwood before it died.

There had been a strong wind the night before. When Linkman carried the old man toward the trees to bury him, he saw a line of rocks, a solid line of them, running from where the dead dog lay to the base of the first dune. It appeared that the crazy old devil had tried at one time to build a dam to catch the floodwaters of Medano Creek in the spring.

The next time Linkman came by the dunes—he was an old man and his riding days were numbered—he observed that the wind had covered the rocks once more.

SERGEANT HOUCK
BY JACK SCHAEFER
(Trooper Hook)

Jack Schaefer's short novel Shane *is an indisputable Western classic; the same is true of the 1953 film version featuring Alan Ladd and Van Heflin. Another Schaefer novel,* Monte Walsh, *which many critics and aficionados feel is his best work and one of the finest Western novels ever written, was filmed in 1970 with Lee Marvin and Jack Palance in the starring roles. Except for "Sergeant Houck," the masterful tale of a man and a woman overcoming racial prejudice on the Western frontier, the only other Schaefer short story to be filmed was "Jeremy Rodock" (see* The Reel West), *which became an excellent 1956 vehicle for the talents of James Cagney, entitled* Tribute to a Bad Man.

Sergeant Houck stopped his horse just below the top of the ridge ahead. The upper part of his body was silhouetted against the skyline as he rose in his stirrups to peer over the crest. He urged the horse on up and the two of them, the man and the horse, were sharp and distinct against the copper sky. After a moment he turned and rode down to the small troop waiting. He reined beside Lieutenant Imler.

"It's there, sir. Alongside a creek in the next hollow. Maybe a third of a mile."

Lieutenant Imler regarded him coldly. "You took your time, Sergeant. Smack on the top too."

"Couldn't see plain, sir. Sun was in my eyes."

"Wanted them to spot you, eh, Sergeant?"

"No, sir. Sun was bothering me. I don't think——"

"Forget it, Sergeant. I don't like this either."

Lieutenant Imler was in no hurry. He led the troop slowly up the hill. He waited until the men were spread in a reasonably straight line just below the ridge top. He sighed softly to himself. The real fuss was fifty-some miles away. Captain McKay was hogging the honors there. Here he was tied to this disgusting sideline detail. Twenty men. Ten would have been enough. Ten, and an old hand like Sergeant Houck with no officer to curb his style. Thank the War Department for sergeants, the pickled-in-salt variety. They could do what no commissioned officer could do. They could forget orders and follow their own thoughts and show themselves on the top of a hill.

Lieutenant Imler sighed again. Even Sergeant Houck must think this had been time enough. He lifted his drawn saber. "All right, men. If we had a bugler, he'd be snorting air into it right now."

Saber pointing forward, Lieutenant Imler led the charge up and over the crest and down the long slope to the Indian village. There were some scattered shots from bushes by the creek, ragged pops indicating poor powder and poorer weapons, probably fired by the last of the old men left behind when the young braves departed in war-paint ten days before. A few of the squaws and children, their dogs tagging, could still be seen running into the brush. They reached cover and faded from sight, disappeared into the surrounding emptiness. The village was silent and deserted and dust settled in the afternoon sun.

Lieutenant Imler surveyed the ground taken. "Spectacular achievement," he muttered to himself. He beckoned Sergeant Houck to him.

"Your redskin friend was right, Sergeant. This is it."

"Knew he could be trusted, sir."

"Our orders are to destroy the village. Send a squad out to round up any stock. There might be some horses around. We're to take them in." Lieutenant Imler waved an arm at the thirty-odd skin-and-pole huts. "Set the others to pulling those down. Burn what you can and smash everything else."

"Right, sir."

Lieutenant Imler rode into the slight shade of the cottonwoods along the creek. He wiped the dust from his face and set his campaign hat at a fresh angle to ease the crease made by the band on his forehead. Here he was, hot and tired and way out at the end of nowhere with another long ride ahead, while Captain McKay was having it out at last with Gray Otter and his renegade warriors somewhere between the Turkey Foot and the Washakie. He relaxed to wait in the saddle, beginning to frame his report in his mind.

"Pardon, sir."

Lieutenant Imler swung in the saddle to look around. Sergeant Houck was afoot, was standing near with something in his arms, something that squirmed and seemed to have dozens of legs and arms.

"What the devil is that, Sergeant?"

"A baby, sir. Or rather, a boy. Two years old, sir."

"How the devil do you know? By his teeth?"

"His mother told me, sir."

"His mother?"

"Certainly, sir. She's right here."

Lieutenant Imler saw her then, close to a neighboring tree, partially behind the trunk, shrinking into the shadow and staring at Sergeant Houck and his squirming burden. He leaned to look closer. She was not young. She might have been any age in the middle years. She was shapeless in the sacklike skin covering with slit-holes for her arms and head. She was sun- and windburned dark, yet not as dark as he expected. And there was no mistaking her hair. It was light brown and long and braided, and the braid was coiled around on her head.

"Sergeant! It's a white woman!"

"Right, sir. Her name's Cora Sutliff. The wagon train she was with was wiped out by a raiding party. She and another woman were taken along. The other woman died. She didn't. The village here bought her. She's been in Gray Otter's lodge." Sergeant Houck smacked the squirming boy briskly and tucked him under one arm. He looked straight at Lieutenant Imler. "That was three years ago, sir."

"Three years? Then that boy——"

"That's right, sir."

Captain McKay looked up from his desk to see Sergeant Houck stiff at attention before him. It always gave him a feeling of satisfaction to see this big slab of cross-grained granite that Nature had hewed into the shape of a man. The replacements they were sending these days, raw and unseasoned, were enough to shake his faith in the Service. But as long as there remained a sprinkling of these case-hardened oldtime regulars, the Army would still be the Army.

"At ease, Sergeant."

"Thank you, sir."

Captain McKay drummed his fingers on the desk. This was a ridiculous proposition. There was something incongruous about it and the solid, impassive bulk of Sergeant Houck made it seem even more so.

"That woman, Sergeant. She's married. The husband's alive, wasn't with the train when it was attacked. He's been located, has a place about twenty miles out of Laramie. The name's right and everything checks. You're to take her there and turn her over with the troop's compliments."

"Me, sir?"

"She asked for you. The big man who found her. Lieutenant Imler says that's you."

Sergeant Houck considered this behind the rock mask of his weather-carved face. "And about the boy, sir?"

"He goes with her." Captain McKay drummed on the desk again. "Speaking frankly, Sergeant, I think she's making a mistake. I suggested she let us see the boy got back to the tribe. Gray Otter's dead, and after that affair two weeks ago there's not many of the men left. But they'll be on the reservation now and he'd be taken care of. She wouldn't hear of it, said if he had to go she would too." Captain McKay felt his former indignation rising again. "I say she's playing the fool. You agree with me, of course."

"No, sir. I don't."

"And why the devil not?"

"He's her son, sir."

"But he's—— Well, that's neither here nor there, Sergeant. It's not our affair. We deliver her and there's an end to it. You'll draw expense money and start within the hour. If you push along, you can make the stage at the settlement. Two days going and two coming. That makes four. If you stretch it another coming back, I'll be too busy to notice. If you stretch it past that, I'll have your stripes. That's all."

"Right, sir." Sergeant Houck straightened and swung about and started for the door.

"Houck."

"Yes, sir."

"Take good care of her—and that damn kid."

"Right, sir."

Captain McKay stood by the window and watched the small cavalcade go past toward the post gateway. Lucky that his wife had come with him, even on this last assignment to this Godforsaken station lost in the prairie wasteland. Without her they would have been in a fix with the woman. As it was, the woman looked like a woman now. And why shouldn't she, wearing his wife's third-best crinoline dress? It was a bit large, but it gave her a proper feminine appearance. His wife had enjoyed fitting her, from the skin out, everything except shoes. Those were too small. The woman seemed to prefer her worn moccasins anyway. And she was uncomfortable in the clothes. But she was decently grateful for them, insisting she would have them returned or would pay for them somehow. She was riding past the window, side-saddle on his wife's horse, still with that strange shrinking air about her, not so much frightened as remote, as if she could not quite connect with what was happening to her, what was going on around her.

Behind her was Private Lakin, neat and spruce in his uniform, with the boy in front of him on the horse. The boy's legs stuck out on each side of the small improvised pillow tied to the forward arch of the saddle to give him a better seat. He looked like a weird, black-haired doll bobbing with the movements of the horse.

And there beside the woman, shadowing her in the mid-morning sun, was that extra incongruous touch, the great granite hulk of Sergeant Houck, straight in his saddle with the military erectness that was so much a part of him that it would never leave him, solid, impassive, taking this as he took everything, with no excitement and no show of any emotion, a job to be done.

They went past, and Captain McKay watched them ride out through the gateway. It was not quite so incongruous after all. As he had discovered on many a tight occasion, there was something comforting in the presence of that big, angular slab of a man. Nothing ever shook him. He had a knack of knowing what needed to be done whatever the shifting circumstances. You might never know exactly what went on inside his close-cropped, hardpan skull, but you could be certain that what needed to be done he would do.

Captain McKay turned back to his desk. He would wait for the report, terse and almost illegible in crabbed handwriting, but he could write off this detail as of this moment. Sergeant Houck had it in hand.

They were scarcely out of sight of the post when the boy began his squirming. Private Lakin clamped him to the pillow with a capable right hand. The squirming persisted. The boy seemed determined to escape from what he regarded as an alien captor. Silent, intent, he writhed on the pillow. Private Lakin's hand and arm grew weary. He tickled his horse forward with his heels until he was close behind the others.

"Beg pardon."

Sergeant Houck shifted in his saddle and looked around. "Yes?"

"He's trying to get away. It'd be easier if I tied him down. Could I use my belt?"

Sergeant Houck held in his horse to drop back alongside Private Lakin. "Kids don't need tying," he said. He reached out and plucked the boy from in front of Private Lakin and laid him, face down, across the withers of his own horse and smacked him sharply. He picked the boy up again and reached out and set him again on the pillow. The boy sat still, very still, making no movement except that caused by the sliding motion of the horse's foreshoulders. Sergeant Houck pushed his left hand into his left side pocket and it came forth with a fistful of small hard biscuits. He passed these to Private Lakin. "Stick one of these in his mouth when he gets restless."

Sergeant Houck urged his horse forward until he was beside the woman once more. She had turned her head to watch, and she stared sidewise at him for a long moment, then looked straight forward again along the wagon trace before them.

They came to the settlement in the same order, the woman and Sergeant Houck side by side in the lead, Private Lakin and the boy tagging at a respectful distance. Sergeant Houck dismounted and helped the woman down and plucked the boy from the pillow and handed him to the woman. He unfastened one rein from his horse's bridle and knotted it to the other, making them into a lead strap. He did the same to the reins of the woman's horse. He noted Private Lakin looking wistfully at the painted front of the settlement's one saloon and tapped him on one knee and handed him the ends of the two straps. "Scat," he said, and watched Private Lakin turn his horse and ride off leading the other two horses. He took the boy from the woman and tucked him under one arm and led the way into the squat frame building that served as general store and post-office and stage stop. He settled the woman on a preserved-goods box and set the boy in her lap and went to the counter to arrange for their fares. When he returned to sit on another box near her, the entire permanent male population of the settlement had assembled just inside the door, all eleven of them staring at the woman.

". . . that's the one . . ."
". . . an Indian had her . . ."
". . . shows in the kid . . ."

Sergeant Houck looked at the woman. She was staring at the floor. The blood was retreating from beneath the skin of her face, making it appear old and leathery. He started to rise and felt her hand on his arm. She had leaned over quickly and clutched his sleeve.

"Please," she said. "Don't make trouble account of me."

"Trouble?" said Sergeant Houck. "No trouble." He rose and confronted the fidgeting men by the door. "I've seen kids around this place. Some of them small. This one now needs decent clothes and the store here doesn't stock them."

The men stared at him, startled, and then at the wide-eyed boy in his clean but patched skimpy cloth covering. Five or six of them went out through the door and disappeared in various directions. The others scattered through the store, finding little businesses to excuse their presence. Sergeant Houck stood sentinel, relaxed and quiet, by his box, and those who had gone out straggled back, several embarrassed and empty-handed, the rest proud with their offerings.

Sergeant Houck took the boy from the woman's lap and stood him on his box. He measured the offerings against the small body and chose a small red flannel shirt and a small pair of faded overalls. He peeled the boy with one quick motion, ripping away the old cloth, and put the shirt and overalls on him. He set the one pair of small scuffed shoes aside. "Kids don't need shoes," he said. "Only in winter." He heard the sound of hooves and stepped to the door to watch the stage approach and creak to a stop, the wheels sliding in the dust. He looked back to see the men inspecting the boy to that small individual's evident satisfaction and urging their other offerings upon the woman. He strode among them and scooped the boy under one arm and beckoned the woman to follow and went out the door to the waiting old Concord coach. He deposited the boy on the rear seat inside and turned to watch the woman come out of the store escorted by the male population of the settlement. He helped her into the coach and nodded up at the driver on his high box seat and swung himself in. The rear seat groaned and sagged as he sank into it beside the woman with the boy between them. The woman peered out the window by her, and suddenly, in a shrinking, experimental gesture, she waved at the men outside. The driver's whip cracked and the horses lunged into the harness and the coach rolled forward, and a faint suggestion of warm color showed through the tan of the woman's cheeks.

They had the coach to themselves for the first hours. Dust drifted steadily through the windows and the silence inside was a persistent thing. The woman did not want to talk. She had lost all liking for it and would speak only when necessary, and there was no need. And Sergeant Houck used words with a natural and unswerving economy, for the sole simple purpose of conveying or obtaining information that he regarded as pertinent to the business immediately in hand. Only once did he speak during these hours and then only to set a fact straight in his mind. He kept his eyes fixed on the dusty scenery outside as he spoke.

"Did he treat you all right?"

The woman made no pretense of misunderstanding him. Her thoughts leaped back and came forward through three years and she pushed straight to the point with the single word. "Yes," she said.

The coach rolled on and the dust drifted. "He beat me once," she said, and the coach rolled on, and four full minutes passed before she finished this in her own mind and in the words: "Maybe it was right. I wouldn't work."

Sergeant Houck nodded. He put his right hand in his right pocket and fumbled there to find one of the short straight straws and bring it forth. He put one end of this in his mouth and chewed slowly on it and watched the dust whirls drift past.

They stopped for a quick meal at a lonely ranchhouse and ate in silence while the man there helped the driver change horses. Then the coach rolled forward and the sun began to drop overhead. It was two mail stops later, at the next change, that another passenger climbed in and plopped his battered suitcase and himself on the front seat opposite them. He was of medium height and plump. He wore city clothes and had quick eyes and features small in the plumpness of his face. He took out a handkerchief and wiped his face and removed his hat to wipe all the way up his forehead. He laid the hat on top of the suitcase and moved restlessly on the seat, trying to find a comfortable position. His movements were quick and nervous. There was no quietness in him.

"You three together?"

"Yes," said Sergeant Houck.

"Your wife, then?"

"No," said Sergeant Houck. He looked out the window on his side and studied the far horizon. The coach rolled on, and the man's quick eyes examined the three of them and came to brief rest on the woman's feet.

"Begging your pardon, lady, but why do you wear those things? Moccasins, aren't they? They more comfortable?"

She looked at him and down again at the floor and shrank back farther in the seat and the blood began to retreat from her face.

"No offense, lady," said the man. "I just wondered——" He stopped. Sergeant Houck was looking at him.

"Dust's bad," said Sergeant Houck. "And the flies this time of year. Best to keep your mouth closed."

He looked again out the window and the coach rolled on, and the only sounds were the running beat of the hooves and the creakings of the old coach.

A front wheel struck a stone and the coach jolted up at an angle and lurched sideways and the boy gave a small whimper. The woman pulled him to her and onto her lap.

"Say," said the man, "where'd you ever pick up that kid? Looks like——" He stopped.

Sergeant Houck was reaching up and rapping a rock fist against the top of the coach. The driver's voice could be heard shouting at the horses and the coach slowed and the brakes bit on the wheels and the coach stopped. One of the doors opened and the driver peered in. Instinctively he picked Sergeant Houck.

"What's the trouble, soldier?"

"No trouble," said Sergeant Houck. "Our friend here wants to ride up on the box with you." He looked at the plump man. "Less dust up there. It's healthy and gives a good view."

"Now, wait a minute," said the man. "Where'd you get the idea——"

"Healthy," said Sergeant Houck.

The driver looked at the bleak, impassive hardness of Sergeant Houck and at the twitching softness of the plump man. "Reckon it would be," he said. "Come along. I'll boost you up."

The coach rolled forward and the dust drifted and the miles went under the wheels. They rolled along the false-fronted one street of a mushroom town and stopped before a frame building tagged "Hotel." One of the coach doors opened and the plump man retrieved his hat and suitcase and scuttled away and across the porch and into the building. The driver appeared at the coach door. "Last meal here before the night run," he said, and wandered off around the building. Sergeant Houck stepped to the ground and helped the woman out and reached back in and scooped up the boy, tucked him under an arm, and led the way into the building.

When they came out, the shadows were long and fresh horses had been harnessed and a bent, footsore old man was applying grease to the axles. When they were settled again on the rear seat, two men emerged from the building lugging a small but heavy chest and hoisted it into the compartment under the high driving seat. Another man, wearing a close-buttoned suitcoat and curled-brim hat and carrying a shotgun in the crook of one elbow, am-bled into sight around the corner of the building and climbed to the high seat. A moment later a new driver, whip in hand, followed and joined him on the seat and gathered the reins into his left hand. The whip cracked and the coach lurched forward and a young man ran out of the low building across the street carrying a saddle by the two stirrup straps swinging and bouncing against his thigh. He ran alongside and heaved the saddle up to fall thumping on the roof inside the guard-rail. He pulled at the door and managed to scramble in as the coach picked up speed. He dropped onto the front seat, puffing deeply.

"Evening, ma'am," he said between puffs. "And you, General." He leaned forward to slap the boy gently along the jaw. "And you too, bub."

Sergeant Houck looked at the lean length of the young man, at the faded levis tucked into short high-heeled boots, the plaid shirt, the brown handkerchief knotted around the tanned neck, the amiable, competent young face. He grunted a greeting, unintelligible but a pleasant sound.

"A man's legs ain't made for running," said the young man. "Just to fork a horse. That last drink was near too long."

"The Army'd put some starch in those legs," said Sergeant Houck.

"Maybe. Maybe that's why I ain't in the Army." The young man sat quietly, relaxed to the jolting of the coach. "Is there some other topic of genteel conversation you folks'd want to worry some?"

"No," said Sergeant Houck.

"Then maybe you'll pardon me," said the young man. "I hoofed it a lot of miles today." He worked hard at his boots and at last got them off and tucked them out of the way on the floor. He hitched himself up and over on the seat until he was resting on one hip. He put an arm on the window sill and cradled his head on it. His eyes closed. They opened and his head rose a few inches. "If I start sliding, just raise a foot and give me a shove." His head dropped down and the dust whirls outside melted into the dusk and he was asleep.

Sergeant Houck felt a small bump on his left side. The boy had toppled against him and was struggling back to sitting position, fighting silently to defeat the drowsiness overcoming him. Sergeant Houck scooped him up and set the small body across his lap with the head nestled into the crook of his right arm. He leaned his head down and heard the soft little last sigh as the drowsiness won. The coach rolled on, and he looked out into the dropping darkness and saw the deeper black of hills far off on the horizon. He looked sidewise at the woman and dimly made out the outline of her head falling forward and jerking back up, and he reached his left arm along the top of the seat until the hand touched her far shoulder. Faintly he saw her eyes staring at him and felt her shoulder stiffen and then relax as she moved closer and leaned toward him. He slipped down lower in the seat so that her head could reach his shoulder and he felt the gentle touch of the topmost strands of the braided coil of brown hair on his neck above his shirt collar. He waited patiently, and at last he could tell by her steady deep breathing that all fright had left her and all her thoughts were stilled.

The coach rolled on and reached a rutted stretch and began to sway and the young man stirred and began to slide on the smooth leather of his seat. Sergeant Houck put up a foot and braced it against the seat edge and the young man's body came to rest against it and was still. Sergeant Houck leaned his head back on the top of the seat and against the wall of the coach. The stars emerged in the clear sky and the coach rolled on, and the running beat of the hooves had the rhythm of a cavalry squad at a steady trot and gradually the great granite slab of Sergeant Houck softened slightly into sleep.

Sergeant Houck awoke as always all at once and aware. The coach had stopped. From the sounds outside fresh horses were being buckled into the traces. The first light of dawn was creeping into the coach. He raised his head and the bones of his neck cracked and he realized that he was stiff in various places, not only his neck but his right arm where the sleeping boy still nestled and his leg stretched out with the foot braced against the opposite seat.

The young man there was awake. He was still sprawled along the hard leather cushion, but he was pulled back from the braced foot and his eyes were open. He was inspecting the vast leather sole of Sergeant Houck's boot. His eyes flicked up and met Sergeant Houck's eyes, and he grinned.

"That's impressive footwear," he whispered. "You'd need starch in the legs with hooves like that." He sat up and stretched, long and reaching, like a lazy young animal. "Hell," he whispered again, "you must be stiff as a branding iron."

He took hold of Sergeant Houck's leg at the knee and hoisted it slightly so that Sergeant Houck could bend it and ease the foot down to the floor without disturbing the sleeping woman leaning against him. He stretched out both hands and gently lifted the sleeping boy from Sergeant Houck's lap and sat back with the boy in his arms.

Sergeant Houck began closing and unclosing his right hand to stimulate the blood circulation in the arm. The coach rolled forward and the first copper streak of sunlight found it and followed it.

The young man studied the boy's face. "Can't be yours," he whispered.

"No," whispered Sergeant Houck.

"Must have some Indian strain."

"Yes."

The young man whispered down at the sleeping boy. "You can't help that, can you, bub?"

"No," said Sergeant Houck suddenly, full voice, "he can't."

The woman jerked upright and pulled over to the window on her side, rubbing at her eyes. The boy awoke, wide awake on the instant, and saw the unfamiliar face above him and began to squirm violently.

The young man clamped his arms tighter. "Morning, ma'am," he said. "Looks like I ain't such a good nursemaid."

Sergeant Houck reached one hand and plucked up the boy by a grip on the small overalls and deposited him in sitting position on the seat beside the young man. The boy stared at Sergeant Houck and sat still, very still.

The sun climbed into plain view and the coach rolled on. It was stirring the dust of a well-worn road now. It stopped where another crossed and the driver jumped down to deposit a little packet of mail in a box on a short post.

The young man inside pulled on his boots. He bobbed his head in the direction of a group of low buildings up the side road. "Think I'll try it there. They'll be peeling broncs about now and the foreman knows I can sit a saddle." He opened a door and jumped to the ground and whirled to poke his head in. "Hope you make it right," he said, "wherever you're heading."

The door closed and he could be heard scrambling up the back of the coach to get his saddle. There was a thump as he and the saddle hit the ground and then voices began outside, rising in tone.

Sergeant Houck pushed his head through the window beside him. The young man and the driver were facing each other over the saddle. The young man was pulling the pockets of his levis inside out.

"Lookahere, Will," he said, "you can see they're empty. You know I'll kick in soon as I have some cash. Hell, I've hooked rides with you before."

"Not now no more," said the driver. "The company's sore. They hear of this they'd have my job. I'll have to hold the saddle."

The young man's voice had a sudden bite. "You touch that saddle and they'll pick you up in pieces from here to breakfast."

Sergeant Houck fumbled for his inside jacket pocket. This was difficult with his head through the window, but he succeeded in finding it. He whistled sharply. The two men swung to see him. His eyes drilled the young man. "There's something on the seat in here. Must have slipped out of your pocket." He saw the young man stare, puzzled, and start toward the door. He pulled his head back and was sitting quietly in place when the door opened.

The young man leaned in and saw the two silver dollars on the hard seat and swiveled his head to look up at Sergeant Houck. Anger blazed in his eyes and he looked at the impassive rock of Sergeant Houck's face and the anger faded.

"You've been in spots yourself," he said.

"Yes," said Sergeant Houck.

"And maybe were helped out of them."

"When I was a young squirt with more energy than brains," said Sergeant Houck. "Yes."

The young man grinned. He picked up the two coins in one hand and swung the other to slap Sergeant Houck's leg, sharp and stinging and grateful. "Age ain't hurting you any, General," he said, and closed the door.

The coach rolled on, and the woman looked at Sergeant Houck and the minutes passed and still she looked at him. He stirred on the seat.

"If I'd had brains enough to get married," he said, "might be I'd have had a son. Might have been one like that."

The woman looked away, out her window. She reached up to pat at her hair and the firm line of her lips softened in the tiny imperceptible beginnings of a smile. The dust drifted and the minutes passed and Sergeant Houck stirred again.

"It's the upbringing that counts," he said, and settled into silent immobility, watching the miles go by.

Fifteen minutes for breakfast at a change stop and the coach rolled on. It was near noon when they stopped in Laramie and Sergeant Houck handed the woman out and tucked the boy under one arm and led the way to the waiting room. He stationed the woman and the boy in two chairs and strode away. He was back in five minutes with sandwiches and a pitcher of milk and two cups. He strode away again and was gone longer and returned driving a light buckboard wagon drawn by a pair of deep-barreled bays. The front part of the wagon bed was well padded with layers of empty burlap bags. He went into the waiting room and scooped up the boy and beckoned to the woman to follow. He deposited the boy on the burlap bags and helped the woman up on the driving seat.

"Straight out the road, they tell me," he said. "About fifteen miles. Then right along the creek. Can't miss it."

He stood by the wagon, staring along the length of the street and the road leading on beyond. The woman leaned from the seat and clutched at his shoulder. Her voice broke and climbed. "You're going with me?" Her fingers clung to the cloth of his service jacket. "Please! You've got to!"

Sergeant Houck put a hand over hers on his shoulder and released her fingers. "Yes, I'm going."

He walked around the wagon and stepped to the seat and took the reins and clucked to the team. The wagon moved forward and curious people along the street stopped to watch, and neither Sergeant Houck nor the woman was aware of them. The wheels rolled silently in the thick dust, and on the open road there was no sound except the small creakings of the wagon body and the muffled rhythm of the horses' hooves. A road-runner appeared from nowhere and raced ahead of them, its feet spatting little spurts of dust, and Sergeant Houck watched it running, effortlessly, always the same distance ahead.

"You're afraid," he said.

The wheels rolled silently in the thick dust and the road-runner swung contemptuously aside in a big arc and disappeared in the low bushes.

"They haven't told him," she said, "about the boy."

Sergeant Houck's hands tightened on the reins and the horses slowed to a walk. He clucked sharply to them and slapped the reins on their backs and they quickened again into a trot, and the wheels unwound their thin tracks endlessly into the dust and the high bright sun overhead crept over and down the sky on the left. The wagon topped a slight rise and the road ahead sloped downward for a long stretch to where the green of trees and tall bushes showed in the distance. A jackrabbit started from the scrub growth by the roadside and leaped high in a spy-hop and leveled out, a gray-brown streak. The horses shied and broke rhythm and quieted to a walk under the firm pressure of the reins. Sergeant Houck kept them at a walk, easing the heat out of their muscles down the long slope to the trees. He let them step into the creek up to their knees and dip muzzles in the clear running water. The front wheels of the wagon were into the current and he reached behind him to find a tin dipper tucked among the burlap bags and leaned far out and down to dip up water for the woman and the boy and himself. He backed the team out of the creek and swung them into the wagon cuts leading along the bank to the right.

The creek was on their left and the sun was behind them, warm on their backs, and the shadows of the horses pushed ahead, grotesque moving patterns always ahead, and Sergeant Houck watched them and looked beside him once and saw that the woman was watching them too. The shadows were longer, stretching farther ahead, when they rounded a bend along the creek and the buildings came in sight, the two-room cabin and the several lean-to sheds and the rickety pole corral.

A man was standing by one of the sheds, and when Sergeant Houck stopped the team, he came toward them and halted about twenty feet away. He was not young, perhaps in his middle thirties, but with the young look of a man on whom the years have made no mark except that of the simple passing of time. He was tall, soft, and loose-jointed in build, and indecisive in manner and movement. His eyes wavered and would not steady as he looked at the woman and the fingers of his hands hanging limp at his sides twitched as he waited for her to speak.

She climbed down her side of the wagon and faced him. She stood straight and the sun behind her shone on and through the escaping wisps of the coiled braid of her hair.

"Well, Fred," she said, "I'm here."

"Cora," he said. "It's been a long time, Cora. I didn't know you'd come so soon."

"Why didn't you come get me? Why didn't you, Fred?"

"I didn't rightly know what to do, Cora. It was all so mixed up. Thinking you were dead. Then hearing about you. And what happened. I had to think about things. And I couldn't get away easy. I was going to try maybe next week."

"I hoped you'd come. Right away when you heard."

His body twisted uneasily, a strange movement that stirred his whole length while his feet remained flat and motionless on the ground. "Your hair's still pretty," he said. "The way it used to be."

Something like a sob caught in her throat and she started toward him. Sergeant Houck stepped down on the other side of the wagon and strode off to the creek and kneeled to bend and wash the dust from his face. He stood, shaking the drops from his hands and drying his face with a handkerchief and watching the little eddies of the current around several stones in the creek. He heard the voices behind him and by the wagon.

"Wait, Fred. There's something you have to know———"

"That kid? What's it doing here with you?"

"It's mine, Fred."

"Yours? Where'd you get it?"

"It's my child. Mine."

Silence, and then the man's voice, bewildered, hurt. "So it's really true what they said. About that Indian."

"Yes. He bought me. By their rules I belonged to him."

Silence, and then the woman's voice again. "I wouldn't be alive and here now, any other way. I didn't have any say about it."

Silence, and then the man's voice with the faint beginning of self-pity creeping into the tone. "I didn't count on anything like this."

Sergeant Houck turned and strode back by the wagon. The woman seemed relieved at the interruption.

"This is Sergeant Houck," she said. "He brought me all the way."

The man nodded his head and raised a hand to shove back the sandy hair that kept falling forward on his forehead. "I suppose I ought to thank you, soldier. All that trouble."

"No trouble," said Sergeant Houck. "Unusual duty. But no trouble."

The man pushed at the ground in front of him with one shoe, poking the toe into the dirt and studying it. "It's silly, just standing around here. I suppose we ought to go inside. It's near suppertime. I guess you'll be taking a meal here, soldier. Before you start back to town."

"Right," said Sergeant Houck. "And I'm tired. I'll stay the night too. Start in the morning. Sleep in one of those sheds."

The man pushed at the ground more vigorously. The little dirt pile in front of his shoe seemed to interest him greatly. "All right, soldier. Sorry there're no quarters inside." He swung quickly and started for the cabin. The woman took the boy from the wagon and followed him. Sergeant Houck unharnessed the horses and led them to the creek for a drink and to the corral and led them through the gate. He walked quietly to the cabin doorway and stopped just outside. He could see the man sitting on a straight-backed chair by the table, turned away from him. The woman and the boy were out of sight to one side.

"For God's sake, Cora," the man was saying, "I don't see why you had to bring that kid with you. You could have told me about it. I didn't have to see him."

Her voice was sharp, startled. "What do you mean?"

"Why, now we've got the problem of how to get rid of him. Have to find a mission or some place that'll take him. Why didn't you leave him where he came from?"

"No! He's mine!"

"Good God, Cora! Are you crazy? Think you can foist off a thing like that on me?"

Sergeant Houck stepped through the doorway. "It's been a time since last eating," he said. "Thought I heard something about supper." He looked around the small room and brought his gaze to bear upon the man. "I see the makings on those shelves. Come along, Mr. Sutliff. She can do without our help. A woman doesn't want men cluttering about when getting a meal. Show me your place before it gets dark."

He stood, waiting, and the man scraped at the floor with one foot and slowly rose and went with him.

They were well beyond earshot of the cabin when Sergeant Houck spoke again. "How long were you married? Before it happened?"

"Six years," said the man. "No, seven. It was seven when we lost the last place and headed this way with the train."

"Seven years," said Sergeant Houck. "And no child."

"It just didn't happen. I don't know why." The man stopped and looked sharply at Sergeant Houck. "Oh! So that's the way you're looking at it."

"Yes," said Sergeant Houck. "Now you've got one. A son."

"Not mine," said the man. "You can talk. It's not your wife. It's bad enough thinking of taking an Indian's leavings." He wiped his lips on his sleeve and spat in disgust. "I'll be damned if I'll take his kid."

"Not his any more. He's dead."

"Look, man. Look how it'd be. A damned little half-breed. Around all the time to make me remember what she did."

"Could be a reminder that she had some mighty hard going. And maybe came through the better for it."

"She had hard going! What about me? Thinking she was dead. Getting used to that. Maybe thinking of another woman. Then she comes back—and an Indian kid with her. What does that make me?"

"Could make you a man," said Sergeant Houck. "Think it over."

He swung away and went to the corral and leaned on the rail, watching the horses roll the sweat-itches out on the dry sod. The man went slowly down by the creek and stood on the bank, pushing at the dirt with one shoe and kicking small pebbles into the water. The sun, holding to the horizon rim, dropped suddenly out of sight and dusk swept swiftly to blur the outlines of the buildings. A lamp was lit in the cabin, and the rectangle of light through the doorway made the dusk become darkness. The woman appeared in the doorway and called and the men came their ways and converged there and went in. There was simple food on the table and the woman stood beside it. "I've already fed him," she said, and moved her head toward the door to the inner room. She sat down and they did and the three of them were intent on the plates.

Sergeant Houck ate steadily and reached to refill his plate. The man picked briefly at the food before him and stopped and the woman ate nothing at all. The man put his hands on the table edge and pushed back and rose and went to a side shelf and took a bottle and two thick cups and returned to set these by his plate. He filled the cups a third full from the bottle and shoved one along the table boards toward Sergeant Houck. He lifted the other chin-high. His voice was bitter. "Happy home-coming," he said. He waited and Sergeant Houck took the other cup and they drank. The man lifted the bottle and poured himself another cup-third.

The woman moved her chair and looked quickly at him and away.

"Please, Fred."

The man paid no attention to the words. He reached with the bottle toward the other cup.

"No," said Sergeant Houck.

The man shrugged. "You can think better on whiskey. Sharpens the mind." He set the bottle down and took his cup and drained it. He coughed and put it carefully on the table in front of him and pushed at it with one forefinger. Sergeant Houck fumbled in his right side pocket and found one of the short straight straws there and pulled it out and put one end in his mouth and chewed slowly on it. The man and the woman sat still, opposite each other at the table, and seemed to forget his quiet presence. They stared at the table, at the floor, at the cabin walls, everywhere except at each other. Yet their attention was plainly concentrated on each other across the table top. The man spoke first. His voice was restrained, carrying conscious patience.

"Look, Cora. You wouldn't want to do that to me. You can't mean what you said before."

Her voice was low, determined. "He's mine."

"Now, Cora. You don't want to push it too far. A man can take just so much. I didn't know what to do after I heard about you. But I remembered you had been a good wife, I was all ready to forgive you. And now you——"

"Forgive me!" She knocked against her chair rising to her feet. Hurt and bewilderment made her voice ragged as she repeated the words. "Forgive me?" She turned and fairly ran into the inner room. The handleless door banged shut and bounced open again inward a few inches and she leaned against it inside to close it tightly.

The man stared after her and shook his head a little and reached again for the bottle.

"Enough's enough," said Sergeant Houck.

The man became aware of him and shrugged in quick irritation. "For you, maybe," he said, and poured himself another cup-third. He thrust his head a little forward at Sergeant Houck. "Is there any reason you should be noseying in on this?"

"My orders," said Sergeant Houck, "were to deliver them safely. Both of them. Safely."

"You've done that," said the man. He lifted the cup and drained it and set it down carefully. "They're here."

"Yes," said Sergeant Houck, "they're here." He rose and stepped to the outside door and looked into the night. He waited a moment until his eyes were accustomed to the darkness and could distinguish objects faintly in the starlight. He stepped on out and went to the strawpile behind one of the sheds and took an armload and carried it back by the cabin and dropped it at the foot of a tree by one corner. He lowered his bulk to the straw and sat there, legs stretched out, shoulders against the tree, and broke off a straw stem and chewed slowly on it. After a while his jaws stopped their slow, slight movement and his head sank forward and his eyes closed.

Sergeant Houck awoke, completely, in the instant, and aware. The stars had swung perhaps an hour overhead. He was on his feet in the swift reflex, and listening. The straw rustled under his shoes and was still. He heard the faint sound of voices in the cabin, indistinct but rising as tension rose in them. He went toward the doorway and stopped just short of the rectangle of light from the still burning lamp.

"You're not going to have anything to do with me!" The woman's voice was harsh with stubborn anger. "Not until this has been settled right!"

"Aw, come on, Cora." The man's voice was fuzzy, slow-paced. "We'll talk about that in the morning."

"No!"

"All right!" Sudden fury shook the man's voice. "You want it settled now! Well, it's settled! We're getting rid of that damn kid first thing tomorrow!"

"No!"

"What gave you the idea you've got any say around here after what you did? I'm the one to say what's to be done. You don't be careful, maybe I won't take you back."

"Maybe I don't want you to take me back!"

"So damn finicky all of a sudden! After being with that Indian and maybe a lot more!"

Sergeant Houck stepped through the doorway. The man's back was to him and he put out his left hand and took hold of the man's shoulder and spun him around, and his right hand smacked against the side of the man's face and sent him staggering against the wall.

"Forgetting your manners won't help," said Sergeant Houck. He looked around and the woman had disappeared into the inner room. The man leaned against the wall rubbing his cheek, and she emerged, the boy in her arms, and ran toward the outer door.

"Cora!" the man shouted. "Cora!"

She stopped, a brief hesitation in flight. "I don't belong to you," she said, and was gone through the doorway. The man pushed out from the wall and started after her and the great bulk of Sergeant Houck blocked the way.

"You heard her," said Sergeant Houck. "She doesn't belong to anybody now. But that boy."

The man stared at him and some of the fury went out of the man's eyes and he stumbled to his chair at the table and reached for the nearly empty bottle. Sergeant Houck watched him a moment, then turned and quietly went outside. He walked toward the corral and as he passed the second shed she came out of the darker shadows and her voice, low and intense, whispered at him.

"I've got to go. I can't stay here."

Sergeant Houck nodded and went on to the corral and opened the gate and, stepping softly and chirruping a wordless little tune, approached the horses. They stirred uneasily and moved away and stopped and waited for him. He led them through the gate to the wagon and harnessed them quickly and with a minimum of sound. He finished buckling the traces and stood straight and looked toward the cabin. He walked steadily to the lighted rectangle of the doorway and stepped inside and over by the table. The man was leaning forward in his chair, elbows on the table, staring at the empty bottle.

"It's finished," said Sergeant Houck. "She's leaving now."

The man shook his head and pushed at the bottle with one forefinger. "She can't do that." He swung his head to look up at Sergeant Houck and the sudden fury began to heat his eyes. "She can't do that! She's my wife!"

"Not any more," said Sergeant Houck. "Best forget she ever came back." He started toward the door and heard the sharp sound of the chair scraping on the floor behind him. The man's voice rose, shrilling up almost into a shriek.

"Stop!" The man rushed to the wall rack and grabbed the rifle there and swung it at his hip, bringing the muzzle to bear on Sergeant Houck. "Stop!" He was breathing deeply and he fought for control of his voice. "You're not going to take her away!"

Sergeant Houck turned slowly. He stood still, a motionless granite shape in the lamplight.

"Threatening an Army man," said Sergeant Houck. "And with an empty gun."

The man wavered and his eyes flicked down at the rifle, and in the second of indecision Sergeant Houck plunged toward him and one huge hand grasped the gun barrel and pushed it aside and the shot thudded harmlessly into the cabin wall. He wrenched the gun from the man's grasp and his other hand took the man by the shirt front and shook him forward and back and pushed him over and down into the chair.

"No more of that," said Sergeant Houck. "Best sit quiet." His eyes swept the room and found the box of cartridges on a shelf and he took this with the rifle and went to the door. "Look around in the morning and you'll find these." He went outside and tossed the gun up on the roof of one of the sheds and dropped the little box by the strawpile and kicked straw over it. He went to the wagon and stood by it and the woman came out of the darkness of the trees by the creek, carrying the boy.

The wagon wheels rolled silently and the small creakings of the wagon body and the thudding rhythm of the horses' hooves were distinct, isolated sounds in the night. The creek was on their right and they followed the tracking of the road back the way they had come. The woman moved on the seat, shifting the boy's weight from one arm to the other, and Sergeant Houck took him by the overalls and lifted him and reached behind to lay him on the burlap bags.

"A good boy," he said. "Has the Indian way of taking things without yapping. A good way."

The thin new tracks in the dust unwound endlessly under the wheels and the late waning moon climbed out of the horizon and its light shone in pale, barely noticeable patches through the scattered bushes and trees along the creek.

"I have relatives in Missouri," said the woman. "I could go there."

Sergeant Houck fumbled in his side pocket and found a straw and put this in his mouth and chewed slowly on it. "Is that what you want?"

"No."

They came to the main road crossing and swung left and the dust thickened under the horses' hooves. The lean dark shape of a coyote slipped from the brush on one side and bounded along the road and disappeared on the other side.

"I'm forty-seven," said Sergeant Houck. "Nearly thirty of that in the Army. Makes a man rough."

The woman looked straight ahead at the far dwindling ribbon of the road and a small smile curled the corners of her mouth.

"Four months," said Sergeant Houck, "and this last hitch is done. I'm thinking of homesteading on out in the Territory." He chewed on the straw and took it between a thumb and forefinger and flipped it away. "You could get a room at the settlement."

"I could," said the woman. The horses slowed to a walk, breathing deeply, and he let them hold the steady, plodding pace. Far off a coyote howled and others caught the signal and the sounds echoed back and forth in the distance and died away into the night silence.

"Four months," said Sergeant Houck. "That's not so long."

"No," said the woman. "Not too long."

A breeze stirred across the brush and took the dust from the slow hooves in small whorls and the wheels rolled slowly and she put out a hand and touched his shoulder. The fingers moved down along his upper arm and curved over the big muscles there and the warmth of them sank through the cloth of his worn service jacket. She dropped the hand again in her lap and looked ahead along the ribbon of the road. He clucked to the horses and urged them again into a trot, and the small creakings of the wagon body and the dulled rhythm of the hooves were gentle sounds in the night.

The wheels rolled and the late moon climbed, and its pale light shone slantwise down on the moving wagon, on the sleeping boy, and on the woman looking straight ahead and the great granite slab of Sergeant Houck.

THE CAPTIVES
BY ELMORE LEONARD
(The Tall T)

Elmore Leonard began writing Western fiction in the late 1940s and selling it regularly in the early 1950s; his first novel, The Bounty Hunters, *appeared in 1953, and several more Westerns followed before he turned to the writing of high-quality (and in recent years, bestselling) crime fiction. "The Captives," which first appeared in* Argosy *in 1955, is one of two Leonard short stories that have been filmed; the other, which we were pleased to reprint in* The Reel West, *is "Three-Ten to Yuma," the basis of the superb 1957 Glenn Ford/Van Heflin movie of the same title. Leonard's novels* Hombre *and* Valdez Is Coming *also made excellent films, the former produced in 1967 with Paul Newman in the lead role, the latter produced in 1971 and starring Burt Lancaster in a memorable performance as the Mexican constable, Valdez.*

He could hear the stagecoach, the faraway creaking and the muffled rumble of it, and he was thinking: It's almost an hour early. Why should it be if it left Contention on schedule?

His name was Pat Brennan. He was lean and almost tall, with a deeply tanned, pleasant face beneath the straight hatbrim low over his eyes, and he stood next to his saddle, which was on the ground, with the easy, hip-shot slouch of a rider. A Henry rifle was in his right hand and he was squinting into the sun glare, looking up the grade to the rutted road that came curving down through the spidery Joshua trees.

He lowered the Henry rifle, stock down, and let it fall across the saddle, and kept his hand away from the Colt holstered on his right leg. A man could get shot standing next to a stage road out in the middle of nowhere with a rifle in his hand.

Then, seeing the coach suddenly against the sky, billowing dust hanging over it, he felt relief and smiled to himself and raised his arm to wave as the coach passed through the Joshuas.

As the pounding wood, iron and three-team racket of it came swaying toward him, he raised both arms and felt a sudden helplessness as he saw that the driver was making no effort to stop the teams. Brennan stepped back quickly, and the coach rushed past him, the driver, alone on the boot, bending forward and down to look at him.

Brennan cupped his hands and called, *"Rintoooon!"*

The driver leaned back with the reins high and through his fingers, his boot pushing against the brake lever, and his body half-turned to look back over the top of the Concord. Brennan swung the saddle up over his shoulder and started after the coach as it ground to a stop.

He saw the company name: HATCH & HODGES, and just below it, Number 42 stenciled on the varnished door; then from a side window, he saw a man staring at him irritably as he approached. Behind the man he caught a glimpse of a woman with soft features and a small, plumed hat and eyes that looked away quickly as Brennan's gaze passed them going up to Ed Rintoon, the driver.

"Ed, for a minute I didn't think you were going to stop."

Rintoon, a leathery, beard-stubbled man in his mid-forties, stood with one knee on the seat and looked down at Brennan with only faint surprise.

"I took you for being up to no good, standing there waving your arms."

"I'm only looking for a lift a ways."

"What happened to you?"

Brennan grinned and his thumb pointed back vaguely over his shoulder. "I was visiting Tenvoorde to see about buying some yearling stock and I lost my horse to him on a bet."

"Driver!"

Brennan turned. The man who had been at the window was now leaning halfway out of the door and looking up at Rintoon.

"I'm not paying you to pass the time of day with"—he glanced at Brennan—"with everybody we meet."

Rintoon leaned over to look down at him. "Willard, you ain't even part right, since you ain't the man that pays me."

"I chartered this coach, and you along with it!" He was a young man, hatless, his long hair mussed from the wind. Strands of it hung over his ears, and his face was flushed as he glared at Rintoon. "When I pay for a coach I expect the service that goes with it."

Rintoon said, "Willard, you calm down now."

"Mr. Mims!"

Rintoon smiled faintly, glancing at Brennan. "Pat, I'd like you to meet Mr. Mims." He paused, adding, "He's a bookkeeper."

Brennan touched the brim of his hat toward the coach, seeing the woman again. She looked to be in her late twenties and her eyes now were wide and frightened and not looking at him.

His glance went to Willard Mims. Mims came out of the doorway and stood pointing a finger up at Rintoon.

"Driver, you're through! I swear to God this is your last run on any line in the Territory!"

Rintoon eased himself down until he was half-sitting on the seat. "You wouldn't kid me."

"You'll see if I'm kidding!"

Rintoon shook his head. "After ten years of faithful service the boss will be sorry to see me go."

Willard Mims stared at him in silence. Then he said, his voice calmer, "You won't be so sure of yourself after we get to Bisbee."

Ignoring him, Rintoon turned to Brennan. "Swing that saddle up here."

"You hear what I said?" Willard Mims flared.

Reaching down for the saddle horn as Brennan lifted it, Rintoon answered, "You said I'd be sorry when we got to Bisbee."

"You remember that!"

"I sure will. Now you get back inside, Willard." He glanced at Brennan. "You get in there too, Pat."

Willard Mims stiffened. "I'll remind you again—this is *not* the passenger coach."

Brennan was momentarily angry, but he saw the way Rintoon was taking this and he said calmly, "You want me to walk? It's only fifteen miles to Sasabe."

"I didn't say that," Mims answered, moving to the coach door. "If you want to come, get up on the boot." He turned to look at Brennan as he pulled himself up on the foot rung. "If we'd wanted company we'd have taken the scheduled run. That clear enough for you?"

Glancing at Rintoon, Brennan swung the Henry rifle up to him and said, "Yes, sir," not looking at Mims; and he winked at Rintoon as he climbed the wheel to the driver's seat.

A moment later they were moving, slowly at first, bumping and swaying; then the road seemed to become smoother as the teams pulled faster.

Brennan leaned toward Rintoon and said, in the noise, close to the driver's grizzled face, "I wondered why the regular stage would be almost an hour early. Ed, I'm obliged to you."

Rintoon glanced at him. "Thank Mr. Mims."

"Who is he anyway?"

"Old man Gateway's son-in-law. Married the boss' daughter. Married into the biggest copper claim in the country."

"The girl with him his wife?"

"Doretta," Rintoon answered. "That's Gateway's daughter. She was scheduled to be an old maid till Willard come along and saved her from spinsterhood. She's plain as a 'dobe wall."

Brennan said, "But not too plain for Willard, eh?"

Rintoon gave him a side glance. "Patrick, there ain't nothing plain about old man Gateway's holdings. That's the thing. Four years ago he bought a half interest in the Montezuma Copper Mine for two hundred and fifty thousand dollars, and he's got it back triple since then. Can you imagine anyone having that much money?"

Brennan shook his head. "Where'd he get it, to start?"

"They say he come from money and made more by using the brains God gave him, investing it."

Brennan shook his head again. "That's too much money, Ed. Too much to have to worry about."

"Not for Willard, it ain't," Rintoon said. "He started out as a bookkeeper with the company. Now he's general manager—since the wedding. The old man picked Willard because he was the only one around he thought had any polish, and he knew if he waited much longer he'd have an old maid on his hands. And, Pat,"—Rintoon leaned closer—"Willard don't talk to the old man like he does to other people."

"She didn't look so bad to me," Brennan said.

"You been down on Sasabe Creek too long," Rintoon glanced at him again. "What were you saying about losing your horse to Tenvoorde?"

"Oh, I went to see him about buying some yearlings—"

"On credit," Rintoon said.

Brennan nodded. "Though I was going to pay him some of it cash. I told him to name a fair interest rate and he'd have it in two years. But he said no. Cash on the line. No cash, no yearlings. I needed three hundred to make the deal, but I only had fifty. Then when I was going he said, 'Patrick'—you know how he talks—'I'll give you a chance to get your yearlings free,' and all the time he's eyeing this claybank mare I had along. He said, 'You bet your mare and your fifty dollars cash, I'll put up what yearlings you need and we'll race your mare against one of my string for the winner.'"

Ed Rintoon said, "And you lost."

"By a country mile."

"Pat, that don't sound like you. Why didn't you take what your fifty would buy and get on home?"

"Because I needed these yearlings plus a good seed bull. I could've bought the bull, but I wouldn't have had the yearlings to build on. That's what I told Mr. Tenvoorde. I said, 'This deal's as good as the stock you're selling me. If you're taking that kind of money for a seed bull and yearlings, then you know they can produce. You're sure of getting your money.'"

"You got stock down on your Sasabe place," Rintoon said.

"Not like you think. They wintered poorly and I got a lot of building to do."

"Who's tending your herd now?"

"I still got those two Mexican boys."

"You should've known better than to go to Tenvoorde."

"I didn't have a chance. He's the only man close enough with the stock I want."

"But a bet like that—how could you fall into it? You know he'd have a pony to outstrip yours."

"Well, that was the chance I had to take."

They rode along in silence for a few minutes before Brennan asked, "Where they coming from?"

Rintoon grinned at him. "Their honeymoon. Willard made the agent put on a special run just for the two of them. Made a big fuss while Doretta tried to hide her head."

"Then"—Brennan grinned—"I'm obliged to Mr. Mims, else I'd still be waiting back there with my saddle and my Henry."

Later on, topping a rise that was thick with jack pine, they were suddenly in view of the Sasabe station and the creek beyond it, as they came out of the trees and started down the mesquite-dotted sweep of the hillside.

Rintoon checked his timepiece. The regular run was due here at five o'clock. From habit, he inspected his watch, and he was surprised to see that it was only ten minutes after four. He remembered then, his mind picturing Willard Mims as he chartered the special coach.

Brennan said, "I'm getting off here at Sasabe."

"How'll you get over to your place?"

"Hank'll lend me a horse."

As they drew nearer, Rintoon was squinting, studying the three adobe houses and the corral in back. "I don't see anybody," he said. "Hank's usually out in the yard. Him or his boy."

Brennan said, "They don't expect you for an hour. That's it."

"Man, we make enough noise for somebody to come out."

Rintoon swung the teams toward the adobes, slowing them as Brennan pushed his boot against the brake lever, and they came to a stop exactly even with the front of the main adobe.

"Hank!"

Rintoon looked from the door of the adobe out over the yard. He called the name again, but there was no answer. He frowned. "The damn place sounds deserted," he said.

Brennan saw the driver's eyes drop to the sawed-off shotgun and Brennan's Henry on the floor of the boot, and then he was looking over the yard again.

"Where in hell would Hank've gone to?"

A sound came from the adobe. A boot scraping—that or something like it —and the next moment a man was standing in the open doorway. He was bearded, a dark beard faintly streaked with gray and in need of a trim. He was watching them calmly, almost indifferently, and leveling a Colt at them at the same time.

He moved out into the yard and now another man, armed with a shotgun, came out of the adobe. The bearded one held his gun on the door of the coach. The shotgun was leveled at Brennan and Rintoon.

"You-all drop your guns and come on down." He wore range clothes, soiled and sun-bleached, and he held the shotgun calmly as if doing this was not something new. He was younger than the bearded one by at least ten years.

Brennan raised his revolver from its holster and the one with the shotgun said, "Gently now," and grinned as Brennan dropped it over the wheel.

Rintoon, not wearing a handgun, had not moved.

"If you got something down in that boot," the one with the shotgun said to him, "haul it out."

Rintoon muttered something under his breath. He reached down and took hold of Brennan's Henry rifle lying next to the sawed-off shotgun, his finger slipping through the trigger guard. He came up with it hesitantly, and Brennan whispered, barely moving his lips, "Don't be crazy."

Standing up, turning, Rintoon hesitated again, then let the rifle fall.

"That all you got?"

Rintoon nodded. "That's all."

"Then come on down."

Rintoon turned his back. He bent over to climb down, his foot reaching for the wheel below, and his hand closed on the sawed-off shotgun. Brennan whispered, "Don't do it!"

Rintoon mumbled something that came out as a growl. Brennan leaned toward him as if to give him a hand down. "You got two shots. What if there're more than two of them?"

Rintoon grunted, "Look out, Pat!" His hand gripped the shotgun firmly.

Then he was turning, jumping from the wheel, the stubby scattergun flashing head-high—and at the same moment, a single revolver shot blasted the stillness. Brennan saw Rintoon crumple to the ground, the shotgun falling next to him, and he was suddenly aware of powder smoke and a man framed in the window of the adobe.

The one with the shotgun said, "Well, that just saves some time," and he glanced around as the third man came out of the adobe. "Chink, I swear you hit him in mid-air."

"I was waiting for that old man to pull something," said the one called Chink. He wore two low-slung, crossed cartridge belts and his second Colt was still in its holster.

Brennan jumped down and rolled Rintoon over gently, holding his head off the ground. He looked at the motionless form and then at Chink. "He's dead."

Chink stood with his legs apart and looked down at Brennan indifferently. "Sure he is."

"You didn't have to kill him."

Chink shrugged. "I would've, sooner or later."

"Why?"

"That's the way it is."

The man with the beard had not moved. He said now, quietly, "Chink, you shut your mouth." Then he glanced at the man with the shotgun and said, in the same tone, "Billy-Jack, get them out of there," and nodded toward the coach.

CHAPTER TWO

Kneeling next to Rintoon, Brennan studied them. He watched Billy-Jack open the coach door, saw his mouth soften to a grin as Doretta Mims came out first. Her eyes went to Rintoon, but shifted away quickly. Willard Mims hesitated, then stepped down, stumbling in his haste as Billy-Jack pointed the shotgun at him. He stood next to his wife and stared unblinkingly at Rintoon's body.

That one, Brennan was thinking, looking at the man with the beard—that's the one to watch. He's calling it, and he doesn't look as though he gets excited. . . . And the one called Chink. . . .

Brennan's eyes went to him. He was standing hip-cocked, his hat on the back of his head and the drawstring from it pulled tight beneath his lower lip, his free hand fingering the string idly, the other hand holding the long-barreled .44 Colt, pointed down but cocked.

He wants somebody to try something, Brennan thought. He's itching for it. He wears two guns and he thinks he's good. Well, maybe he is. But he's young, the youngest of the three, and he's anxious. His gaze stayed on Chink and it went through his mind: Don't even reach for a cigarette when he's around.

The one with the beard said, "Billy-Jack, get up on top of the coach."

Brennan's eyes raised, watching the man step from the wheel hub to the boot and then kneel on the driver's seat. He's number-three man, Brennan thought. He keeps looking at the woman. But don't bet him short. He carries a big-gauge gun.

"Frank, there ain't nothing up here but an old saddle."

The one with the beard—Frank Usher—raised his eyes. "Look under it."

"Ain't nothing there, either."

Usher's eyes went to Willard Mims, then swung slowly to Brennan. "Where's the mail?"

"I wouldn't know," Brennan said.

Frank Usher looked at Willard Mims again. "You tell me."

"This isn't the stage," Willard Mims said hesitantly. His face relaxed then, almost to the point of smiling. "You made a mistake. The regular stage isn't due for almost an hour." He went on, excitement rising in his voice, "That's what you want, the stage that's due here at five. This is one I chartered." He smiled now. "See, me and my wife are just coming back from a honeymoon and, you know—"

Frank Usher looked at Brennan. "Is that right?"

"Of course it is!" Mims' voice rose. "Go in and check the schedule."

"I'm asking this man."

Brennan shrugged. "I wouldn't know."

"He don't know anything," Chink said.

Billy-Jack came down off the coach and Usher said to him, "Go in and look for a schedule." He nodded toward Doretta Mims. "Take that woman with you. Have her put some coffee on, and something to eat."

Brennan said, "What did you do with Hank?"

Frank Usher's dull eyes moved to Brennan. "Who's he?"

"The station man here."

Chink grinned and waved his revolver, pointing it off beyond the main adobe. "He's over yonder in the well."

Usher said, "Does that answer it?"

"What about his boy?"

"He's with him," Usher said. "Anything else?"

Brennan shook his head slowly. "That's enough." He knew they were both dead and suddenly he was very much afraid of this dull-eyed, soft-voiced man with the beard; it took an effort to keep himself calm. He watched Billy-Jack take Doretta by the arm. She looked imploringly at her husband, holding back, but he made no move to help her. Billy-Jack jerked her arm roughly and she went with him.

Willard Mims said, "He'll find the schedule. Like I said, it's due at five o'clock. I can see how you made the mistake"—Willard was smiling—"thinking we were the regular stage. Hell, we were just going home . . . down to Bisbee. You'll see, five o'clock sharp that regular passenger-mail run'll pull in."

"He's a talker," Chink said.

Billy-Jack appeared in the doorway of the adobe. "Frank, five o'clock, sure as hell!" He waved a sheet of yellow paper.

"See!" Willard Mims was grinning excitedly. "Listen, you let us go and we'll be on our way"—his voice rose—"and I swear to God we'll never breathe we saw a thing."

Chink shook his head. "He's somethin'."

"Listen, I swear to God we won't tell *anything!*"

"I know you won't," Frank Usher said. He looked at Brennan and nodded toward Mims. "Where'd you find him?"

"We just met."

"Do you go along with what he's saying?"

"If I said yes," Brennan answered, "you wouldn't believe me. And you'd be right."

A smile almost touched Frank Usher's mouth. "Dumb even talking about it, isn't it?"

"I guess it is," Brennan said.

"You know what's going to happen to you?" Usher asked him tonelessly.

Brennan nodded, without answering.

Frank Usher studied him in silence. Then, "Are you scared?"

Brennan nodded again. "Sure I am."

"You're honest about it. I'll say that for you."

"I don't know of a better time to be honest," Brennan said.

Chink said, "That damn well's going to be chock full."

Willard Mims had listened with disbelief, his eyes wide. Now he said hurriedly, "Wait a minute! What're you listening to him for? I told you, I swear to God I won't say one word about this. If you don't trust him, then keep him here! I don't know this man. I'm not speaking for him, anyway."

"I'd be inclined to trust him before I would you," Frank Usher said.

"He's got nothing to do with it! We picked him up out on the desert!"

Chink raised his .44 waist-high, looking at Willard Mims, and said, "Start running for that well and see if you can make it."

"Man, be reasonable!"

Frank Usher shook his head. "You aren't leaving, and you're not going to be standing here when that stage pulls in. You can scream and carry on, but that's the way it is."

"What about my wife?"

"I can't help her being a woman."

Willard Mims was about to say something, but stopped. His eyes went to the adobe, then back to Usher. He lowered his voice and all the excitement was gone from it. "You know who she is?" He moved closer to Usher. "She's the daughter of old man Gateway, who happens to own part of the third richest copper mine in Arizona. You know what that amounts to? To date, three-quarters of a million dollars." He said this slowly, looking straight at Frank Usher.

"Make a point out of it," Usher said.

"Man, it's staring you right in the face! You got the daughter of a man who's practically a millionaire. His only daughter! What do you think he'd pay to get her back?"

Frank Usher said, "I don't know. What?"

"Whatever you ask! You sit here waiting for a two-bit holdup and you got a gold mine right in your hands!"

"How do I know she's his daughter?"

Willard Mims looked at Brennan. "You were talking to that driver. Didn't he tell you?"

Brennan hesitated. If the man wanted to bargain with his wife, that was his business. It would give them time; that was the main thing. Brennan nodded. "That's right. His wife is Doretta Gateway."

"Where do you come in?" Usher asked Willard Mims.

"I'm Mr. Gateway's general manager on the Montezuma operation."

Frank Usher was silent now, staring at Mims. Finally he said, "I suppose you'd be willing to ride in with a note."

"Certainly," Mims quickly replied.

"And we'd never see you again."

"Would I save my own skin and leave my wife here?"

Usher nodded. "I believe you would."

"Then there's no use talking about it." Mims shrugged and, watching him, Brennan knew he was acting, taking a long chance.

"We can talk about it," Frank Usher said, "because if we do it, we do it my way." He glanced at the house. "Billy-Jack!" Then to Brennan, "You and him go sit over against the wall."

Billy-Jack came out, and from the wall of the adobe, Brennan and Willard watched the three outlaws. They stood in close, and Frank Usher was doing the talking. After a few minutes Billy-Jack went into the adobe again and came out with the yellow stage schedule and an envelope. Usher took them, and against the door of the Concord, wrote something on the back of the schedule.

He came toward them folding the paper into the envelope. He sealed the envelope and handed it with the pencil to Willard Mims. "You put Gateway's name on it and where to find him. Mark it personal and urgent."

Willard Mims said, "I can see him myself and tell him."

"You will," Frank Usher said, "but not how you think. You're going to stop on the main road one mile before you get to Bisbee and give that envelope to somebody passing in. The note tells Gateway you have something to tell him about his daughter and to come alone. When he goes out, you'll tell him the story. If he says no, then he never sees his daughter again. If he says yes, he's to bring fifty thousand in U.S. script divided in three saddle bags, to a place up back of the Sasabe. And he brings it alone."

Mims said, "What if there isn't that much cash on hand?"

"That's his problem."

"Well, why can't I go right to his house and tell him?"

"Because Billy-Jack's going to be along to bring you back after you tell him. And I don't want him some place he can get cornered."

"Oh . . ."

"That's whether he says yes or no," Frank Usher added.

Mims was silent for a moment. "But how'll Mr. Gateway know where to come?"

"If he agrees, Billy-Jack'll give him directions."

Mims said, "Then when he comes out you'll let us go? Is that it?"

"That's it."

"When do we leave?"

"Right this minute."

"Can I say good-bye to my wife?"

"We'll do it for you."

Brennan watched Billy-Jack come around from the corral, leading two horses. Willard Mims moved toward one of them and they both mounted. Billy-Jack reined his horse suddenly, crowding Mims to turn with him, then slapped Mims' horse on the rump and spurred after it as the horse broke to a run.

Watching them, his eyes half closed, Frank Usher said, "That boy puts his wife up on the stake and then he wants to kiss her good-bye." He glanced at Brennan. "You figure that one for me."

Brennan shook his head. "What I'd like to know is why you only asked for fifty thousand."

Frank Usher shrugged, "I'm not greedy."

CHAPTER THREE

Chink turned as the two horses splashed over the creek and grew gradually smaller down the road. He looked at Brennan and then his eyes went to Frank Usher. "We don't have a need for this one, Frank."

Usher's dull eyes flicked toward him. "You bring around the horses and I'll worry about him."

"We might as well do it now as later," Chink said.

"We're taking him with us."

"What for?"

"Because I say so. That reason enough?"

"Frank, we could run him for the well and both take a crack at him."

"Get the horses," Frank Usher said flatly and stared at Chink until the gunman turned and walked away.

Brennan said, "I'd like to bury this man before we go."

Usher shook his head. "Put him in the well."

"That's no fit place!"

Usher stared at Brennan for a long moment. "Don't push your luck. He goes in the well, whether you do it or Chink does."

Brennan pulled Rintoon's limp body up over his shoulder and carried him across the yard. When he returned, Chink was coming around the adobe with three horses already saddled. Frank Usher stood near the house and now Doretta Mims appeared in the doorway.

Usher looked at her. "You'll have to fork one of these like the rest of us. There ain't no lady's saddle about."

She came out, neither answering nor looking at him.

Usher called to Brennan, "Cut one out of that team and shoo the rest," nodding to the stagecoach.

Minutes later the Sasabe station was deserted.

They followed the creek west for almost an hour before swinging south toward high country. Leaving the creek, Brennan had thought: Five more miles and I'm home. And his eyes hung on the long shallow cup of the Sasabe valley until they entered a trough that climbed winding ahead of them through the hills, and the valley was no longer in view.

Frank Usher led them single file—Doretta Mims, followed by Brennan, and Chink bringing up the rear. Chink rode slouched, swaying with the movement of his dun mare, chewing idly on the drawstring of his hat, and watching Brennan.

Brennan kept his eyes on the woman much of the time. For almost a mile, as they rode along the creek, he had watched her body shaking silently and he knew that she was crying. She had very nearly cried mounting the horse—pulling her skirts down almost desperately, then sitting, holding onto the saddle horn with both hands, biting her lower lip and not looking at them. Chink had side-stepped his dun close to her and said something, and she had turned her head quickly as the color rose from her throat over her face.

They dipped down into a barranca thick with willow and cottonwood and followed another stream that finally disappeared into the rocks at the far end. And after that they began to climb again. For some time they rode through the soft gloom of timber, following switchbacks as the slope became steeper, then came out into the open and crossed a bare gravelly slope, the sandstone peaks above them cold pink in the fading sunlight.

They were nearing the other side of the open grade when Frank Usher said, "Here we are."

Brennan looked beyond him and now he could make out, through the pines they were approaching, a weather-scarred stone-and-log hut built snugly against the steep wall of sandstone. Against one side of the hut was a hide-covered lean-to. He heard Frank Usher say, "Chink, you get the man making a fire and I'll get the woman fixing supper."

There had not been time to eat what the woman had prepared at the stage station and now Frank Usher and Chink ate hungrily, hunkered down a dozen yards out from the lean-to where Brennan and the woman stood.

Brennan took a plate of the jerky and day-old pan bread, but Doretta Mims did not touch the food. She stood next to him, half turned from him, and continued to stare through the trees across the bare slope in the direction they had come. Once Brennan said to her, "You better eat something," but she did not answer him.

When they were finished, Frank Usher ordered them into the hut.

"You stay there the night . . . and if either of you comes near the door, we'll let go, no questions asked. That plain?"

The woman went in hurriedly. When Brennan entered he saw her huddled against the back wall near a corner.

The sod-covered hut was windowless, and he could barely make her out in the dimness. He wanted to go and sit next to her, but it went through his mind that most likely she was as afraid of him as she was of Frank Usher and Chink. So he made room for himself against the wall where they had placed the saddles, folding a saddle blanket to rest his elbow on as he eased himself to the dirt floor. Let her try and get hold of herself, he thought; then maybe she will want somebody to talk to.

He made a cigarette and lit it, seeing the mask of her face briefly as the match flared, then he eased himself lower until his head was resting against a saddle, and smoked in the dim silence.

Soon the hut was full dark. Now he could not see the woman though he imagined that he could feel her presence. Outside, Usher and Chink had added wood to the cook fire in front of the lean-to and the warm glow of it illuminated the doorless opening of the hut.

They'll sit by the fire, Brennan thought, and one of them will always be awake. You'd get about one step through that door and *bam*. Maybe Frank would aim low, but Chink would shoot to kill. He became angry thinking of Chink, but there was nothing he could do about it and he drew on the cigarette slowly to make himself relax, thinking: Take it easy: you've got the woman to consider. He thought of her as his responsibility and not even a doubt entered his mind that she was not. She was a woman, alone. The reason was as simple as that.

He heard her move as he was snubbing out the cigarette. He lay still and he knew that she was coming toward him. She knelt as she reached his side.

"Do you know what they've done with my husband?"

He could picture her drawn face, eyes staring wide-open in the darkness. He raised himself slowly and felt her stiffen as he touched her arm. "Sit down here and you'll be more comfortable." He moved over to let her sit on the saddle blanket. "Your husband's all right," he said.

"Where is he?"

"They didn't tell you?"

"No."

Brennan paused. "One of them took him to Bisbee to see your father."

"My father?"

"To ask him to pay to get you back."

"Then my husband's all right." She was relieved, and it was in the sound of her voice.

Brennan said, after a moment, "Why don't you go to sleep now? You can rest back on one of these saddles."

"I'm not tired."

"Well, you will be if you don't get some sleep."

She said then, "They must have known all the time that we were coming."

Brennan said nothing.

"Didn't they?"

"I don't know, ma'am."

"How else would they know about . . . who my father is?"

"Maybe so."

"One of them must have been in Contention and heard my husband charter the coach. Perhaps he had visited Bisbee and knew that my father . . ." Her voice trailed off because she was speaking more to herself than to Brennan.

After a pause Brennan said, "You sound like you feel a little better."

He heard her exhale slowly and he could imagine she was trying to smile.

"Yes, I believe I do now," she replied.

"Your husband will be back sometime tomorrow morning," Brennan said to her.

She touched his arm lightly. "I *do* feel better, Mr. Brennan."

He was surprised that she remembered his name. Rintoon had mentioned it only once, hours before. "I'm glad you do. Now, why don't you try to sleep?"

She eased back gently until she was lying down and for a few minutes there was silence.

"Mr. Brennan?"

"Yes, ma'am."

"I'm terribly sorry about your friend."

"Who?"

"The driver."

"Oh. Thank you."

"I'll remember him in my prayers," she said, and after this she did not speak again.

Brennan smoked another cigarette, then sat unmoving for what he judged to be at least a half hour, until he was sure Doretta Mims was asleep.

Now he crawled across the dirt floor to the opposite wall. He went down on his stomach and edged toward the door, keeping close to the wall. Pressing his face close to the opening, he could see, off to the right side, the fire, dying down now. The shape of a man wrapped in a blanket was lying full-length on the other side of it.

Brennan rose slowly, hugging the wall. He inched his head out to see the side of the fire closest to the lean-to, and as he did he heard the unmistakable click of a revolver being cocked. Abruptly he brought his head in and went back to the saddle next to Doretta Mims.

CHAPTER FOUR

In the morning they brought Doretta Mims out to cook; then sent her back to the hut while they ate. When they had finished they let Brennan and Doretta come out to the lean-to.

Frank Usher said, "That wasn't a head I seen pokin' out the door last night, was it?"

"If it was," Brennan answered, "why didn't you shoot at it?"

"I about did. Lucky thing it disappeared," Usher said. "Whatever it was." And he walked away, through the trees to where the horses were picketed.

Chink sat down on a stump and began making a cigarette.

A few steps from Doretta Mims, Brennan leaned against the hut and began eating. He could see her profile as she turned her head to look out through the trees and across the open slope.

Maybe she *is* a little plain, he thought. Her nose doesn't have the kind of a clean-cut shape that stays in your mind. And her hair—if she didn't have it pulled back so tight she'd look a little younger, and happier. She could do something with her hair. She could do something with her clothes, too, to let you know she's a woman.

He felt sorry for her, seeing her biting her lower lip, still staring off through the trees. And for a reason he did not understand, though he knew it had nothing to do with sympathy, he felt very close to her, as if he had known her for a long time, as if he could look into her eyes—not just now, but any time—and know what she was thinking. He realized that it was sympathy, in a sense, but not the feeling-sorry kind. He could picture her as a little girl, and self-consciously growing up, and he could imagine vaguely what her father was like. And now—a sensitive girl, afraid of saying the wrong thing; afraid of speaking out of turn even if it meant wondering about instead of knowing what had happened to her husband. Afraid of sounding silly, while men like her husband talked and talked and said nothing. But even having to listen to him, she would not speak against him, because he was her husband.

That's the kind of woman to have, Brennan thought. One that'll stick by you, no matter what. And, he thought, still looking at her, one that's got some insides to her. Not just all on the surface. Probably you would have to lose a woman like that to really appreciate her.

"Mrs. Mims."

She looked at him, her eyes still bearing the anxiety of watching through the trees.

"He'll come, Mrs. Mims. Pretty soon now."

Frank Usher returned and motioned them into the hut again. He talked to Chink for a few minutes and now the gunman walked off through the trees.

Looking out from the doorway of the hut, Brennan said over his shoulder, "One of them's going out now to watch for your husband." He glanced around at Doretta Mims and she answered him with a hesitant smile.

Frank Usher was standing by the lean-to when Chink came back through the trees some time later. He walked out to meet him.

"They coming?"

Chink nodded. "Starting across the slope."

Minutes later, two horses came into view crossing the grade. As they came through the trees, Frank Usher called, "Tie up in the shade there!" He and Chink watched the two men dismount, then come across the clearing toward them.

"It's all set!" Willard Mims called.

Frank Usher waited until they reached him. "What'd he say?"

"He said he'd bring the money."

"That right, Billy-Jack?"

Billy-Jack nodded. "That's what he said." He was carrying Rintoon's sawed-off shotgun.

"You didn't suspect any funny business?"

Billy-Jack shook his head.

Usher fingered his beard gently, holding Mims with his gaze. "He can scare up that much money?"

"He said he could, though it will take most of today to do it."

"That means he'll come out tomorrow," Usher said.

Willard Mims nodded. "That's right."

Usher's eyes went to Billy-Jack. "You gave him directions?"

"Like you said, right to the mouth of that barranca, chock full of willow. Then one of us brings him in from there."

"You're sure he can find it?"

"I made him say it twice," Billy-Jack said. "Every turn."

Usher looked at Willard Mims again. "How'd he take it?"

"How do you think he took it?"

Usher was silent, staring at Mims. Then he began to stroke his beard again. "I'm asking you," he said.

Mims shrugged. "Of course, he was mad, but there wasn't anything he could do about it. He's a reasonable man."

Billy-Jack was grinning. "Frank, this time tomorrow we're sitting on top of the world."

Willard Mims nodded. "I think you made yourself a pretty good deal."

Frank Usher's eyes had not left Mims. "You want to stay here or go on back?"

"What?"

"You heard what I said."

"You mean you'd let me go . . . now?"

"We don't need you any more."

Willard Mims' eyes flicked to the hut, then back to Frank Usher. He said, almost too eagerly, "I could go back now and lead old man Gateway out here in the morning."

"Sure you could," Usher said.

"Listen, I'd rather stay with my wife, but if it means getting the old man out here faster, then I think I better go back."

Usher nodded. "I know what you mean."

"You played square with me. By God, I'll play square with you."

Mims started to turn away.

Usher said, "Don't you want to see your wife first?"

Mims hesitated. "Well, the quicker I start traveling, the better. She'll understand."

"We'll see you tomorrow then, huh?"

Mims smiled. "About the same time." He hesitated. "All right to get going now?"

"Sure."

Mims backed away a few steps, still smiling, then turned and started to walk toward the trees. He looked back once and waved.

Frank Usher watched him, his eyes half-closed in the sunlight. When Mims was almost to the trees, Usher said, quietly, "Chink, bust him."

Chink fired, the .44 held halfway between waist and shoulders, the long barrel raising slightly as he fired again and again until Mims went down, lying still as the heavy reports faded into dead silence.

CHAPTER FIVE

Frank Usher waited as Billy-Jack stooped next to Mims. He saw Billy-Jack look up, nodding his head.

"Get rid of him," Usher said, watching now as Billy-Jack dragged Mims' body through the trees to the slope and there let go of it. The lifeless body slid down the grade, raising dust, until it disappeared into the brush far below.

Frank Usher turned and walked back to the hut.

Brennan stepped aside as he reached the low doorway. Usher saw the woman on the floor, her face buried in the crook of her arm resting on one of the saddles, her shoulders moving convulsively as she sobbed.

"What's the matter with her?" he asked.

Brennan said nothing.

"I thought we were doing her a favor," Usher said. He walked over to her, his hand covering the butt of his revolver, and touched her arm with his booted toe. "Woman, don't you realize what you just got out of?"

"She didn't know he did it," Brennan said quietly.

Usher looked at him, momentarily surprised. "No, I don't guess she would, come to think of it." He looked down at Doretta Mims and nudged her again with his boot. "Didn't you know that boy was selling you? This whole idea was his, to save his own skin." Usher paused. "He was ready to leave you again just now . . . when I got awful sick of him way down deep inside."

Doretta Mims was not sobbing now, but still she did not raise her head.

Usher stared down at her. "That was some boy you were married to, would do a thing like that."

Looking from the woman to Frank Usher, Brennan said, almost angrily, "What he did was wrong, but going along with it and then shooting him was all right!"

Usher glanced sharply at Brennan. "If you can't see a difference, I'm not going to explain it to you." He turned and walked out.

Brennan stood looking down at the woman for a few moments, then went over to the door and sat down on the floor just inside it. After a while he could hear Doretta Mims crying again. And for a long time he sat listening to her muffled sobs as he looked out at the sunlit clearing, now and again seeing one of the three outlaws.

He judged it to be about noon when Frank Usher and Billy-Jack rode out, walking their horses across the clearing, then into the trees, with Chink standing looking after them.

They're getting restless, Brennan thought. If they're going to stay here until tomorrow, they've got to be sure nobody's followed their sign. But it would take the best San Carlos tracker to pick up what little sign we made from Sasabe.

He saw Chink walking leisurely back to the lean-to. Chink looked toward the hut and stopped. He stood hip-cocked, with his thumbs in his crossed gun belts.

"How many did that make?" Brennan asked.

"What?" Chink straightened slightly.

Brennan nodded to where Mims had been shot. "This morning."

"That was the seventh," Chink said.

"Were they all like that?" he asked.

"How do you mean?"

"In the back."

"I'll tell you this: yours will be from the front."

"When?"

"Tomorrow before we leave. You can count on it."

"If your boss gives you the word."

"Don't worry about that," Chink said. Then, "You could make a run for it right now. It wouldn't be like just standing up gettin' it."

"I'll wait till tomorrow," Brennan said.

Chink shrugged and walked away.

After a few minutes Brennan realized that the hut was quiet. He turned to look at Doretta Mims. She was sitting up, staring at the opposite wall with a dazed expression.

Brennan moved to her side and sat down again. "Mrs. Mims, I'm sorry—"

"Why didn't you tell me it was his plan?"

"It wouldn't have helped anything."

She looked at Brennan now pleadingly. "He could have been doing it for all of us."

Brennan nodded. "Sure he could."

"But you don't believe that, do you?"

Brennan looked at her closely, at her eyes puffed from crying. "Mrs. Mims, you knew your husband better than I did."

Her eyes lowered and she said quietly, "I feel very foolish sitting here. Terrible things have happened in these two days, yet all I can think of is myself. All I can do is look at myself and feel very foolish." Her eyes raised to his. "Do you know why, Mr. Brennan? Because I know now that my husband never cared for me; because I know that he married me for his own interest." She paused. "I saw an innocent man killed yesterday and I can't even find the decency within me to pray for him."

"Mrs. Mims, try and rest now."

She shook her head wearily. "I don't care what happens to me."

There was a silence before Brennan said, "When you get done feeling sorry for yourself I'll tell you something."

Her eyes came open and she looked at him, more surprised than hurt.

"Look," Brennan said. "You know it and I know it—your husband married you for your money; but you're alive and he's dead and that makes the difference. You can moon about being a fool till they shoot you tomorrow, or you can start thinking about saving your skin right now. But I'll tell you this —it will take both of us working together to stay alive."

"But he said he'd let us—"

"You think they're going to let us go after your dad brings the money? They've killed four people in less than twenty-four hours!"

"I don't care what happens to me!"

He took her shoulders and turned her toward him. "Well, I care about me, and I'm not going to get shot in the belly tomorrow because you feel sorry for yourself!"

"But I can't help!" Doretta pleaded.

"You don't know if you can or not. We've got to keep our eyes open and we've got to think, and when the chance comes we've got to take it quick or else forget about it." His face was close to hers and he was still gripping her shoulders. "These men will kill. They've done it before and they have nothing to lose. They're going to kill us. That means we've got nothing to lose. Now you think about that a while."

He left her and went back to the door.

Brennan was called out of the hut later in the afternoon, as Usher and Billy-Jack rode in. They had shot a mule deer and Billy-Jack carried a hindquarter dangling from his saddle horn. Brennan was told to dress it down, enough for supper and the rest to be stripped and hung up to dry.

"But you take care of the supper first," Frank Usher said, adding that the woman wasn't in fit condition for cooking. "I don't want burned meat just 'cause she's in a state over her husband."

After they had eaten, Brennan took meat and coffee into Doretta Mims.

She looked up as he offered it to her. "I don't care for anything."

He was momentarily angry, but it passed off and he said, "Suit yourself." He placed the cup and plate on the floor and went outside to finish preparing the jerky.

By the time he finished, dusk had settled over the clearing and the inside of the hut was dark as he stepped inside.

He moved to her side and his foot kicked over the tin cup. He stooped quickly, picking up the cup and plate, and even in the dimness he could see that she had eaten most of the food.

"Mr. Brennan, I'm sorry for the way I've acted." She hesitated. "I thought you would understand, else I'd never have told you about—about how I felt."

"It's not a question of my understanding," Brennan said.

"I'm sorry I told you," Doretta Mims said.

He moved closer to her and knelt down, sitting back on his heels. "Look. Maybe I know how you feel, better than you think. But that's not important. Right now you don't need sympathy as much as you need a way to stay alive."

"I can't help the way I feel," she said obstinately.

Brennan was momentarily silent. He said then, "Did you love him?"

"I was married to him!"

"That's not what I asked you. While everybody's being honest, just tell me if you loved him."

She hesitated, looking down at her hands. "I'm not sure."

"But you wanted to be in love with him, more than anything."

Her head nodded slowly. "Yes."

"Did you ever think for a minute that he loved you?"

"That's not a fair question!"

"Answer it anyway!"

She hesitated again. "No, I didn't."

He said, almost brutally, "Then what have you lost outside of a little pride?"

"You don't understand," she said.

"You're afraid you can't get another man—is that what it is? Even if he married you for money, at least he married you. He was the first and last chance as far as you were concerned, so you grabbed him."

"What are you trying to do, strip me of what little self-respect I have left?"

"I'm trying to strip you of this foolishness! You think you're too plain to get a man?"

She bit her lower lip and looked away from him.

"You think nobody'll have you because you bite your lip and can't say more than two words at a time?"

"Mr. Brennan—"

"Listen, you're as much woman as any of them. A hell of a lot more than some, but you've got to realize it! You've got to do something about it!"

"I can't help it if—"

"Shut up with that I-can't-help-it talk! If you can't help it, nobody can. All your life you've been sitting around waiting for something to happen to you. Sometimes you have to walk up and take what you want."

Suddenly he brought her to him, his arms circling her shoulders, and he kissed her, holding his lips to hers until he felt her body relax slowly and at the same time he knew that she was kissing him.

His lips brushed her cheek and he said, close to her, "We're going to stay alive. You're going to do exactly what I say when the time comes, and we're going to get out of here." Her hair brushed his cheek softly and he knew that she was nodding yes.

CHAPTER SIX

During the night he opened his eyes and crawled to the lighter silhouette of the doorway. Keeping close to the front wall, he looked out and across to the low-burning fire. One of them, a shadowy form that he could not recognize, sat facing the hut. He did not move, but by the way he was sitting Brennan knew he was awake. You're running out of time, Brennan thought. But there was nothing he could do.

The sun was not yet above the trees when Frank Usher appeared in the doorway. He saw that Brennan was awake and he said, "Bring the woman out," turning away as he said it.

Her eyes were closed, but they opened as Brennan touched her shoulder, and he knew that she had not been asleep. She looked up at him calmly, her features softly shadowed.

"Stay close to me," he said. "Whatever we do, stay close to me."

They went out to the lean-to and Brennan built the fire as Doretta got the coffee and venison ready to put on.

Brennan moved slowly, as if he were tired, as if he had given up hope; but his eyes were alive and most of the time his gaze stayed with the three men—watching them eat, watching them make cigarettes as they squatted in a half-circle, talking, but too far away for their voices to be heard. Finally, Chink rose and went off into the trees. He came back with his horse, mounted, and rode off into the trees again but in the other direction, toward the open grade.

It went through Brennan's mind: He's going off like he did yesterday morning, but this time to wait for Gateway. Yesterday on foot, but today on his horse, which means he's going farther down to wait for him. And Frank went somewhere yesterday morning. Frank went over to where the horses are. He suddenly felt an excitement inside of him, deep within his stomach, and he kept his eyes on Frank Usher.

A moment later Usher stood up and started off toward the trees, calling back something to Billy-Jack about the horses—and Brennan could hardly believe his eyes.

Now. It's now. You know that, don't you? It's now or never. God help me. God help me think of something! And suddenly it was in his mind. It was less than half a chance, but it was something, and it came to him because it was the only thing about Billy-Jack that stood out in his mind, besides the shotgun: *He was always looking at Doretta!*

She was in front of the lean-to, and he moved toward her, turning his back to Billy-Jack sitting with Rintoon's shotgun across his lap.

"Go in the hut and start unbuttoning your dress." He half whispered it and saw her eyes widen as he said it. "Go on! Billy-Jack will come in. Act surprised. Embarrassed. Then smile at him." She hesitated, starting to bite her lip. "Damn it, go on!"

He poured himself a cup of coffee, not looking at her as she walked away. Putting the coffee down, he saw Billy-Jack's eyes following her.

"Want a cup?" Brennan called to him. "There's about one left."

Billy-Jack shook his head and turned the sawed-off shotgun on Brennan as he saw him approaching.

Brennan took a sip of the coffee. "Aren't you going to look in on that?" He nodded toward the hut.

"What do you mean?"

"The woman," Brennan said matter-of-factly. He took another sip of the coffee.

"What about her?" Billy-Jack asked.

Brennan shrugged. "I thought you were taking turns."

"What?"

"Now, look, you can't be so young. I got to draw you a map—" Brennan smiled. "Oh, I see . . . Frank didn't say anything to you. Or Chink . . . Keeping her for themselves . . ."

Billy-Jack's eyes flicked to the hut, then back to Brennan. "They were with her?"

"Well, all I know is Frank went in there yesterday morning and Chink yesterday afternoon while you were gone." He took another sip of the coffee and threw out what was left in the cup. Turning, he said, "No skin off my nose," and walked slowly back to the lean-to.

He began scraping the tin plates, his head down, but watching Billy-Jack. Let it sink through that thick skull of yours. But do it quick! Come on, move, you animal!

There! He watched Billy-Jack walk slowly toward the hut. God, make him move faster! Billy-Jack was out of view then beyond the corner of the hut.

All right. Brennan put down the tin plate he was holding and moved quickly, noiselessly, to the side of the hut and edged along the rough logs until he reached the corner. He listened first before he looked around. Billy-Jack had gone inside.

He wanted to make sure, some way, that Billy-Jack would be looking at Doretta, but there was not time. And then he was moving again—along the front, and suddenly he was inside the hut, seeing the back of Billy-Jack's head, seeing him turning, and a glimpse of Doretta's face, and the sawed-off shotgun coming around. One of his hands shot out to grip the stubby barrel, pushing it, turning it up and back violently, and the other hand closed over the trigger guard before it jerked down on Billy-Jack's wrist.

Deafeningly, a shot exploded, with the twin barrels jammed under the outlaw's jaw. Smoke and a crimson smear, and Brennan was on top of him wrenching the shotgun from squeezed fingers, clutching Billy-Jack's revolver as he came to his feet.

He heard Doretta gasp, still with the ringing in his ears, and he said, "Don't look at him!" already turning to the doorway as he jammed the Colt into his empty holster.

Frank Usher was running across the clearing, his gun in his hand.

Brennan stepped into the doorway leveling the shotgun. "Frank, hold it there!"

Usher stopped dead, but in the next second he was aiming, his revolver coming up even with his face, and Brennan's hand squeezed the second trigger of the shotgun.

Usher screamed and went down, grabbing his knees, and he rolled to his side as he hit the ground. His right hand came up, still holding the Colt.

"Don't do it, Frank!" Brennan had dropped the scattergun and now Billy-Jack's revolver was in his hand. He saw Usher's gun coming in line, and he fired, aiming dead center at the half-reclined figure, hearing the sharp, heavy report, and seeing Usher's gun hand raise straight up into the air as he slumped over on his back.

Brennan hesitated. Get him out of there, quick. Chink's not deaf!

He ran out to Frank Usher and dragged him back to the hut, laying him next to Billy-Jack. He jammed Usher's pistol into his belt. Then, "Come on!" he told Doretta, and took her hand and ran out of the hut and across the clearing toward the side where the horses were.

They moved into the denser pines, where he stopped and pulled her down next to him in the warm sand. Then he rolled over on his stomach and parted the branches to look back out across the clearing.

The hut was to the right. Straight across were more pines, but they were scattered thinly, and through them he could see the sand-colored expanse of the open grade. Chink would come that way, Brennan knew. There was no other way he could.

CHAPTER SEVEN

Close to him, Doretta said, "We could leave before he comes." She was afraid, and it was in the sound of her voice.

"No," Brennan said. "We'll finish this. When Chink comes we'll finish it once and for all."

"But you don't know! How can you be sure you'll—"

"Listen, I'm not sure of anything, but I know what I have to do." She was silent and he said quietly, "Move back and stay close to the ground."

And as he looked across the clearing his eyes caught the dark speck of movement beyond the trees, out on the open slope. There he was. It had to be him. Brennan could feel the sharp knot in his stomach again as he watched, as the figure grew larger.

Now he was sure. Chink was on foot leading his horse, not coming straight across, but angling higher up on the slope. He'll come in where the trees are thicker, Brennan thought. He'll come out beyond the lean-to and you won't see him until he turns the corner of the hut. That's it. He can't climb the slope back of the hut, so he'll have to come around the front way.

He estimated the distance from where he was lying to the front of the hut —seventy or eighty feet—and his thumb eased back the hammer of the revolver in front of him.

There was a dead silence for perhaps ten minutes before he heard, coming from beyond the hut, "Frank?" Silence again. Then, "Where the hell are you?"

Brennan waited, feeling the smooth, heavy, hickory grip of the Colt in his hand, his finger lightly caressing the trigger. It was in his mind to fire as soon as Chink turned the corner. He was ready. But it came and it went.

It went as he saw Chink suddenly, unexpectedly, slip around the corner of the hut and flatten himself against the wall, his gun pointed toward the door. Brennan's front sight was dead on Chink's belt, but he couldn't pull the trigger. Not like this. He watched Chink edge slowly toward the door.

"Throw it down, boy!"

Chink moved and Brennan squeezed the trigger a split second late. He fired again, hearing the bullet thump solidly into the door frame, but it was too late. Chink was inside.

Brennan let his breath out slowly, relaxing somewhat. Well, that's what you get. You wait, and all you do is make it harder for yourself. He could picture Chink now looking at Usher and Billy-Jack. That'll give him something to think about. Look at them good. Then look at the door you've got to come out of sooner or later.

I'm glad he's seeing them like that. And he thought then: How long could you stand something like that? He can cover up Billy-Jack and stand it a little longer. But when dark comes . . . If he holds out till dark he's got a chance. And now he was sorry he had not pulled the trigger before. You got to make him come out, that's all.

"Chink!"

There was no answer.

"Chink, come on out!"

Suddenly gunfire came from the doorway and Brennan, hugging the ground, could hear the swishing of the bullets through the foliage above him.

Don't throw it away, he thought, looking up again. He backed up and moved over a few yards to take up a new position. He'd be on the left side of the doorway as you look at it, Brennan thought, to shoot on an angle like that.

He sighted on the inside edge of the door frame and called, "Chink, come out and get it!" He saw the powder flash, and he fired on top of it, cocked and fired again. Then silence.

Now you don't know, Brennan thought. He reloaded and called out, "Chink!" but there was no answer, and he thought: You just keep digging your hole deeper.

Maybe you did hit him. No, that's what he wants you to think. Walk in the door and you'll find out. He'll wait now. He'll take it slow and start adding up his chances. Wait till night? That's his best bet—but he can't count on his horse being there then. I could have worked around and run it off. And he knows he wouldn't be worth a damn on foot, even if he did get away. So the longer he waits, the less he can count on his horse.

All right, what would you do? Immediately he thought: I'd count shots. So you hear five shots go off in a row and you make a break out the door, and while you're doing it the one shooting picks up another gun. But even picking up another gun takes time.

He studied the distance from the doorway to the corner of the hut. Three long strides. Out of sight in less than three seconds. That's if he's thinking of it. And if he tried it, you'd have only that long to aim and fire. Unless . . .

Unless Doretta pulls off the five shots. He thought about this for some time before he was sure it could be done without endangering her. But first you have to give him the idea.

He rolled to his side to pull Usher's gun from his belt. Then, holding it in his left hand, he emptied it at the doorway. Silence followed.

I'm reloading now, Chink. Get it through your cat-eyed head. I'm reloading and you've got time to do something.

He explained it to Doretta unhurriedly—how she would wait about ten minutes before firing the first time; she would count to five and fire again, and so on until the gun was empty. She was behind the thick bole of a pine and only the gun would be exposed as she fired.

She said, "And if he doesn't come out?"

"Then we'll think of something else."

Their faces were close. She leaned toward him, closing her eyes, and kissed him softly. "I'll be waiting," she said.

Brennan moved off through the trees, circling wide, well back from the edge of the clearing. He came to the thin section directly across from Doretta's position and went quickly from tree to tree, keeping to the shadows until he was into thicker pines again. He saw Chink's horse off to the left of him. Only a few minutes remained as he came out of the trees to the off side of the lean-to, and there he went down to his knees, keeping his eyes on the corner of the hut.

The first shot rang out and he heard it *whump* into the front of the hut. One . . . then the second . . . two . . . he was counting them, not moving his eyes from the front edge of the hut . . . three . . . four . . . be ready. . . . Five! Now, Chink!

He heard him—hurried steps on the packed sand—and almost immediately he saw him cutting sharply around the edge of the hut, stopping, leaning against the wall, breathing heavily but thinking he was safe. Then Brennan stood up.

"Here's one facing you, Chink."

He saw the look of surprise, the momentary expression of shock, a full second before Chink's revolver flashed up from his side and Brennan's finger tightened on the trigger. With the report, Chink lurched back against the wall, a look of bewilderment still on his face, although he was dead even as he slumped to the ground.

Brennan holstered the revolver and did not look at Chink as he walked past him around to the front of the hut. He suddenly felt tired, but it was the kind of tired feeling you enjoyed, like the bone weariness and sense of accomplishment you felt seeing your last cow punched through the market chute.

He thought of old man Tenvoorde, and only two days ago trying to buy the yearlings from him. He still didn't have any yearlings.

What the hell do you feel so good about?

Still, he couldn't help smiling. Not having money to buy stock seemed like such a little trouble. He saw Doretta come out of the trees and he walked on across the clearing.